Garfield's Train

A Novel

Feather Schwartz Foster

PublishAmerica
Baltimore

First printing

ISBN: 1-4137-6915-2
PUBLISHED BY PUBLISHAMERICA, LLLP
www.publishamerica.com
Baltimore

Printed in the United States of America

Acknowledgments

Grateful thanks are due to the following people who have helped bring *Garfield's Train* to life.

To the Long Branch Public Library, and its reference librarian Janet Birkenhead, for allowing me to research through all their clippings, photos, drawings, etc.

To Jim Foley of the Long Branch Historical Society for his help in collecting information about the "old days."

To Karen Schnitzpahn, author of *Victorian Summers*, who was kind enough to answer some of my questions, and whose book on "old Long Branch" became my foundation stone.

To John Kilbride, a bona fide railroad maven, for his assistance in getting my train rides reasonably correct.

To Colleen Fantini, Randi Grunstein and Dave McNelis for being my "readers" and plowing through an early and often tedious version of *Garfield's Train*. Their comments and suggestions were invaluable.

To the entire staff of the Scotch Plains Public Library, my home base, for not only making me feel welcome, but for taking a sincere interest in the progress of my book.

To my parents, Harold and Helen Schwartz for my past…and to my daughter Alexandra, for my future.

And, finally, to my husband, Steve Foster, for everything.

Garfield's Train

A Novel

Prologue

I am seventy-nine years old.

I remember clearly the day Franklin Roosevelt died. I was working for my Uncle Henry in the office of his tool and die plant in Pittsburgh. When the news came over the radio, everyone was stunned. Uncle Henry made the announcement over the loud speaker, and we all recited the Lord's Prayer. Then all two hundred employees went outside and Uncle Henry lowered the flag to half-staff as tears ran down everybody's cheeks. Mr. Elberson, who was a deacon in his church, recited the Twenty-Third Psalm. Funny how I can remember little details like Mr. Elberson's name after all these years. Then Uncle Henry told everyone to go home. Nobody felt like working.

Of course I remember when Kennedy was shot. I was at the supermarket with Cap, my youngest son. The store manager made the announcement on the microphone, and you could hear him choking back tears as he told us the awful news. We were truly shocked this time. Kennedy was a young man in the prime of health. Assassination was the furthest thing from our minds. Then the manager asked everyone to finish their shopping as quickly as possible because the store would be closing.

So now I am the same age as my grandmother was when we went across the country by train to bury her dear friend Mollie

Brown. I am in good health, and my marbles are still rattling around in fair order. I take after Gran, and she lived to be eighty-six. Seventy-nine doesn't seem that old today, but in my advancing age, I am amazed how much I've been thinking about her, twining the pieces of her life into their proper order in my life, and into the lives of my children and grandchildren and now, great-grandchildren. I have two. There will be more. I want to pass down our sliver of history. I think it is important. When I think of history, I think of Michelangelo and I can visualize each generation passing along its history to the next, with an outstretched, almost-touching finger. Lately, I wonder if those fingers shouldn't actually be touching, or grabbing, or even pounding with fists. Today's generations don't understand subtlety at all, and history can be such a subtle thing.

The truth is, I really never knew Gran—my maternal grandmother—until that train trip so long ago. I was twenty-three in 1947. Gran lived within an hour's drive from us in Pittsburgh, but she and my mother never saw eye-to-eye, and the only times I remember seeing her, other than at family milestones, were at Christmas, when the entire family made the trek. My mother said it was because Gran didn't care for Daddy, who she thought was a snob since his family owned a good portion of the Pittsburgh Paint Company. Actually, Daddy was a gem and I adored him. It was Mother who was the snob. But frankly, after I got to know Gran, I think she and Mother didn't see eye-to-eye long before Daddy arrived on the scene. Gran had been very active with the Suffragettes, and I think it embarrassed my mother, who preferred the country club set. I think they just plain didn't get on. It must be one of those family genes about mothers and daughters not seeing eye-to-eye. I never saw eye-to-eye with my mother either.

They say that when you get old (and I suppose, whether I like it or not, I am old), you remember things long past far better than you remember things that happened yesterday. I find myself thinking about that trip with Gran so very long ago, and how I

8

have become a conduit for well over a hundred years of living and maybe even a little piece of history itself.

Names have always been important in our family. We tend to give our children the names of people we loved and admired, in the hope that their fine qualities will resurface in their namesakes. I have two older sisters: Margaret Ophelia, named for Gran's mother and favorite aunt, and who was nine years older than I. She has been dead for fifteen years. We always called her Margie. My sister Marlene (actually Mary Charlene) is six years older than I am. She is beginning to fail. Gran had wanted Marlene to be named for her best friend Mollie Brown (actually a Mary as well), who was also my mother's godmother. The Charlene part was for "Pops," my maternal step-grandfather. Mother agreed to "Mary," since it was also Daddy's mother's name, but calling my sister "Mollie" was out of the question. First of all, Mother seldom saw her godmother, who lived in California, and other than birthday presents when she was small, a nice wedding present—and the Mollie-cups when her children were born—she had little contact with her. Moreover, it was an old-fashioned name back in 1918, when my sister was born, and "Marlene" seemed more in keeping with the image Mother wanted for her daughters. And thirdly, I don't think Mother was over-anxious to please Gran. There had been a brother, John Milton, but he died of scarlet fever when he was two—before I was born.

I am the youngest. I was born in 1924. I was called Katherine Louise, for Daddy's older sister and for Gran. Daddy would always "sing" my name when I was little. "K-K-K-Katie, Beautiful Lady…." It's funny how those memories creep back. He died when I was fifteen, and I miss him every day of my life.

My two sisters were married and out of the house when Daddy had his heart attack. He wasn't even fifty-five and we were all devastated. I imagine it was tough on Mother, but in the callowness of a fifteen-year-old adolescent, I don't think I paid too much attention to what she was going through. I was much too absorbed with my own grief. Daddy's family, as I said, were very well fixed, and even though they lost a great deal during the Depression, they were still far better off than most people in town. Mother always got along with them very well, and there was never anything for her to worry about financially. I remember (incredible what you remember!), she went out right before the funeral, and bought some jet jewelry. A necklace, earrings, bracelet, ring and a brooch. "Mourning jewelry," she called it. I was horrified that she would even think of having new jewelry, mourning or not. She wore it with everything for a year. Marlene's granddaughter has it now. It is supposedly worth several thousand dollars.

Mother remarried when I was twenty-eight. Delton Trent was a nice man, a few years older than Mom. He was a widower, and they were both lonely. We all liked him. I liked him better than I liked my mother. Margie and Marlene were busy with their families, and I was starting my own. History was repeating itself: We saw Mother and Dell every Christmas. He died in 1969, right after the moon landing. Mother went to the funeral wearing all the jet jewelry. She lived to be eighty-five years old.

Fate was kind enough to provide me with three sons. Getting along with daughters-in-law was far easier for me than getting along with daughters was for my mother. We had a cordial affection, but maintained a respectful distance. And now I have six fine grandsons. I also have two little great-granddaughters, who I hope will have a chance to know their great-grandma, at least for a little while.

My own life has been uneventful for the most part. I have been an observer of history, rather than a participant, and that is fine, too. But I think, before I die, or before I get too old to stop the silly babbling, I should write down, for my great-grandchildren, the pinprick of history that included our family.

Chapter 1

In August, 1947, I traveled by train across the country with my grandmother. The telegram had come two days before. Mollie Brown was dying and calling for Gran, her oldest and dearest friend. Gran was going, willy or nilly. She made it plain and clear, seventy-nine years old or not, she would not deny Mollie's last wish. But Uncle Henry was adamant: No seventy-nine-year-old mother of his would travel from Pittsburgh to Pasadena by herself. Since I had six weeks till college started, I was dispatched. It was a free trip for me, and I had never been West before. Uncle Henry had originally suggested that we fly to California, and I was thrilled! But Gran said she would walk first before flying in the air, so the train it was. Besides, Gran always had a fondness for trains, she claimed.

She was anything but frail, and except for a few aches and pains and the reading glasses that she resented bitterly, she could have deducted ten years or more. I was happy to carry the luggage and hail the taxicabs. I considered it a long overdue vacation, and besides, I had never been far from home before. For four long years after I graduated high school, I worked in the office of Uncle Henry's tool and die plant. His business was considered essential to the war effort, and Uncle Henry insisted he needed a smart gal to handle the paperwork that never ended. I wanted to go away to college, mainly to get away from living with my mother, but Uncle Henry said he needed me, and he promised that once the war was over and the men came home, I could go to college. He even said he'd pay for it, although I had my trust fund money from Daddy, and from my Pittsburgh Paint grandparents. Money wasn't the problem: manpower, or perhaps I should say "woman power" was. Anyway, true to his word, I started school in the fall of 1945, and Uncle Henry was footing the bill. He told me to keep my money for a time when I might need it. Twenty-three wasn't so old to be in college in 1947; thousands of young men my age were going back to school. Hal—Major Harry Brown—was twenty-seven, and he was back in school. Hal was Mollie Brown's grandson and an unexpected benefit of the trip to bury Gran's friend.

I had heard about Mollie Brown on and off all my life. Gran and Mollie had been friends since they were twelve or so. She was Mother's godmother; Gran was godmother to Mollie's son Rudy. In more than fifty years, they had seen each other only once or twice a decade, since Mollie had moved to California back when Theodore Roosevelt was President. But hardly a month passed that long letters didn't cross in the mail, catching them up on each other's lives. And every child and grandchild and great-grandchild in our family received a monogrammed silver cup from Tiffany's when they were born—from Mollie Brown. The same, by the way, was true for Mollie's family: monogrammed silver cups from Tiffany's from Gran. The only difference was that Mollie preferred script, and Gran chose block lettering.

I remember the five silver cups lined up in my mother's china cabinet: hers, mine, my two sisters', and the brother's who died when he was two. Cups had been sent to my sisters a few years ago—for Gran's great-grandchildren. Uncle Henry's side had cups—so did Uncle Walter's. Quite a collection of Mollie-cups, as we called them. Now that Mollie was dying, there would be no more cups for my nieces or nephews on the way. Both my sisters were expecting again.

When we started our trip, Gran was silent, and I could sense the concern she undoubtedly felt about her old friend. Twice— once in Chicago where we changed trains for the "Super Chief," that marvel of luxurious transportation, and again in Flagstaff, Arizona—she had me send a telegram to Mollie's daughter saying where she was and to "tell Mollie to wait."

At breakfast neither of us talked. We had that in common: no chatter before coffee, and we both drank copious amounts. I respected her silence, especially since I was inclined to lapse into long periods of introspection myself. I kept busy with *For Whom the Bell Tolls*, which was on the reading list for fall semester.

Over chicken pot pies at lunch in the dining car, she asked me about college; I was enjoying it. I had made a good decision going to Susquehanna College. It was small enough to give me the opportunities I needed without getting lost. Uncle Walter was a professor of English Lit there and having him and Aunt Harriet around was good too, especially during spring holidays. Mother liked traveling, and I think she was relieved that I would be with family and not tying up her Easter.

I told Gran I was majoring in journalism, but I didn't have any real driving ambition. Maybe I would work for a local newspaper. She very sternly reminded me that I was the first girl in her family to have a college education, and I had better shape up and appreciate it.

Then Gran told me she had wanted very much to go to college herself, or at least to a Normal School where they trained teachers.

"I had a wonderful teacher for eighth grade," she said. "Miss MacClure. Amelia MacClure. Funny how you remember names from so long ago! She would be over a hundred years old today, I'd bet. She was a remarkable woman. Most women teachers only taught children up to the age of ten. Then we had men teachers for the harder work. But Miss MacClure taught us science and botany and geography and algebra. And she made it so interesting! I still remember learning about cirrus and cumulus clouds," Gran said as she laughed and closed her eyes, and disappeared into one of her reveries, so I kept my ongoing date with Ernest Hemingway. I had little interest in clouds.

"Now where was I?" Gran said as she woke with a start about ten minutes later. "Oh yes. I thought about being a teacher. My father, however, thought it was foolish, since I would likely marry, raise a family and never teach. Waste of money, that's what he said. Waste of money. Can you imagine? My mother was more encouraging. We shall see, she said. Who knows what will be in five years?

"One night I overheard them talking about the Normal School. My mother said, 'Suppose Louise isn't married by the time she's twenty. What if she never marries?' That, of course, was unthinkable to my father. 'We will wait and see,' advised my mother. And, of course, that's exactly what happened. We waited, and I married. Time takes care of itself, I think."

My grandmother was suddenly becoming very talkative. "I wanted to send your mother to college, Kate, but Clara had other ideas. She was never more than an indifferent student. She liked socializing better than studying. Then she met your father when she was graduating high school. I begged her to wait and think it over, since she was only eighteen. But you know your mother when she sets her mind to something. She got married. I like to think she was happy."

Frankly, I think Gran would have much preferred to think that Mother shed bitter tears regretting her early marriage, but Gran would have been wrong. Dad loved Mother dearly, and she was very happy socializing and becoming a first-class society grande dame. I'm just sorry Gran never got to know Daddy better. He was aces. He was tall, dark and handsome, just like in the romance magazines. And he had a grin that lit up his face, and a dimple in his chin. He played polo and golf, was a superb marksman and had the softest heart of anyone I ever

14

knew. Both my parents were very charitable. And Daddy always had plenty of time for me.

Neither of my sisters went to college, and I suppose if it weren't for my trust fund and Uncle Henry's encouragement, neither would I. Mother had very old-fashioned ideas about women and education. "A college education makes for an unhappy wife," she claimed. "An overeducated woman is always dissatisfied at home."

Of course that's nonsense. Or is it? Today's women are educated and have every modern convenience to avoid household drudgery; they have nannies and daycare to tend the children, and thousands of opportunities my mother never even heard of. But they don't seem especially happy to me. I don't think people are especially happy in general, and I think children are downright miserable.

Mother insisted there were only "certain" women who should go to college: the very brainy and talented ones, like Madame Curie, I suppose; the homely ones, who didn't seem likely to be snapped up early on; and the ones from small towns where opportunities to meet eligible prospects were slim. I didn't qualify on any count. I was above average as a student, but I was no Madame Curie. I was more-pretty than not-pretty, and had my share of dates. And Pittsburgh isn't exactly the wilderness. Mother had hopes for her third daughter.

Gran became downright gabby by dinnertime. Maybe she was bored. Or maybe she truly believed that Mollie Brown would wait to die until after we arrived. As we sat at a comfortable table for two, set with a linen cloth and elegant china, monogrammed with the railroad's insignia, she started to tell me little tidbits about herself when she was small. "You should know your family history, Kate," she said. "It's important. You can have all the pictures and family albums, but if you don't know who the people are and what they did, it becomes meaningless.

"I know Mollie is eighty, and eighty is a good long life and I mustn't be too sad," Gran said over coffee that first night, "but I love her in a way I have never loved anyone else, and I shall miss her with my whole heart."

I don't think I have ever had a friend I cared for that much.

"I'm not originally from Pittsburgh," she began out of nowhere. "I moved there with Charlie Stanfield. He was my second husband, you know. Your real grandfather—Henry Cobbs—died, and three years later I married Pops. Your Uncle Walter is your mother's half-brother." That part I knew.

Gran continued, "Pops loved your mother and your Uncle Henry as if they were his own blood, and when Walter was born, he formally adopted them. Charlie wanted us all to have the same last name. I think Clara was around nine then.

"No," she said, "I grew up in New Jersey, by the ocean, in a little town called Long Branch. It was a beautiful seashore town, especially in the summer when all the wealthy people would come. This was right after the Civil War, when a lot of people had become extremely rich. We weren't rich; we were comfortable. My father owned a dry-goods store and some property in the area. He was also our mayor when I was a girl."

I vaguely remembered a sepia-toned photograph on Gran's mantel with a picture of a medium-sized stiff man of about forty, with a dark handlebar moustache that looked waxed at the tips, and a derby hat. He was standing straight, with his right hand down at his side, and his left hand tucked under his armpit in a popular pose of the era. He was next to and slightly behind a small, dark-eyed pretty woman with dark hair piled atop her head. She was seated. Standing next to her on the other side was a girl of about fifteen. That was Gran.

"My father's name was John Milton Dunbar," Gran continued. "His parents, James and Louisa Dunbar, had come from Ireland in the mid-1840s, a few years before the famous potato famine, when my father, your great-grandfather was around five. We weren't Catholic, you know. The Dunbars were from a town near Belfast, in Northern Ireland, and we were

Protestant. Very unusual for the Irish at the time, but Protestant we were. The Dunbars came first to New York City, and then to Elizabeth, New Jersey. My grandfather was a carpenter by trade, but in those days, people didn't care for the Irish, Protestant or not, so he earned a living doing odd jobs or manual labor. According to my father, James Dunbar was always up to taking a risk and a gamble, and one of those gambles paid off. He won a lottery—several hundred dollars, I'm told. So he bought a horse and wagon and became a wagoneer. That's someone who leases himself and his horse and wagon to anyone who needs his services. It was a paltry living, but they managed to raise six sons and three daughters to maturity."

I remember Gran telling a story when I was little about how the Dunbars got their names. It seems that my great-great-grandmother Dunbar, whose first name was Louisa (Gran's namesake), had a literary bent, and hoping to inspire her offspring to lofty aims, named her sons after her favorite authors. An immigrant Irish woman who could read in the 1840s was about as unlikely as a Protestant Irishman, but Gran intimated that the Dunbars "married up" when James married Louisa, who was half-English, and had had some schooling.

Anyway, according to Gran, there was Walter Scott Dunbar, the eldest, Alexander Pope Dunbar, Daniel Defoe Dunbar, Homer Dunbar (the only one without a middle name), John Milton Dunbar (my great-grandfather), and Alexander Dumas Dunbar. Since Alexander Pope was older and had claim to "Alex," they used the middle name for the youngest, and called him "Dumas." But they always pronounced it "Doomis," and Uncle Doomis adopted the spelling when he was ten, since he bitterly resented the children at school calling him "Dum-ass Dum-bar." Gran loved telling that story.

My great-great-aunts were Penelope, Rowena and Ophelia, after their mother's favorite literary heroines. There had been another boy somewhere in that lineup, William Shakespeare Dunbar, but he died when he was three or four. Unfortunately, no Dunbar ever inherited literary tendencies, although Great-Great-Grandmother Louisa always insisted that Will was the one with all the talent. I expect she would be pleased that my Uncle Walter was at least a professor of English literature.

Gran went on to say that the only ones she knew well were Uncle Walter and Aunt Ophelia, since she saw them often. "My grandparents had been long dead by the time I was born and I never met Aunt Rowena either, since she died years before. Uncle Alex—that's Alexander Pope Dunbar—and Uncle Homer went west after the Civil War for the free land. We would hear from them on occasion, with letters posted from Colorado Territory or Dakota Territory. When I was around six or seven, Uncle Doomis went West to seek his fortune, too, but he was killed in a mining accident.

"Uncle Dan had stayed with my grandfather in the wagoneering business in Elizabeth, and after the war, he bought a few surplus wagons, horses and mules, and began renting them out to anyone who needed machinery or furniture moved. He did remarkably well and became partners with a man named Amos Smith. Anyway, Amos Smith wound up marrying my Aunt Nell—that was Penelope. Aunt Nell had been married before to a man named McDonough who was killed at Gettysburg. She was left with two children, James and Louisa, named for her parents. They were a lot older than I was. We saw Uncle Smith and Aunt Nell occasionally, usually on holidays or at weddings."

I was reeling, trying to keep track of that litany of Dunbars I was learning about. We took our coffee from the dining car into the parlor car, and she continued her narrative of my family's history.

"When John Milton, your great-grandfather Dunbar, was fourteen, his father died, so his formal schooling ended. Uncle Dan could barely make ends meet with the wagoneering business, and the other brothers were starting lives of their own. My father felt responsible for his mother, plus Ophelia and Doomis, who were only twelve and ten. He tried for weeks to find employment, but 'no Irish were wanted.'

"Finally a harness-maker named Isaac Warren put him to work. He got tired of seeing my father show up two or three times a week asking if there were any openings yet. Young Johnny Dunbar was a persistent fellow. 'Maybe someone died or went West. Maybe business has improved and you need an extra man,' he kept saying. Mr. Warren admired my father's willingness to work hard and learn, so he said he could sweep up and keep things tidy.

"My father dusted everything in that shop—even the high shelves that hadn't been dusted in ten years. The place fairly sparkled! Mr. Warren was impressed and decided the lad was worth training. So he taught him everything about harness making, but especially about the business itself: how to stock the merchandise and deal with the customers and the suppliers. My father took to it like a duck to water. It was his idea to tie ribbons and bells on a harness and drive a team around town just before Christmas—with a sign saying 'Special price on Christmas harnesses.' They did very well that year. By the time he was eighteen, Mr. Warren had put him in charge of the place.

"But most importantly, my father never forgot Mr. Warren's kindness—or the fact that he took in an Irishman when nobody else would.

"When my father was twenty-one, the Civil War started; he was quick to enlist. He was made a sergeant right off, since he had been a foreman and knew how to supervise. Then he took a bullet in his right arm in a skirmish near Harper's Ferry, a few days before the battle of Antietam. He was on a scouting expedition and a few in his party were killed, including the lieutenant. Somehow, despite his great pain, my father managed to lead the rest of the men back to camp. They promoted him to lieutenant on the spot. My father was considered fortunate his arm wasn't cut off, and always said it was because he was wounded *before* Antietam. The doctors weren't so busy and could take time to probe for the bullet. At

Antietam, everything was amputated. It was quicker. His arm was pretty useless, however. He couldn't raise it more than a few inches or hold anything heavier than the coffeepot. It should have ended his military career, but he was full of spit and vinegar and wanted to stay, so they sent him to the Quartermaster's Division to help with the paperwork. My father was very good with numbers, and since he was left-handed, could still work with a pencil. As a matter of fact," Gran said, between sips of coffee, "he was so good at managing supplies, within six months he was promoted up to captain."

The Captain, as he was commonly called after that, mustered out at the end of the war. He had expected to become partners with Isaac Warren, but the man had died and his daughters sold the place. So he settled at the seashore at the urging of his oldest brother, Gran's Uncle Walter Scott Dunbar, who ran a hotel in Long Branch. Opening a store was natural for the quartermaster's adjutant, and John Milton Dunbar proved so adept that he was soon able to marry his childhood sweetheart and buy a house. He also loved politics. "What Irishman doesn't?" Gran commented rhetorically. His prominence in the community was recognized and rewarded by his election as mayor year after year. He had very little competition. Long Branch thrived under his jurisdiction.

"My mother was named Margaret Coyne," Gran said, continuing her narrative. "She was born near Dublin in 1842 and came to America when she was two or three years old. Her mother died coming over. Some kind of fever, they said. Anyway, she and her father came directly to Elizabeth, New Jersey where there were some relatives on her mother's side."

The porter wheeled in a cart with a silver coffee urn and all the accoutrements so we could refill our cups. I could understand why my grandmother enjoyed train travel. The "Super Chief" was one of those wonderful new streamliner trains that were the height of luxurious travel back then. It featured every modern convenience — including soft cushioned seats and electric fans overhead. It was definitely a civilized way to travel.

"'Miss Peg,' as her father started calling her early on because she had big, dark, serious eyes and seemed so wise beyond her years, wound up staying for a while with a great aunt and uncle until her father could get settled, but they still didn't want the Irish, and it was hard times for them. When Miss Peg (the nickname stuck) was seven or eight, they discovered gold in California. So her father packed up all her things, deposited her back with the great aunt, and took off for the West and swore he would send for her as soon as he struck it rich. She never heard from him again. She insisted he must have died en route because she believed he truly loved her, and would never have abandoned her.

"Her great aunt and uncle were kind and raised her as their own granddaughter. She was sent to school—through the eighth grade, which was quite an accomplishment in those days, when schooling, for a girl at least, was over by age ten. It was at school that she struck up a fast friendship with Ophelia Dunbar, the little girl who shared her desk. They seated you in alphabetical order. Coyne and Dunbar. The friendship lasted till the end of her life. It was only a matter of time until the serious, dark-eyed girl met Ophelia's brother John Milton. He was a couple of years older, and for whatever reason, decided that this serious, dark-eyed girl needed a protector, so he took it upon himself to make sure this orphaned friend of his sister had another friend—one who was bigger and of the opposite sex.

"When Miss Peg was thirteen and done with schooling, her great-uncle, who was a hatmaker, began teaching her the millinery trade. Every girl learned to sew by the time she was six. My mother was good at it and enjoyed it, especially the fancy-work as they used to call it. The embroidery and trim. She liked being a milliner, and during the Civil War, right after her great-uncle died, and her "protector" John Milton Dunbar had enlisted, she quickly found employment at a hat shop, where she was encouraged to create some of her own designs. She developed a nice following, and even managed to set aside $300 as a nest-egg for when she and John Milton would marry. They wrote to each other throughout the war. It was just a question of time and money—and if The Captain survived.

"After the war ended and she married my father and moved to Long Branch, she expected to open a millinery shop. However, my birth and her subsequent fragile health put an end to her plans to be an entrepreneur. There were two other millinery shops in town anyway: Madame Lili's, and Milady's. Curiously enough, they were good friends with each other—and with Miss Peg. It always surprised me that there was so little competitive spirit between them, but they specialized in different types of hats, so perhaps they didn't really compete. Lili created fancy expensive hats for formal and special occasions; Milady's catered to everyday summer hats. Neither of them did a thriving business in winter.

"A year and a half after their wedding, I was born, and a year and a half later, a stillborn brother, also named John Milton." Gran paused for a moment. "That put an end to my mother's ability to bear children. In truth, my mother was lucky to have lived. My Aunt Ophelia told me many years later that Miss Peg was close to death for several weeks. She was frail for the rest of her life, which was not a long one. She died when I was twenty. She was only forty-five.

"My parents had a nice, roomy house five or six blocks inland on Chelsea Avenue. Not nearly as big or as fancy as the cottages over near the bluff for the wealthy summer folks, but a nice house. Ten or twelve rooms, as I recall. With a big sprawling porch. All the houses had big porches then. There was the front parlor and the back parlor, the dining room, The Captain's study, kitchen, several bedrooms, and even a room in the cellar fitted out with washtubs for laundry. And on the top floor, the servants' rooms.

"We had two who lived in. There was the cook, who also did

all the shopping and serving. We had a lot of cooks over the years. A Dora and a Nora, and several Marys. Finally, my father announced that the cook would be called 'Mary' regardless of her given name. It was easier that way. I don't know why they never stayed with us very long. Maybe since there were only the three of us, The Captain didn't pay that well. Cooks were usually the best-paid servants in Long Branch. The folks with big families and a lot of servants paid a cook at least two or three times what my father ever paid any of the Marys.

"Then there was Aggie, our maid. She took charge of the house, since Miss Peg was frail and not supposed to be on her feet for long. Aggie was with us forever. Even after my Mother died and I got married, she stayed on to look after The Captain. Then we had Hester who lived in town and came three times a week to help with the sweeping and the laundry. She was a colored woman, born free, and honest and reliable. Her son Marcellus was a couple of years older than I was, and my father had him helping out in the back room of the dry-goods store when he wasn't in school.

"My Aunt Ophelia and Uncle Cork were particularly close to us," continued Gran. "Uncle Cork seldom talked about his youth. He said it was hard and sad and hungry. He was born Daniel Patrick Corcoran in 1838, in County Cork, Ireland. By the time he was ten or twelve, he had lost four younger siblings and his mother to whatever diseases were caused by starvation. His father was an out-of-work laborer of some kind, who usually drank whatever wages he might have earned long before he brought them home—if and when he ever came home.

"When his mother died, Uncle Cork packed up whatever was left in the house, and walked all the way to Dublin, sleeping wherever it was dry, and hiring himself out to do odd-jobs. One man who hired him to sweep up or move boxes suggested he might go to America. His cousin was a brick-layer and might want an apprentice. Since Uncle Cork was always a believer that if something falls in your lap, you should sit down and make a lap, he saved whatever he could, asked his kind patron to write to his cousin, and sure enough, within the year, passage money had been advanced to him by one Samuel Clancy of Elizabeth, New Jersey.

"My Uncle Cork came to America all alone. He had a name and address paper pinned to his coat, since his ability to read and write was limited. He knew his basic ABCs, and could write his name, but it was an effort for him to do more.

"The Clancys liked the skinny fourteen-year-old redheaded fellow with the sly grin and map of Ireland stamped on his face, and were happy to let him board with them as part of his apprenticeship agreement. Uncle Cork wasn't in town for two weeks before he wound up in a fight with a scrappy fellow a year or so younger and half-a-head shorter who lived three doors down. But right after they exchanged black eyes, Daniel Patrick Corcoran and John Milton Dunbar became best of friends till their dying days. Neither one of them could remember what they originally fought about.

"For them too, it was only a matter of time before Uncle Cork (between Corcoran and County Cork, it was natural for the nickname to stick) met the rest of the literary-named Dunbars, a fact completely lost on him.

But Ophelia, with her saucy manners and dark hair appealed to him from the start, even though she was only nine or ten. And she thought her brother's friend, with hair the color of an Irish setter and whose brogue became thicker each year he was away from the Auld Sod, was the handsomest young man she had ever seen. She took it upon herself—when she was fifteen, and he close to twenty—to teach him (secretly) how to read and write better. She was obviously a good teacher, since my uncle not only learned well, but actually enjoyed reading, except his tastes ran to dime-novels and the *Police Gazette*. Aunt Phee said she didn't really care what he read so long as he learned from it. I suppose Uncle Cork learned that he wanted a more exciting trade than brick-laying, so after the war (he had enlisted and eventually became a sergeant), he applied for a position on the Jersey City Police Force, which he believed would be a big step up. The day his application was accepted, he asked Aunt Phee to marry him.

"I suppose lifelong friendship runs in my family, Kate. My aunt and uncle were much more than just relatives in our house. They were also my father and mother's best friends—long before they became related by marriage. They were like second parents to me. They stayed with us almost every weekend during the summer, and always came for holidays. And they were always bringing me dolls and games and velvet capes and an enormous amount of candy. They spoiled me thoroughly, since they never had children of their own. Once I was married, Aunt Phee confided she had always had problems. Her 'monthlies' were more like once-or-twice 'yearlies,' and three different doctors told her if she ever had children, it would be a miracle.

"My mother was born a Catholic, and so was Uncle Cork, but I don't think either of them cared for religion very much. My mother said that she went to church, prayed hard for her father's return, lit candles every day for nearly two years and he never came back. When she prayed in her bedroom for Captain Johnny Dunbar to return from the war, her prayers were answered. She lost faith in churches and candles.

"But when my father became mayor, he realized it was important to be a regular church-goer, so we joined the Lutheran Church, mainly to keep the family together. My Aunt Elizabeth, Uncle Walter's wife was Lutheran, and very active in the church. So I went to Sunday School, and we did all the things we were supposed to do, but I don't think we were especially religious. Or active."

After two days on the train, I had discovered something interesting about my grandmother: she was a fine storyteller,

25

and could lapse into her Uncle Cork's Irish brogue as if it were her own. I was learning my family history and being entertained simultaneously.

There were things about Gran that never showed up in the photographs. Like the way she watched you when she thought you weren't looking. Like her posture—which was excellent. Even at 79 years old, she retained her full height of nearly five-foot-five and insisted on wearing high-heeled shoes every day. She never wore slacks or pedal pushers. Never owned a pair of sneakers. Never wore a turtleneck sweater or Bermuda shorts. Wouldn't be caught dead leaving the house without a hat and gloves, and positively refused to carry a shoulder-strap pocketbook. She claimed a lady only carried a handbag. But she stopped wearing corsets as soon as brassieres were introduced, while most women her age remained true to their stiff undergarments with laces, hooks and stays. Of course she wore a girdle. Every woman did. I did.

Her brown hair was mostly gray, even from my earliest memory, but her brown eyes were always lively, and she had a way of seeing past the question you asked, and answering the three other questions you hadn't gotten around to posing yet. She claimed she had lovely teeth until she had children. Then they grew soft and began to rot. By the time she was fifty she had had enough, so she had them all removed and replaced with dentures, and never regretted it. She said she got tired of monthly visits to the dentist.

My mother, on the other hand, had more bridges than the East River, and swore she did not want to die with her teeth in a glass. Eventually, she needed a complete set of dentures too. It was either teeth in a glass, or pieces of teeth in a glass. Either way, nothing original was left. At 79, I still have all my own teeth and am grateful that they give me little trouble.

"But if you think Long Branch was a sleepy little seashore village, you are sadly mistaken, Kate," she said as she continued her story. "It was a fast town. A sporting town." She explained that on one end was Monmouth Racetrack, built not long after she was born. On the other end, near the ocean, were all the fancy hotels, each with its own whiskey bar and casino. And in between were dozens of hotels, whiskey bars and casinos. Anyone who wished could find a card or dice game or a roulette wheel on which to lose his money.

But it was General Grant who put Long Branch on the map as a summer resort.

After the Civil War, Ulysses Grant was the most famous person in the country: the Hero of Appomattox. From a rather ignoble existence in Illinois, clerking in his father's leather shop, he was now feted by every wealthy capitalist vying for his attention. Mrs. Grant had been a Southern belle from Missouri before she married, and it was said Grant accepted all the invitations from the high-living millionaires in an effort to please her, or maybe to make up for being a poor provider for most of their marriage.

Several Eastern bankers and merchants and industrialists had "cottages" in Long Branch. "That was an understatement, if ever there was one," said Gran. "Like calling Buckingham Palace a house in town." The "cottages" could be twenty or thirty rooms, designed in mid-Victorian splendor. They had turrets and porches, balconies and widow's walks, and pillars and tons—literally tons—of wrought iron railings and "gingerbread." There were square windows, rectangular windows, round windows, arched windows, and most popularly, floor-to-ceiling windows that could open out onto the porch or second-story balcony. It also let in the cool ocean breezes. On the inside, everything was done in ornate gold leaf, even for a summer place.

"It wasn't called the Gilded Age for nothing," she said, "and if it was a Gilded Age, Long Branch was the Gilded Strand."

Anyway, Gran went on to say that one of those wealthy industrialists had invited the Grants to spend a fortnight as their guests. This was before he was President, but it was no secret that he was expected to run — and win — in the next election. The Grants had a lovely time, being entertained by everybody who was anybody, and even a few nobodies.

The Grants enjoyed themselves so much, the story went, that some of their wealthy friends decided once he became President, that it would be splendid for the town if he had a cottage there himself. Grant declined. He said a suitable "cottage" might cost forty or fifty thousand dollars, and he did not have that kind of money. His friends, not to be discouraged, offered to buy a cottage for him as a gift.

It was well known that the Grants were accustomed to receiving and accepting expensive gifts. After the war, "a grateful nation" supplied him with three fine houses: one in Galena, Illinois, where he had lived before the war, one in Philadelphia, which he promptly sold, and one in Washington. And he had been given thousands and thousands of dollars worth of silver and gold swords and trays and cups and artwork and jewelry gifts for Mrs. Grant. Then there were the carriages and horses. Grant was a fine one for horses. He had a keen sense of horse quality and his team was always the best in town. Then, of course, he received hundreds of boxes of the finest cigars in the world.

Grant, in a rare moment of moral conscience, said no, he could not accept such a lavish and expensive gift. It wouldn't be right. But his friends, who were accustomed to having their way, were undeterred in their efforts to make the President of the United States a bona fide resident of Long Branch. They came up with the novel idea of presenting the "cottage" to *Mrs.* Grant as a gift. It was also a well known fact that *she* never had a problem accepting expensive gifts either. So there it was. *Mrs.* Grant owned the "cottage" — a modest one, by Long Branch standards. Only fifteen rooms or so, in a prime location. Right on the bluff overlooking the ocean, just set back enough from Ocean Avenue so the President could have some privacy. It was a wonderful investment for Grant's friends. They bought up additional lots, and just as they surmised, people began to flock to Long Branch, even for a day, to have the chance to see and possibly shake hands with the President. Property values soared. Everyone benefited.

Gran was enjoying her reminiscences, and I found myself enjoying them as well. "I remember once when I was around seven or eight," she said, "I was walking with my mother, and General Grant passed us on the street. He was President of the United States then, but he never seemed to mind being referred to as 'General.' Naturally he tipped his hat to Mother and nodded, and she nodded and smiled, and nudged me to make a curtsey, which I did. It must have tickled him, since he had a fondness for children, and he came over to us, removed his hat, bowed deeply to me, and kissed my hand. I nearly fell over! Mother nearly fell over! But the best and most endearing part was that the general always remembered me after that, and would invariably bow and smile to me, and once, when he was driving in his carriage and saw me, he winked and blew me a kiss!" Gran beamed from ear to ear reliving that memory from seventy years before, and I grinned back. "Wow," I thought, "Gran had her hand kissed by General Grant."

"Now that I think about it, Kate, my father idolized General Grant," my grandmother continued. "Do you remember the photograph I have on the mantel?" My great-grandfather was standing next to General Grant, who was wearing civilian clothes. It was inscribed in a bold handwriting, "To Captain Dunbar with sincere regard, Ulysses S. Grant." "It was my father's proudest possession. One of mine, too," she said.

"I never knew him except in passing—and I was just a little girl and the memories are little-girl memories. Sometimes my mother and I would see him on the street or driving his carriage. He liked to drive himself—hated having a driver. He would always tip his hat and smile at us. He knew who were. The mayor's family. Sometimes he even greeted my mother by name. Miss Peg, he would call her. Everybody called her Miss Peg. I don't think anyone ever called her Mrs. Dunbar. Aunt *Elizabeth* was Mrs. Dunbar. Mrs. Grant would usually nod pleasantly to my mother, but I doubt they ever spoke. She was more inclined to put on airs. Besides, we—my family—were the natives. We lived there all year round. There was always a strict dividing line between the natives and the opulent visitors.

"The general cut a fine figure in Long Branch," Gran continued. "All us 'natives' were very used to seeing him sitting on his porch smoking a cigar, or walking with Mrs. Grant along the bluff in the evening or driving his carriage along Ocean Avenue. He had such a splendid team. Four jet black horses. The Captain said they were Arabians, bred for speed. And the general was certainly a speeder. He would race down the street at a gallop most of the time—unless there was a great deal of traffic, which seemed to irritate him no end.

"One time, an old soldier who had been hired as one of the town constables, gave him a ticket for speeding. Grant was President of the United States at the time and was appalled at the effrontery. 'Don't you know who I am?' he said as he glowered at the old man. 'I do indeed, General,' said the old soldier, 'but it's my duty to give a ticket to speeders. You were speeding, and I was doing my duty.' Well, if nothing else, Grant was a fair man, and he knew that the old soldier was absolutely right. He paid his $2 fine right then and there, and commended the constable for doing his duty. Afterwards, he would occasionally drive down to where the old soldier was usually posted, and pass the time of day with him, talking over old times at Petersburg."

My grandmother continued her saga of the Grants in Long Branch. Grant's oldest son, Colonel Fred Grant, also bought a "cottage," but for him money was not a problem. Col. Grant had married extremely well. "His wife was from Chicago, and was the sister of Mrs. Potter Palmer, you know." Gran paused as if she expected me to know something. I looked at her blankly. "Your mother would know about Mrs. Potter Palmer," Gran said assuredly. "She was to Chicago what Mrs. Astor was to New York." With that statement, I was convinced that my mother would know every detail about the life of Mrs. Potter Palmer. She cared about those things.

"General Sherman and General Sheridan also bought 'cottages' down the street from the Grants. They were all very good friends," Gran said. "We would see Phil Sheridan riding down the street. He seldom walked. They said it was because he was so short. Whatever it was, he rode very tall. Like Napoleon. And he barely ever nodded or tipped his hat to anyone. He had this air about him—like the wind was blowing in from the stables.

"General Sherman also had a fondness for children," Gran continued. "When I was in the 3rd or 4th grade, there was a story about town that a couple of the older boys had been playing ball near Sherman's cottage. The ball was thrown poorly and landed in the hedges near the porch, where the great man was relaxing and reading his newspaper. He rose slowly, marched down the steps, retrieved the ball, and looked very sternly at two twelve-year-old boys who must have been shaking in their shoes.

"'Front and center, men,'" said Gran in a gruff voice doing her best imitation of General Sherman. "The boys very cautiously slinked forward into the yard and stood facing the general, who hitched his shoulders a bit, to encourage the boys to stand at attention." I found myself grinning and sitting-at-attention. "'Identify yourselves,'" said Gran-as-the-general, "and the boys replied in very small voices, 'I'm Willie So-and-So' and 'I'm Johnny Such-and-Such...sir.' 'Well, lads,' Sherman said in his deep voice, 'it seems your artillery is badly aimed.' And with that, he spent the next fifteen or twenty minutes helping the boys throw the ball straighter, harder and faster. And when he was done, he told them to come back for inspection when they thought they had sufficiently improved.

Well," said Gran, with a smile on her face reminiscing about that half-forgotten incident, "when word spread through school, nearly every boy in town started walking by Sherman's cottage tossing a ball in the air, hoping the general would come out to play. And from time to time, he did.

"But I'll tell you this, Kate, when General Grant was dying some years later—he had throat cancer, you know—it nearly broke the town's heart. Grant had lost all his money in some stock swindle, and about the only thing he had left was the cottage. It was the one thing he wouldn't sell. Actually, since it was in *Mrs.* Grant's name, he *couldn't* sell it. The wealthy businessmen who bought it for him did him more of a favor than he knew. He was writing his memorials then so he could provide for his family. We would see him on his porch with a pad and pen.

"A committee of us natives would send over biscuits and pies and bread, and leave them for the general with their compliments, that last year before he died. Aunt Elizabeth sent jams and preserves. She was a marvelous cook. The Captain was still mayor so he arranged for the flower shops to deliver fresh flowers twice a week. And when anyone from the Grant household went to our dry-goods store, my father only charged the wholesale price.

"And I remember when my cousin Edna got finally got married. (She was Uncle Walter's youngest daughter and gave piano lessons in town. Her young man was a salesman at the music store, and they had been keeping company for nearly ten years while he saved up enough money for a house. He was very proud and refused to take help from Uncle Walter.) Anyway, Dunbars came from all over and we had them to dinner. There must have been twenty of us! Mother had hired extra kitchen help, and one of the Marys made a delicious custard dessert. When The Captain saw it, he sent his plate back to the kitchen with instructions to send it to General Grant, since it was soft and would not irritate his diseased throat. With that, everyone else offered to send their desserts to the general, too. So Miss Peg stood up and insisted that fresh custard would be made in the morning for General Grant, and we should please enjoy ours.

"Oh yes, my father loved General Grant. The whole town did. After he died, my father stopped running for mayor. The Captain and Uncle Cork took the train to New York City to march in his funeral cortege with his old regiment. Years later, when Sherman died, there was a big funeral procession for him in New York too. I remember the day. It was in January or February. Miserable weather. Cold and rainy. The Captain and Uncle Cork took the train and marched with the Grand Army of the Republic. They were getting on in years by then. Past fifty, I would imagine. And a half-dozen younger men in town, maybe thirty years old—just babies when Sherman marched to the sea—also took the train to New York City to pay their respects to a great man who wasn't so great that he couldn't spare a few minutes to teach some young boys how to throw a ball.

"Long Branch loved General Grant, but the boys idolized General Sherman. Nobody cared too much for General Sheridan. I don't think anybody remembered when he died."

"Of course the best thing about Long Branch was the beach. Ah, Kate," Gran continued, "you've grown up with photographs of Betty Grable wearing a skimpy bathing suit, showing off everything she owns. She would have been run out of town when I was a girl. We wore more at the beach than half the women today wear in the middle of the winter. Back then, very few women actually owned a bathing costume. Even people who lived at the beach all year long like we did. People rented them."

I looked at my grandmother in disbelief at the thought of wearing something on intimate parts of my body that had been worn by complete strangers.

She must have noticed my shock and grinned, "Oh, indeed they did, Kate." She went on to tell me about people at the beach who operated bathhouses, and rented you a bathing costume for a small fee. Of course I knew about bathhouses. Even in 1947, people still went there to change into bathing suits and rent lockers for their regular clothes.

Gran continued, "I don't know exactly what they did about sizes. I was only a child. I imagine they were more like small, medium and large, and the man in charge would look at you, size you up, literally, and hand you a costume. It didn't matter how well or how badly it fit, since there were so many layers, everything was covered except your face and your hands." She enumerated on her fingers. "There were bloomers, a skirt, a blouse, a vest, stockings and shoes, and a hat. They would call it their nine-piece costume. Maybe there were more pieces I've forgotten. And everything was made of wool."

"Wool!" I exclaimed, "It must have been dreadful!"

"Actually," Gran commented, "I think the worst part was getting it wet. The wool soaked up the water, and you would come out of the ocean so water-logged you could hardly stand up. I think that's why most women did little more than wade in up to their ankles or knees. No woman I ever knew would venture into the water past her waist without a strong man holding her hand. Between the undertow and the weight of all that wet wool, she could sink like a rock!"

My eyes widened. "But it was so unsanitary," I began. "Renting suits that somebody else—"

Gran shook her head and cut me off. "We didn't know very much about hygiene in those days," she said. "Germs hadn't been discovered. Doctors didn't even wash their hands before they operated. That renting a bathing suit might be unsanitary was about the last thing we thought about."

Gran's mouth twitched, suppressing a chuckle as she noticed my incredulous expression. "Beach blankets hadn't been discovered either, dear. If you got tired, you plopped yourself right down on the sand, wet bathing outfits or not. And even the men and women who strolled up and down the beach in their fine clothes would think nothing of plunking themselves right on the sand. No wonder the hotels would hire people to do nothing except sweep."

My mouth was open at the thought of elegant ladies and gentlemen sitting directly in the sand. Edison had already invented the light bulb; Bell had invented the telephone. Who was the genius that suggested bringing a blanket to the beach?

"But just listen to me," Gran said. "Rambling on about old-fashioned bathing suits and sweeping. I must be boring you silly, Kate. An old lady and all her babbling."

"Not at all, Gran," I said very sincerely. "I don't know very much about you or your side of the family. I hardly saw you when we were growing up. It's interesting." The truth was, it was *very* interesting, and I was enjoying her ramblings about her childhood and her family and how she lived a lot more than she could have imagined. Or I could have imagined, for that matter. I liked it better than Hemingway.

Chapter 2

It hadn't dawned on me that I might actually enjoy taking this trip with my seventy-nine year-old grandmother. I figured I was doing a good deed. I also figured that it was a free trip, and that I might get some time to see Pasadena—or even Los Angeles. Maybe even the Pacific Ocean. I had never seen an ocean before. And a train trip across the country would have wonderful scenery, anyway.

But here I was, enjoying my grandmother's company and hearing about her youth so long ago. Once or twice I mentioned Mollie Brown, but she shrugged me off. She wasn't ready to talk about it. Now that I am that age myself, it occurs to me that goodbyes are just another step along the way, and the older we get, the less frightening it becomes. It is also a "freeing" experience. It becomes a part of your past, and once the goodbye is said, you are free to move on. And if you are wise, or strong, or healthy, or whatever the word is, you take the good of that person with you, and let the bad be "interred with their bones," like Shakespeare said. Gran would talk about Mollie Brown if and when she was ready. I would not press.

"Did I ever tell you about your grandfather, Kate? Your real grandfather, Henry Cobbs?" she asked the afternoon we were crossing the flat expanse of northern New Mexico. I could see the outline of the Rocky Mountains far off in the distance but we were on the southern route and wouldn't be crossing them according to the conductor. I shook my head. I knew Gran had been married twice, and that her first husband had died when my mother was three and Uncle Henry was a baby. Neither had memories of their real father. Charlie Stanfield had raised them and legally adopted them, so their last names were Stanfield, and they both adored "Pops."

"I don't know very much about Henry's father, except that his name was Francis Cobbs and he had been a school teacher in New York," Gran began. "He enlisted during the war, and came down with malaria or typhoid. Some kind of war fever, I suppose. He was always sickly after that, and died when Henry was five. His mother's name was Clara. She died when your mother was twelve. I was very fond of her, even though I didn't see her often. Your mother was named for them both: Clara Frances. Anyway, since your great-grandmother Cobbs had also taught school earlier in her life, she took a position as governess with the Mills family, who lived in Yonkers. Mr. Mills was a vice president or something with the railroads, and they had eight or nine children.

"From what Henry told me, the Millses were kind folks and were very good to his mother and to him. They had a little house on the Mills' property, and when he wasn't in school, Henry would help out in the stable or the yard or wherever he could be useful.

"I don't ever remember meeting Henry Cobbs. He was just 'there.' He was six years older than I was, and had been coming to Long Branch each summer with his mother and the rest of the Mills family for quite some time. Mr. Mills had a cottage and came every summer for years and years. It must have had at least twenty-five rooms, and good-sized ones at that. With the eight or nine children, plus the mister and missus, plus the tutor and the governess and the nanny and all the servants, they probably used every nook and cranny in that house. I remember Henry telling me that they had two whole rooms just for storing their trunks."

She continued. "Henry's mother came down with the family every summer to take care of the younger Mills children. There were always plenty of them. One would grow too old for a governess, and another would be on the way. By the time the last ones were done needing a governess, the older ones had married and had children of their own who were exactly the right age for Clara Cobb's services.

"Henry would tag along when he was little, and when he got to be around ten, he went down to the railroad station to run errands for the rich folks when they arrived. He would hail their carriages, or help load their trunks on the wagons, or send off telegrams, and they would usually give him a nickel for his efforts. Sometimes he would make twenty or thirty cents in a day if the train was crowded or if it rained. Henry loved when it rained. He'd borrow his mother's big black umbrella and race down to the station, a dozen blocks away, and when the train came in, he would go up to one of the women and escort her inside the station under his big umbrella so she wouldn't get wet. Then he would run back to the train, and escort another woman inside. Then, when their carriages came, or the station wagons came from the hotels, he would escort them out to the carriage or wagon—under his umbrella. Sometimes he might even get a dime for it. One rainy day, he made eighty cents. That was a LOT of money in those days, especially for a ten-year-old boy. Hmmpf, fifty cents could nearly buy out my father's entire candy counter.

"Anyway, when Henry was about twelve, he found himself with extra time on his hands at the Mills' cottage, and was tired of running errands at the station, so he marched into my father's dry-goods store and asked to see The Captain. He looked my father right in the eye and asked if he could use a likely young fellow to work in the store. Well, The Captain always had a warm place in his heart for an enterprising lad, having been one himself, and with his bad arm, he always needed someone to help stock the shelves.

"So Henry started at the store every afternoon for three or four hours, and was paid fifty-cents a day. That was extremely generous back then, when the head clerk only made $7 or $8 week during the peak summer season. But my father knew that Henry and his mother could use the money, and like I said, he had a warm spot for an orphan boy who could hustle. All the Dunbars admired enterprise, and if nothing else, Henry was a hustler! Besides, the Mills family, with the eight or nine children, were very good customers at the store. It didn't hurt to hire Henry.

"He sent us a Christmas card that year. And in March, he wrote to The Captain and said that the Mills family would be arriving in mid-June, and mightn't he work at the store again? And so on and so on every summer. Henry made himself very useful. He not only stocked shelves, but made deliveries, helped the customers load their carriages or wagons, took inventory, maintained the order book. By the time he was seventeen, he could practically run the store himself.

"When Henry announced he planned to attend City College in New York City, The Captain was delighted, and suggested he study business. I think my father offered to help him with the tuition, but Mr. Mills had already done that. He was very well off, and had always treated Henry and his mother generously. But Henry said City College was free, and all he had to do was keep up his grades, which wasn't too hard for him since he was a bright fellow with a strong drive to get ahead.

"All through his college days, Henry would spend the summer working with The Captain, taking on more and more responsibilities, and receiving appropriately raised salaries. He didn't stock the shelves anymore—they hired another "likely young fellow" of around twelve for those duties, and Marcellus had been promoted to maintaining the stockroom and driving the wagon. My father could be a demanding man to work for sometimes, but if you had hustle, he was always ready to help you along. He said it was a lesson he had learned from Isaac Warren.

"Right before Henry started his senior year, my father invited him to dinner. Henry had been in our house a hundred times over the years, but never for dinner. Mostly he came to help out with the heavy work like moving furniture, or to drop something off for The Captain. But this time was different. I will never forget it! My mother used our white lace tablecloth, and one of the Marys made a roast with all the trimmings. I was only fifteen at the time, but I was starting to look at Henry like you young girls look at Tyrone Power.

"I was at that awkward age, Kate, when a girl gets the giggles when she sees a young fellow she likes. I had been manufacturing dozens of reasons to go to my father's store that summer, but the truth was I had such a crush on Henry! But I behaved so silly then—fits of giggles as soon as he said hello.

"Henry Cobbs was a fine looking young man. Tall and slim, with dark hair. Your mother and Uncle Henry both favor him a little. And Henry had grown a fantastic moustache! It came out straight at the sides, and then dropped down to his bottom lip like a festoon." Gran's finger drew a picture on her upper lip. "But to Henry, I was still The Captain's little girl. I hadn't yet put my hair up or lowered my skirts.

"After dinner, my father invited Henry to sit with him in the front parlor while he smoked his evening cigar and had a wee-drop of whatever spirits he was in the mood for that night. This time he offered some to Henry, who, by that time, also smoked cigars and enjoyed a whiskey. I had a feeling it must have been a very special occasion for him to treat Henry like that."

I smiled when Gran talked about her father treating my grandfather-to-be as an equal. I remember when I was about ten, how my father had had a talk with Margie's husband-to-be, and wanted him to study business and come into *our* family business, which was, in some way, connected to the Pittsburgh Paint Company. We didn't own it, but there was a strong connection.

My paternal great-grandfather had started an investment company shortly after the Civil War and had made a fortune by buying a large number of shares of Pittsburgh Paint, some of the steel company stocks and other Pittsburgh-connected industries. My great-grandfather Atcheson, they said, was on very good terms with Carnegie and Frick, and once had even sat at a banquet table with John D. Rockefeller. By the time Daddy was born, our family was very wealthy. Daddy was sent to the finest prep school in Pittsburgh and went to Brown University. Then he came home and went right into the family business, which demanded little on his part, and left him plenty of time for polo and golf and skeet shooting. Margie's husband, however, preferred to study civil engineering.

Gran continued, "The gist of the their conversation was that The Captain was planning to open another dry-goods store in Asbury Park, about a half-hour's drive away, and figured he would need somebody to run Long Branch. Henry thought it was a good opportunity. Shore towns were growing and dry-goods stores provided the staples. He envisioned a whole chain of them. Chain stores were becoming rather popular.

"The next summer I was sixteen—nearly seventeen—and Henry stopped looking at me like The Captain's little girl. I had reached my full height, and I put my hair up and started wearing grownup clothes—with a bustle. Do you remember when you were little, Kate, and everyone would come for Christmas? I would let you and your sisters put on some of my clothes from the 'olden days.' You girls had such a grand time!"

Even today I love thinking back to those days years ago when I would put on one of Gran's old dresses from the 18-somethings, with the bustles and the flounces, and the brocades and buttons—and the hats! Oh, those hats! Gran had more hats than anyone I ever knew! Hats with feathers and flowers, and birds and ribbons. I remember one hat was so large I nearly disappeared under it. Actually, I don't really remember it at all from memory, but Daddy took a picture of me. I was around four. If you stood the hat on its end it might have been as tall as I was! That photo has been in our family albums since before the

Depression! One day I will to show it to my little great-granddaughters.

Gran went on. "When a girl reached sixteen, she was considered old enough to attend a hop. Those were the dances the hotels gave for the younger set. Miss Peg had bought me three new summer party-dresses and a pair of high-heeled slippers. I practiced wearing them for a month so I wouldn't wobble or trip. And she let me wear her pearl necklace, too. So there I was at my first hop, feeling very shy, sitting with my friends at the edge of the ballroom looking mostly at the floor, worried that nobody would ask me to dance and that I would be a wallflower. Then I saw two patent leather shoes pointing directly in front of me, and when I looked up, there was Henry Cobbs looking especially handsome in his pearl gray summer suit. 'May I have the pleasure of this dance, Miss Dunbar?' he asked. I think I must have blushed from head to toe, partly because none of my friends had been asked to dance yet, but mostly because he was the young man I had admired for a long time. I took his hand and we danced. He was not a very good dancer, but I was. My mother and Aunt Phee taught me all the latest steps, and I had a good sense of rhythm.

"'You are all grown up now and very beautiful,' Henry said rather formally, 'so I suppose I ought to call you Miss Dunbar, or Miss Louise.' 'Oh don't be silly, Henry, you've known me since I was six,' I said. 'And I've been waiting for you to grow up,' he answered very sincerely.

"At first I assumed he was just looking after his boss' daughter, or maybe just being kind. I wasn't permitted to actually keep company with a young man until I was seventeen. The Captain was very strict about that. But Henry kept showing up at the different hops and parties, and by the time I was seventeen and he began to court me in earnest, it was like we had known each other forever, which, in fact, we had.

"We married when I was twenty—six months after my mother passed. She loved Henry dearly, and of course he was like a son to The Captain. Nobody in the family thought it would be disrespectful to Miss Peg's memory to postpone the wedding, although it was a small one and somewhat subdued. Just family and close friends, like the Millses. You remember my silver tea service on the hall table?" I nodded, remembering Gran's beautiful silver tray with the teapot and coffee pot and cream pitcher and sugar bowl. "That was their wedding gift to Henry and me. It was very expensive at the time, so I imagine it must be worth a thousand dollars or more now. I used it very sparingly. I am quite sure it was polished many more times than it was used.

"Henry and I bought a small house on Fourth Avenue, a half dozen blocks from the store, and we were very happy. I loved him dearly, and he was crazy about me. He died when your mother was a little past three, Kate. Uncle Henry was a year old, and I was twenty-five. It was February '93, and we were having a spell of the most terrible weather. There was one of those dreadful nor'easter storms, where the winds were fifty, sixty miles an hour and the rain and sleet came in waves. And of course, since we lived by the sea, it was even worse.

"Anyway, the storm was so bad that Henry closed the store early. Nobody was out shopping and his clerks were just as anxious to get home as he was. When he came home, he put on dry clothes and we sat by the fire and had cocoa and played with the babies. Then the fire bell and the whistle sounded. We knew what that meant. The ocean was dangerously close to the bluff, and several cottages might be swept away if something wasn't done immediately. Henry quickly changed into work clothes, his warm sweater and his heavy oilcloth coat, hat and boots and rushed down to the fire station along with every other able-bodied man in town.

"My father went too, although he couldn't do much with his bad arm, and he was past fifty, besides. But since he had been mayor for so long, he knew every inch of Long Branch and just about every person in town as well. So he handed out the sandbags and shovels and ropes, and sent the younger men out to build a barricade. He stayed up all night at the firehouse, making sure the men had sandwiches and hot coffee and whatever dry clothing was on hand.

"Henry came home at four in the morning. I had put the children to bed, and I even tried sleeping, but it wasn't much use. I stayed on Henry's side of the bed to keep it warm, since I knew he'd be chilled. He was. Chilled to the bone. I gave him a little brandy, and put him straight to bed. The next morning, he had a raging fever. The doctor came and said it was pneumonia. That was a killer in those days, Kate. Now they give you a miracle drug and you're fine in a week. But not then. Henry died three days later."

Gran looked at me wistfully. It had probably been years since she talked to anyone about her first husband, dead for more than fifty years. "He would have been thirty-two that June, Kate." I didn't know what to say, so I said nothing, but I smiled back wistfully and reached over and placed my hand over hers. It was the perfect gesture. Gran smiled. "It was such a long, long time ago, Kate. I think Mollie and I may be the only ones left who remember him. The children have no memory of him at all.

"I was devastated," she continued after a long pause. "I loved Henry dearly and my heart was broken. But I was young and I had two little children to raise. So my father suggested, insisted, actually, that I sell our little house and move back with him. He was all alone except for Aggie, and he missed Henry almost as much as I did. I tell you, Kate, the death of my mother and Henry hit him very hard. Henry was like his own son. My father was never the same afterwards. So I moved back with him. Aunt Phee and Uncle Cork were happy about it, since they worried about The Captain being alone so much. He sold the store in Asbury Park. He couldn't handle both, he said, and his heart wasn't in it anymore. Our old house was plenty big for everyone, including Miss Cray, the nurse I had hired to tend the children."

Gran's elbow was resting on the window ledge of the parlor car, and she slapped her face in amazement and said, "Lord, Lord! How have I managed to dredge up Miss Cray?" She shook her head and laughed. "You cannot believe the silly little details that come back to you in old age! But then again, Miss Cray was one of those people who are hard to forget." She frowned, thinking hard. "I don't think she had a first name. For sure I didn't know it, and even if I did, I would never have ventured to use it. She was one of those women who would be born Miss-Something and die Miss-Something with no trace of familiarity in between. I think today she would have been in the WACs, or maybe a matron in a women's prison.

"Miss Cray was a tall, thin woman, flat as a board all the way around, like Olive Oyl in the funny papers. She ran our house. She ran the children and for certain, she ran me—then. For whatever reason, she was kindly disposed to Henry's authority, and when we lived with The Captain, she pampered him like a puppy dog. Needless to say, she and Aggie didn't get on since Aggie had unquestionably been in charge of The Captain's house—and The Captain. Aggie threatened to leave every other day, but of course we wouldn't hear of it.

"I suppose I could have been my own nanny," Gran mused, "but it wasn't proper in those days. If you were of a certain station, you were expected to have a nurse for the children. And since I never was inclined to goo and gurgle over babies, I was grateful to have Miss Cray, flat and bossy as she was. And she was very good with the children. She was strict, and she made them mind, but I don't think they were afraid of her. I, on the other hand, was petrified.

"Since I had idle hours to fill, I began going to the store to handle the books. I am a pretty fair bookkeeper. And sometimes, if it was busy, or if we were shorthanded, I helped out in front. It was something to do, and I needed to keep busy."

I was amazed at how little I knew about my grandmother. Mother had told me practically nothing about her family, except that Charlie Stanfield was her stepfather. Mother was first and always an Atcheson. She was never a Stanfield or Cobbs or Dunbar. She never used her maiden name unless it was absolutely required, preferring to sign Clara F. (for Frances) Atcheson.

Gran continued her story. "Some of my friends began introducing me to eligible young men after a decent time. I went out on occasion, but there was no one to interest me. Time passed, and in the summer of '96, Charlie Stanfield walked into our store." Gran smiled. She was obviously enjoying a much happier memory after the past half-hour of poignancy.

"I was in the front, folding and stocking a shipment of towels on the shelves. Charlie walked in, saw me, nodded, and asked if we had straw hats. I nodded back and pointed to a counter right in smack front of him where there were a dozen or more straw hats on display. Charlie never stopped talking! He talked to me, to the other clerks, to the other customers, but mostly to me. Oh, Pops was always a talker. You know that, Kate."

I knew Pops the same way I knew Gran. Perhaps even better. He was more accessible. And like Gran said, he loved to talk. Pops died only three years ago, and everybody loved him. During this last war, when he was well past seventy, he would come down to Uncle Henry's plant (actually it was Pops' plant originally and Uncle Henry went to work with him after he graduated Lehigh) to check on things and make sure we were all doing our jobs. He talked to everybody from the janitor on up. He remembered all their names, and they loved him for it.

I could see a sparkle in my grandmother's eyes as she relived those old memories. "Here he was," she said, "a total stranger in our shop, and he starts telling me—or anyone who would listen—how some fat lady sat on his hat on the train to Philadelphia and crushed it. Then he announced that his doctor insisted he relax for a fortnight because he was working too hard. Said he had never seen the ocean before. Said he was staying at the Ocean House Hotel and asked me if their food was any good. He never let me answer, all the while trying on straw hats. Then, when he had found a hat he liked, he asked me if I liked it. He didn't let me answer that either, and announced that he preferred derbies, but they made him sweat in the summer. I found myself laughing, and so did the other clerks and the customers, and he laughed, too. And you know yourself, Kate, Pops had the merriest eyes and that one dimple that nobody could resist.

"Finally, as he was paying for his new straw hat, he looked straight at me. I was still behind a counter full of towels. 'What I would really like is some company at supper,' he said. 'Would you care to join me Miss...Miss...?' I looked him right in the eye and said, 'Louise Cobbs. *Mrs.* Louise Cobbs.' I paused for effect, and Charlie blushed from ear to ear. 'Oh, I am sorry, madam, I hope I haven't offended you.' 'Not at all, Mister...Mister...' 'Charlie Stanfield,' he said, still embarrassed. 'Well, Mr. Stanfield,' I said, 'I am not offended. I am a widow.' I paused again to see how he would react. He looked up at me shyly, and I laughed and added, 'and I think I would enjoy joining you for supper.' That was it, Kate. That's how I met Pops."

My own memories of Pops were always as an old man. He had to be nearly sixty when I was born. But in the old family albums, indeed, all around Gran's house, and in a few places in our house, I saw pictures of "young" Charlie Stanfield. He was definitely not a handsome man, but he was one of the most pleasant-looking people I've ever seen. He was of average height, perhaps five-foot-nine or so, and since he was mostly bald as an older man, I suspect his hair was thinning when Gran met him. But you could still tell in the old pictures that he was outgoing and gregarious—surprising for a mechanical-type.

My grandmother went on. "We had supper together just about every night for two weeks. The Captain liked him, especially when he told us about his tool-and-die plant in Pittsburgh, and the three patents he had in his own name. The Captain always admired a man with hustle." Gran paused. She was telling me something important, I sensed, but I wasn't exactly sure what it was or why she paused. "Aunt Phee and Uncle Cork liked him," she added. "He was one of the few people who could out-blarney Uncle Cork. The children liked him—he loved children. Even Aggie and Miss Cray managed to agree about how much they liked 'Miss Louise's new beau.' And I was perfectly wild for him. By the end of his vacation, we had an understanding.

"Charlie went back to Pittsburgh, and a week later I got a letter from Miss Fanny Stanfield, Charlie's maiden aunt who had raised him since he was a child. His parents died by the time he was thirteen, and the older brother Charlie barely remembered had gone West years before. Everyone 'went West' in those days. There were great fortunes to be made.

"Aunt Fanny wrote the sweetest note, saying that Charlie had raved about his new friend Mrs. Cobbs, and that we must meet. She invited me for a week—at my convenience. I wired Aunt Phee to come and stay with The Captain and the children. I wanted someone in the house who would tuck Clara and Henry in at night. Between Miss Cray and The Captain, I was afraid they'd be forlorn. Of course she came right away. She adored your mother and Uncle Henry. And I adored Aunt Fanny!

"She was a plump, bustling, merry lady, with Charlie's single dimple. Rumor was that she had been engaged to a fellow who was killed at Antietam and she never married. But she wasn't a mournful soul. She went places and did things! Miss Peg would have loved her. Aunt Phee certainly did.

"After my father and Uncle Cork had died, I insisted she come to Pittsburgh to be near us, and she and Aunt Fanny got on like a house afire! They went to concerts and lectures and exhibits, and even went out west one summer to see the Grand Canyon. They must have been well past sixty by then! Gives you an idea of how enterprising they were.

"Anyway Charlie took me all over Pittsburgh, and I don't mind telling you that I hated it, Kate! I loved the quiet and fresh salt air of the seashore, and here I was in a noisy, soot-gray city of smoke with not a blade of grass or a flower to be seen. I found it hard to breathe sometimes, and my clothes never seemed clean."

I laughed. Having been born and raised in Pittsburgh, I thought nothing of the smoke and soot and noise. They didn't call it pollution then, but obviously it was the worst polluted city in the country. People had been cracking jokes about Pittsburgh for years, so I understood how my grandmother felt.

She went on. "But I met some lovely people—Aunt Fanny saw to that—and Charlie took me around to some of the nicer sections so I could see for myself that Pittsburgh had some gentility, and even places with gardens.

"We married on Christmas Day in The Captain's front parlor. That's why I always insist that Christmas be celebrated at our house. It was our wedding anniversary. Aunt Fanny came for the occasion of course. Since she was the closest thing to a mother-in-law I was going to have, it behooved me to have a good relationship with her. She made it easy, but then again, I always got on well with my older women relatives. Clara Cobbs even came all the way from Yonkers for our wedding. She liked Charlie and was grateful that her grandchildren would have a fine new father. It pleased all of us to have her blessing.

"It's important to get on with a mother-in-law, Kate—especially for a woman. And daughters-in-law, too." She paused and reflected. "You know, child, your blood kin will love you and stand by you no matter what, and no matter how irksome they may be. I love Clara dearly, even though we are oil and water sometimes. And I have no doubt if I needed her, she would be by my side in a minute."

Gran was right. I remember overhearing Mom and Daddy talking about how wonderful Gran was when Mom miscarried—three times before Margie was born. And when baby John Milton died. And when Daddy died, Gran and Pops stayed for a week to help Mother get through her grief. Mother would be there for Gran, too. I had no doubt.

"In-laws are different, Kate," she went on. "They don't have to love you and they don't have to like you either, and, if they don't want to, they don't even have to try to get along with you. Don't look to anyone else to do it for you. You must set the tone yourself. And if you are fortunate enough to have them meet you halfway, your chances for success in your marriage are greatly improved."

This was the opening I had wanted, so I took a deep breath and asked, "Why didn't you like my father, Gran?" She looked at me in great surprise and said, "I always liked Phil Atcheson. So did Pops. It would be hard *not* to like him. He was outgoing and charming. Very pleasant. Of course we liked him."

Something wasn't being said. Gran could be a real clam sometimes with any subject she didn't wish to discuss. But I pressed. Who knew if or when I would have the chance again.

"Mother always hinted that we didn't come to visit much because you didn't like Daddy," I said, adding quickly, "and he was tops, Gran! A lot nicer than Mother." Oops, I thought, holding my breath. I just insulted Gran's daughter. But she laughed.

"Clara was always difficult. Much more so than Henry or Walter. But I suppose the answer is not that we didn't *like* Phil. We thought Clara was too young, of course, only eighteen. But we also didn't care for Phil's complete lack of enterprise." She took her own deep breath; now she would insult my father.

"There is nothing wrong with great wealth, Kate. Charlie and I were far from having the money of the Atchesons, but we did have a thriving company with more than two hundred employees—and eighteen patents is nothing to sneeze at. But with all your father's wealth, charm, good looks, education and opportunities, he never did a solid day's work in his life. I know he didn't need to, but it would have been nice if he had made an effort."

Gran was right about that part. Daddy seldom worked, although he and Mom were very active in behalf of several charities, and sat on boards of countless organizations. Daddy was not a snob. He was likeable, but he didn't have the "Dunbar hustle." Gran did not admire him, and to her, admiration was more important than liking.

It has been a half-century since that conversation with my grandmother, but I never forgot what she said about hustle. I never forgot what she said about in-laws either.

I tried to be affectionate to my parents-in-law and welcoming to my daughters-in-law. In all cases, I was more successful than most. They have all had a special and dear place in my life. And we are also a family of hustlers. Not a lazy one in the bunch.

Chapter 3

We arrived in Los Angeles just before noon. We found a redcap, hailed a taxi, and went directly to the Ritz Carlton, the best hotel in Pasadena. Actually, it was the best hotel I had ever been in, and to this day, it still ranks in my top ten. Uncle Henry had made all the arrangements, and nothing but the best would do for his elderly mother and favorite niece. Pasadena is a colorful place, only a half-hour from Los Angeles. Bright sun, blue skies, stucco and white houses, and the most gorgeous trees and flowers! It was the direct opposite to gray Pittsburgh. I was entranced from the moment we left the station.

The Ritz Carlton was magnificent, with a lobby full of tropical flowers I had never seen before. The California climate, I supposed. The stucco walls were covered with photographs, drawings, oil paintings, water-colors and other works of art—all depicting the Rose Parades that had been the trademark of Pasadena since 1884. I came to learn that just about every public place in Pasadena had photographs of the Rose Parade, the football teams that played in the Rose Bowl, action photos taken during the games themselves or famous people who had come to watch the aforementioned. Not being a football enthusiast, I had little interest.

Our room was large, sunny, and had a view of a huge swimming pool surrounded by palm trees, gazebos, sunbathers and some of the flowers that I had seen in the lobby. There was a covered walkway from the hotel to the pool, with enormous mural paintings depicting the history of California. The entire location was breathtaking, and I hoped to have a chance to sun myself during the however-many-days we might be staying. The length of our stay, of course, depended on Mollie Brown, and how long it would take before she finally expired. In the trip from the station, I saw enough to make me hope Mollie would have a lengthy demise.

Gran was understandably anxious to get to the hospital. Mollie was waiting for her, she insisted, and her days, more likely her hours, were numbered. I unpacked our suitcases quickly and set a bundle of clothes outside the room for laundry service, just as our bell captain instructed. Three days on a train wrinkled everything—and wash-and-wear was still in the future. I also insisted we have lunch. Neither of us were big breakfast eaters, and it might be several more hours before we would eat again. A tuna sandwich and a cold drink (it was too hot for coffee) and we took a taxi to the hospital.

The hospital was one of the few public buildings without Rose Parade memorabilia in the waiting room. I was told the memorabilia, which included photographs of all the football players who were treated there for injuries, was in the hospital director's office. The receptionist said Mrs. Brown was in a private room on the fourth floor, so up we went.

As the elevator doors opened onto the solarium, I saw a well-dressed woman about my mother's age browsing through a magazine. She looked up, smiled, and rose quickly to greet my grandmother.

"Louise!" she said, as she rushed over to us and hugged Gran, "It's so wonderful that you came!"

"Ruth, dear," murmured Gran, returning the embrace. They were silent for a moment or two, and I saw the genuine affection between them.

"I can't believe it's been what? Ten years? It was before the war...."

"At least that," said Gran. "Charlie was still alive, and I think so was your father."

"Mom has been waiting for you," said Ruth quietly. "I checked with the station. They said you'd be arriving around noon, so I've been here for the past hour. Mother was relieved when I said the train was in and that you should be along shortly. She's napping now. The uncles arrived yesterday."

Gran embraced Ruth again, and then pulled back abruptly and drew me forward. "Where are my manners? This is Kate, Clara's youngest," she told the woman.

Ruth nodded pleasantly to me. "And how is Clara?" she asked sincerely. "I haven't seen her, dear Lord, it has to be thirty years. When *my* grandmother died. We were both young women then. And she was pregnant at the time. Was that you?"

I had no idea, but Gran answered quickly, "That was in '18, I believe. It must have been Marlene. Kate was born in '24."

I smiled, feeling completely out of place and stupid. I knew nothing about this person who seemed to know my grandmother—and my mother—so well.

"I want to see Mollie now. I don't want her to wait any longer," insisted Gran.

"She's in Room 428. It's the best room here, of course. She and my father contributed enough money when they built this place," Ruth added. "It's down the hall on the left."

I offered to wait in the solarium, but Gran said no, she wanted to introduce me, so I trudged along down the hall after a seventy-nine-year-old woman who walked at a very rapid clip for a seventy-nine-year-old woman.

She opened the door to a sterile looking room, with bed, nightstand, two chairs and a long table by the window that held at least a dozen different floral arrangements. I don't think they allow flowers in a room with a "heart" patient now, but back then, they didn't know or care about flowers and oxygen need. Anyway, Mollie Brown was propped up at a tilt, dozing. I could hear her labored breathing all the way to the door.

She must have heard us come in, since she opened her eyes, and recognizing Gran, extended her arms outward and boomed out, "Louise! Dear, dear Louise! I have been waiting for you!"

Her voice was not that of an elderly woman on her deathbed. Her eyes lit up as if she could have done handsprings across the floor. My grandmother rushed to her side, and I could see tears welling in her eyes as she bent over and kissed her old friend on the forehead, and grasped her hand with both of hers. Then she reached for the little box of tissues on the nightstand, sniffed hard and wiped her tears.

"I knew you wouldn't go anywhere until we could have a good visit," said Gran, with fresh tears streaming down her cheeks.

"Of course not," said the dying woman, in a voice that could have been heard in the solarium. It was hard for me to believe there was such strength in someone who was not long for this world.

Gran dried her eyes for a second time, took a deep breath and said, "This is Kate. Clara's youngest."

The dying woman looked at me and beamed, "And how is your dear mother? She is my god-daughter, you know."

I nodded, "Yes I know, ma'am. She is well and sends her love." I did not know then, nor do I know now, what to say to a dying person.

Mollie Brown was oblivious to my discomfort, and continued, "Those flowers there, with the bird-of-paradise and the white gladiolus. They are from Clara," she said, pointing to a huge arrangement on the window table. My mother, of course, would never have failed to send flowers to the godmother she hadn't seen in ten or twenty or even thirty years. Mother was like that.

About the time I was awkwardly acknowledging the flowers, the door opened and the day nurse entered, and very sternly advised that "Mrs. Brown should not be disturbed. She needs her rest. One visitor, and only if it is family. And only for five minutes."

Mollie Brown looked at the nurse with condescension that even my mother couldn't match, and said, in a voice that could have been heard across the Rose Bowl, "My oldest and closest friend has come all the way across the country to see me, and she will not leave until both of us are good and ready. I am dying and I know it. I will be resting long enough, God knows, so I intend to spend whatever I have left enjoying myself."

Day nurses are not easily intimidated. I don't think any nurse is easily intimidated; however, this one was obviously put in her place, and departed quickly.

There was absolutely no reason for me to be in the room, and Ernest Hemingway was waiting in my purse. I excused myself, murmuring something about being glad to have met Mollie Brown at last, and retired to the solarium. Ruth was gone.

The solarium looked like somebody tried hard to make it pleasant by painting the walls a pale green. Restful, they said. Better than the old whitewash they used to paint hospital walls before the war. And they had hung a few mediocre oil paintings of flowers and woods and playful kittens. These were never going to be museum pieces. The furniture was a conglomeration of whatever was available and cheap, and the lighting was poor: Three large overhead globes with chains attached, and four small tables each with a lamp reminiscent of the gaslit lamps of the 1880s, except they were electric. The chairs and small settees were not exactly comfortable, but after three sleepless nights in the upper berth, I was used to being uncomfortable. The magazines were months old. I was grateful that Hemingway engrossed me enough to forget how fidgety I was.

I spent the better part of an hour reading in the solarium. Gran told me that I might stay at the hotel while she sat with Mollie, but I knew Uncle Henry would want me nearby, so Hemingway it was, along with the uncomfortable chairs. Gran promised we'd leave by five o'clock, which would still give me plenty of time for a swim.

Then "the uncles," as Ruth called them, arrived. It was easy to figure that out: Three elderly men, two of whom were at least six-feet tall, the third, perhaps only five-foot ten. None of them were frail. There had been another brother, equally as tall, but he had died a few years earlier. Naturally they had no idea who I was or why I was there, but they seemed to know their way to Mollie's room, so down the hall they pattered.

A half hour later, Ruth came back with her son Joe and his wife, who seemed to be around my age. Gran and the uncles left Mollie to her new set of visitors for a little while and returned to the solarium, where I was formally introduced to the elderly trio. It was obvious they adored my grandmother and were thrilled that she had come all the way from Pittsburgh. They had come cross-country as well, from New York and Chicago, but they were family. It's expected.

It just so happened that Gran was in the solarium with the uncles when Hal Brown stepped off the elevator. He made a striking appearance, probably because of those steel blue eyes and the fact that he was six-foot-two. He recognized his great-uncles immediately and grinned. Three rather tall old men are not exactly inconspicuous, especially when nobody else is in the room. They didn't recognize him, but since they hadn't seen him since he was twelve, it was forgivable.

"Uncle Abe!" he exclaimed, and shortest of the old men looked around. "Uncle Irv? Uncle Jim?"

They turned and clasped the young man by the shoulders. "Which one are you?" the one called Uncle Jim asked.

"I'm Hal. Rudy's oldest son. I haven't seen you in what, fifteen years? At my dad's funeral."

"Ah, yes, Rudy's son," said one of the uncles. "Has it been that long?"

They embraced and shook hands and Uncle Jim introduced Gran. "And this is Louise Dunbar, I mean, Louise Stanfield. Your grandmother's dear friend."

Hal grinned at Gran and kissed her on the cheek. "I remember you too, from Dad's funeral," he said, "and I want you to know that Mother still has my baby cup somewhere." Those silver cups were part of his family lore, too.

From what Hal told me afterwards, his side of the family was not on the best of terms with Mollie. Actually, he said, all three of Mollie's children were somewhat distant from their mother, and even when Mollie gave up her old house and moved in with Ruth, she kept to herself a good deal of the time.

"I don't think my grandmother liked children very much," Hal said. "When I was little, we'd go to visit every so often, but it was always a hands-off atmosphere. It's not that she didn't love us all; I just don't think we interested her. Grandma preferred being with her friends, and she had a great many of them."

I also learned that Uncle Jim's wife had died a few years before, Uncle Abe's wife was an invalid of sorts, and Uncle Irv's wife didn't care for Mollie, and decided it would be best if Irv visited by himself. It was becoming apparent that Mollie Brown was one of those people you either adored or hated. Nothing in between. That usually makes for a more interesting person.

For three days Gran and I were at the hospital by nine o'clock and stayed most of the day. The Uncles were there too, and from time to time, I would hear gales of laughter emanate all the way down the hall from Room 428. Everyone in that family had stentorian voices. It was hard to believe that five elderly people could generate such genuine merriment—and noise.

I was flabbergasted one morning to hear a loud, off-key rendition of *Glory, Glory Hallelujah* coming from the room, followed by another burst of hearty laughter. This, of course, was immediately followed by the patter of the nurse's footsteps scurrying down the hall to "shush" the death-vigil. They were disturbing the other patients.

Ruth, who was as dutiful a daughter as my mother was, checked in every day for a half hour or so, collected cards and telegrams to be answered, and departed. It was obvious the elderly woman preferred to spend her remaining hours with her brothers and dearest friend, reminiscing about times long past. In more than ten years, the only times they were together was at funerals.

Every morning baskets of flowers would arrive, as did dozens of cards with each mail. Then a nurse would wheel a cart of flowers out to the elevator; Mrs. Brown had directed them to give "yesterday's arrangements" to the indigent in the women's ward. In the afternoon, two or three fairly elderly women would get off the elevator and look around, asking for Room 428. Five minutes later Gran and her three escorts would be back in the solarium to wait ten or fifteen minutes until Mollie's latest batch of visitors left.

And every day around noon, Hal Brown showed up. It would be a lie to say that he was so devoted to his dying grandmother he felt the need for a daily visit. He had come the first day to pay respects for his side of the family, since neither his mother nor sisters planned to make the trip. They had sent flowers and decided it was sufficient. But Hal lived only a half hour away, and it would be a deliberate snub to the old woman for imagined slights of twenty years ago that he didn't even know or care about. Then, of course, he met me. Thereafter, he came to see me, take me to lunch in the hospital cafeteria, and pop a perfunctory nose in to see Mollie. He said he saw her more in those three days than he had since he was twelve.

Gran decided she would much rather have dinner with the uncles (who were delighted for her company) than with me. They were also aware of Hal's increasing attentions and endeavored to help things along, so when he asked me to dinner, Gran was quick to encourage it.

"Don't worry about me, dear," she told me, "you should have some time to see the sights and enjoy yourself." When she told Mollie of Hal's interest in her granddaughter, the two old women beamed from ear to ear.

The day before Mollie died, Gran decided to take a taxi to the hospital by herself, and suggested that Hal might enjoy spending the day with me at the hotel pool. After assuring myself that she really meant it, and grateful for the respite from the solarium, I telephoned Hal, who was happy for the respite from the hospital cafeteria. He came over by eleven. That day at the poolside of the Ritz Carlton was one of the most delightful afternoons in my memory.

This was a time before the hundreds of posh hotels that abound today in the sunny resorts of the Caribbean or Florida. But California, mainly due to Hollywood, had some of the most magnificent luxury hotels in the world. In 1947, my resort experience had been limited to Lake Erie and one trip to Niagara Falls, and this was a far cry from anything I had ever seen before. Young waiters and waitresses, probably aspiring actors and actresses, were on hand bringing tropical rum punches to guests stretched out on padded lounge chairs by the pool. The scenery was indescribable. And of course, the company was terrific.

Hal filled me in on what little he knew about his grandmother, and I told him what little I knew about Gran. He said that his father, Rudy, was the oldest of Mollie's children. He died when Hal was twelve. Rudy, it seemed, had always been a little in awe of his parents. Joe Brown was domineering and strict, and Mollie, despite her size (she was five-foot-eight) and largeness-of-voice, deferred to her husband assiduously. It didn't appear that his grandparents were an especially loving couple. Hal's guess was they went their own ways a lot.

He also said his mother didn't care for Mollie or Joe either. Maybe it was mutual. Whatever the problem, it was a poor relationship, and after Rudy died, Hal's mother and sisters only saw Mollie and Aunt Ruth once more—six years before, when Joe Brown died. Hal was away at college at the time. Then there was nothing except the customary Christmas cards. When Hal enlisted in the Army in early '42, Mollie had sent him a letter, her best wishes, and a generous check, which he decided was a fine gesture and promptly acknowledged.

Since my history with Gran was similarly sparse, Hal and I decided that our "meeting" was divinely inspired, and vowed to make the most of it. We spent whatever time we had in Pasadena together.

On the fourth morning, the telephone in our hotel room rang at a quarter to eight. It was one of the uncles, who asked in a quiet voice to speak with Gran. I knew instinctively what had happened, and handed the phone to my grandmother, who also seemed to know why the phone rang so early.

The tears ran down her cheeks. "Mollie is gone. She expired in the night. Peacefully in her sleep. The way I want to go." She went into the bathroom for tissues, and returned, wiping her eyes. "I mustn't be sad," she sniffed. "It was exactly how she wanted it; time for a good visit with all of us. She saw her brothers as seldom as she saw me, and wrote them even less. But she loved them dearly, and they adored her. She died with a happy heart, I know it."

We put on the black dresses and hats we had brought for the expected funeral, and I remarked that I was surprised she hadn't borrowed Mother's jet jewelry. "I'm sure she would have been glad to lend it to you," I added.

Gran looked at me and said sharply, "I am here to mourn, not show off." In that moment, I understood the difference between Gran and my mother, and the distance between their eye-to-eyes.

Room service sent up breakfast, and at noon, we took a taxi to Ruth's house, where the uncles had already gathered. Mollie had been living with her daughter for the past five years—since her first heart attack, when the doctors insisted she must no longer live alone. Her second heart attack, by the way, was the reason Mollie didn't come east for Pops' funeral two years ago. It occurred less than a month before Pops died, and she was still confined to bed. She had sent flowers of course, and called long distance twice.

From what I learned later, Mollie wanted to live with Ruth about as much as Gran would want to live with Mom, but her choices were limited: Either live with her daughter, or in-laws who would be adamantly opposed, or hire a trained nurse. Or go to an old-folks home, which was totally out of the question. Ruth's house was the least of the evils. Fortunately, it was a large house and Mollie could come and go as she pleased. Ruth didn't mind when Mollie commandeered the living room for her various meetings, since Ruth was out a great deal herself. They seldom even dined together, except for breakfast or special holidays. Mollie had many friends and socialized an enormous amount for an old woman with a bad heart. Since both women were well-to-do, it was easy to hire a gardener-chauffeur to drive Mollie wherever she wanted to go. And Mollie had insisted that she would check into the hospital when she became too weak to leave her room. She would not burden her daughter.

I remember very little about the funeral except it was large and was reported in the newspapers. Gran cut out the clipping and tucked it away before I could read it. Mollie Brown was a stranger to me, so I felt no personal tie. She was also eighty years old. The funeral was not sad. Somber, but not sad. Even Ruth didn't seem overly grieved. Gran was invited to sit with the uncles, which left me free to sit with Hal. Neither of us minded.

Ruth had been kind enough to open her house to Gran and the uncles (who, I came to learn, she liked much better than she liked her mother—perhaps because she saw them so seldom). Otherwise they would have been left to sit in hotel lobbies. And, thinking back on memories of more than fifty years ago, Gran and Mollie's brothers were enjoying themselves immensely. Ruth's house was indeed large, and she had a full-time maid who was directed to see that Gran and the uncles had every comfort, including the use of her well-stocked bar. They were all inclined to enjoy a little nip on occasion.

In the few days between the funeral and the reading of Mollie's will, they enjoyed Ruth's hospitality, went to dinners, took a trip to Knott's Berry Farm and Graumann's Chinese Theatre, toured the Rose Bowl, and walked in the parks and gardens that Pasadena is famous for. Gran insisted Mollie would have wanted them to make the most of their time together, since it would not happen again. They didn't waste a moment.

Hal and I also made the most of our time together. We went to dinner, to the Pasadena Playhouse, spent time at the Ritz Carlton swimming pool, and drove all around Hollywood to see where Tyrone Power and Clark Gable lived.

We did not see too much of Ruth.

Mollie's will was read the day before we left for home. I wasn't there, of course, nor was Hal. Mollie had divided a generous sum amongst her grandchildren and great-grandchildren, but from what Gran said, most of her considerable estate went to her considerable charities. Ruth seemed to be aware of those provisions, and since she was financially well-fixed, raised no objections. She had been left property when her father died, and naturally, due to their ages and their own comfortable circumstances, Gran and the uncles were not left monetary gifts either.

Gran came back to our hotel room later that afternoon with three heavy hat boxes containing almost seventy years of correspondence. She was also wearing an elegant gold brooch set with three rose-cut diamonds, which is now in my possession. "It was Mollie's favorite pin," she explained, "and she wanted me to have a memento."

I said my own tearful goodbye to Hal late that night, after a long dinner and a longer drive in the California moonlight. We promised to write often, and maybe even call for special occasions. He mentioned coming East after the fall semester. Gran said more tearful goodbyes to the uncles. She would never see them again, although they would exchange Christmas cards with affectionate notes to the end of their individual lives.

Our return trip began quietly. We were taking the northern route this time. First to San Francisco, and then over the Rockies to Chicago, where we would change trains for the last leg home. We left early in the morning, and since neither of us were chatterboxes till at least three cups of coffee, we remained silent for a long time. I reverted to Ernest Hemingway, but my mind was full of Hal Brown, and my deliciously steamy episodes of the past week.

Finally, after a quiet luncheon in the dining car, Gran suggested we finish our coffee in the parlor car where it was more comfortable.

"I suppose I ought to tell you a little about Mollie Brown," she said.

Chapter 4

"I was eleven years old, sitting on our porch with my mother the afternoon we met," my grandmother said. "Miss Peg was crocheting and I was cutting paper dolls. I looked up and saw a little girl across the street, with a doll slung across her shoulders like a sack of potatoes. She had a very irritable expression on her face. I couldn't tell whether she was angry or bored or both, since I was also known to have had that same expression from time to time."

I smiled, knowing all too well that angry-bored look that young girls have when they are midway between childhood and adult.

"Out of the corner of my eye, I could tell this little girl was glancing at me and quickly turning away," Gran went on. "I was doing the same thing. You know how it is when children are sizing each other up." I smiled. I knew that too.

"So my mother, who was watching everything, said, 'That little girl looks about your age, Louise. Perhaps she'd like to cut paper dolls with you. I have a spare pair of scissors.' Thus armed with an excuse, I walked down the stairs and called over to the girl, 'My *mother* wants to know if you'd like to come over and cut paper dolls.'"

Gran wiped her lips with her napkin and settled in.

"Obviously she came over," I ventured.

"Obviously," said Gran as she smiled. "She was thrilled for some girl-company, since she was surrounded by brothers. Two older and two younger. We spent the next hour cutting paper dolls and their fancy dresses, and she chattered nonstop. She was one of the few people who could out-talk Charlie once she got going! Then Aggie brought us lemonade and jelly sandwiches. Mollie said she couldn't remember having such a nice time.

"She told us she was staying at the West End Hotel, several blocks down the street, and that she was very angry with Lulu Rockwell, the daughter of her parents' friends. She said Lulu bored her silly and never wanted to do anything interesting, so she marched off for a long walk. Then she told me—and Mother—that her parents were both very studious, and insisted that all five children work hard at their books. Her older brothers—Hal, the one who died a few years ago, and Jim, whom you met, Kate—hated studying. Mollie said they were always sneaking out to play ball when they were supposed to be doing their Latin or Greek."

I shuddered. Thank goodness I never had to learn that. Nobody speaks Latin anymore except maybe the priests, and Father Colligan, the only priest I knew, spoke English all the time.

"Mollie babbled away all afternoon," Gran went on. "I was thrilled, since I was shy as a girl. Maybe it's from being an only child, but I was positively in awe of this girl who seemed to be so comfortable with us—complete strangers. She told us her family lived near Cleveland, but that they spent most of the time in Washington, since her father was in Congress."

"I didn't know that," I said with renewed interest. "Mollie's father was a congressman? Gran nodded. "Long Branch was full of congressmen during the summer. Congressmen and senators and secretaries of this-and-that. Probably because of General Grant.

"Anyway, the very next morning, a messenger came with a letter for Miss Louise Dunbar. Mollie's mother invited me for luncheon and croquet that day at the West End Hotel. I was very excited. My mother seemed pleased and sent for the phaeton. She had decided to accompany me to meet my new friend again.

"Mollie's mother was polite and gracious. She was a petite woman, which was amusing, since Mollie was already bigger than she was, and eventually would tower over her. All five children were tall and well built—including Mollie. She was half-a-head taller than I am, and as you can see, I'm not especially short. Mollie's mother was also somewhat delicate looking. I always thought she had a lot in common with my mother—at least in looks. But they never seemed to be any more than courteous.

"'How do you do, Mrs. Dunbar,' she said to my mother, 'we are very pleased that Mollie has made a new friend.' 'We were delighted to have had her play with Louise yesterday,' Mother replied with a smile, 'and please call me Miss Peg. Everybody does.' 'Ummm,' said Mollie's mother uncomfortably.

"I'm not sure why they never became better friends, or even better acquaintances, but I'm positive it wasn't because of my mother," Gran said. "Miss Peg had a reputation all her life for being endearing. I think Mollie's mother just didn't warm to people easily. Both Mollie's parents were born poor and had to struggle for a long time, so they were not snobs. Mollie's mother was distant by nature.

"She was always very nice to me in her own remote way, but while I knew her till she died some forty years later, I felt no real affection or warmth on her part. We maintained a sporadic correspondence throughout her life, and whenever she would see me, she was kindness itself. She had every charming quality one wanted, but she was just cool. We would embrace always, but I always felt the Mississippi River was between us. There was no closeness. Do you remember how affectionate Mollie's brothers were? Hugging you and immediately insisting you call them Uncle So-and-So? Mollie's mother was never like that. I think it was just her nature to keep every feeling to herself and every person at arm's distance.

"On the other hand, Mollie adored Miss Peg. My mother would fix Mollie's hair—it was naturally very curly, so it wasn't conducive to the fashions of the time, but Mother tried. Sometimes she'd let us put on some of her hats and all three of us would chatter away over the latest *Harper's Magazine* fashions. And Mollie would confide thoughts to Miss Peg that she would never have told her own mother. I'm sure of it.

"I think I told you that my mother died when I was twenty," Gran said. "She wasn't particularly ill. Just tired. Then more tired. And finally, too tired to get out of bed. The doctor said it was her heart. She died two weeks after taking to her bed. Mollie was married by then, Rudy about two. He was my godson. I think she was carrying Ruth at the time. She was living in Cleveland, so I telegraphed that Miss Peg was failing rapidly and the doctor had given up hope. I got a return wire saying she was on her way, and to 'tell Miss Peg to wait.' She left little Rudy with their nurse and even though it was the middle of January, and she was pregnant and feeling poorly, she took the train by herself and came at once. She dropped everything for a last goodbye with Mother and to comfort me in my grief, which was intense. It was hard to tell which of us grieved more. Mollie loved my mother dearly, too.

"Anyway, I got to meet Mollie's brothers that second day. We got on famously from the start! Harry—they called him Hal— and Jim didn't stay after luncheon. They were fourteen and fifteen, and were going to the beach. It was a beautiful day. Not too hot, if I recall. Perfect for the beach or croquet. Irv and Abe didn't play croquet. They were too small, but they were cute and wild and ran all over the place, exactly like eight- and nine-year-olds ought to do. And I even met Mollie's friend Lulu."

I laughed, conjuring up an image of the popular cartoon character with the pear-shaped face and the silly corkscrew curls.

"Lulu Rockwell was an only child around my age," continued Gran. "Her parents were old and close friends with Mollie's parents, and they often traveled together. I think the

Rockwells thought since Lulu was an only child, and Mollie was surrounded by brothers, they would be boon companions. Not so. She was the original little Miss Priss according to Mollie, who could not abide her. Afraid to get her feet wet or her hands dirty; afraid to do anything without permission; afraid to run and jump because she might fall down. Always needed to have her hand held. And she always wore dressy clothes, even when she was playing croquet. I like people well enough, Kate, but in this I agreed with Mollie. Lulu was a pill.

"So for the rest of that week, Mollie and I were inseparable. We went walking along the bluff, and down to the beach, took the streetcar to Broadway for ice cream, and walked the iron pier down and back. Sometimes as much as two or three times. Oh, that was something, that iron pier!"

Gran closed her eyes remembering those old days. "Funny how I can picture it from so long ago," she said. "It jutted out more than a quarter-mile into the ocean, held up by huge iron pilings. And at the very end was a clam restaurant. Uncle Cork would take us all there sometimes. The steamships from New York would tie up to the Iron Pier. They came two or three times a day in the summer, each trip bringing hundreds of day tourists. Watching them getting on and off was almost as much fun as going to the train station—at least for a child. I think the boys preferred the trains—they were grimier. We girls liked the steamship.

"The week flew by, and we both cried when it was time for Mollie and her folks to go back to Cleveland. We promised to write to each other often, and," Gran added wryly, "you can see that we did. Two weeks later I received a letter—with a picture postal card enclosed that said 'Greetings from Cleveland.' They were all the rage, then. Of course I wrote her back and told her whatever news I had. Then she wrote back, and so it went. Later, when Mollie's family went to Washington, she enclosed another postal card that said 'Greetings from the Nation's Capital.' I think I still have those old postcards pasted in the family album with the birth announcements and obituaries."

I always smile when I think of Gran's family albums. Every Christmas when I was little, I made a beeline for those old scrapbooks, poring over them again and again, enjoying the old pictures and all the other memorabilia she crammed into them. Gran saved everything: ticket stubs, invitations, dried flowers, magazine articles that interested her, pieces of ribbon and cloth from favorite clothing—even a swizzle stick that said "This drink's on us" from a party she and Pops attended at the repeal of Prohibition.

"Anyway," she continued, "I think it was in March or April that Mollie wrote me big news! She said the biggest news was that her father had been elected senator. In those days, senators were not elected on the ballot, but by their state legislatures. That was definitely big news! Mollie said her father brought home a big box of candy for the children and a beautiful new hat for her mother—to celebrate! My father was duly impressed. A senator was a lot more important than a congressman."

I was impressed. Scratch congressman. Mollie's father had been a senator! My grandmother had a lot of secrets, it seemed. Or at least they were secret to me. I only knew that Mollie Brown was Gran's childhood friend and they exchanged long letters and monogrammed sterling silver cups from Tiffany's to commemorate the birth of children.

"But she also wrote the *best* news," Gran went on. "Her family had loved Long Branch so much, they were planning to spend a fortnight during the summer at the brand new Elberon Hotel. It had just been built over the winter, and was supposed to be the height of elegance. It was smaller than the grand hotels on the bluff, and a little farther south, but it afforded important people the luxury and privacy they wanted.

Mollie wasn't sure exactly when they would be coming, since the dates for the Republican convention weren't set yet, but she thought it would be after the 4th of July. Mollie's father was a staunch Republican, another mark in his favor, according to The

Captain. I could hardly wait! I made lists of things we would do that summer. Maybe with her father's new position, she would be able to buy her own bathing costume so she wouldn't need to rent one from those damp, ugly bathhouses.

"It turned out the Republican Convention was held in early June in Chicago. My father was not one of the delegates. That honor was reserved for more important politicians, and besides, it was enormously expensive, and The Captain couldn't afford to leave the store for so long anyway. But he was very interested in the outcome, and I think we took three newspapers every day that spring! One from New York, one from Philadelphia, and of course, our own Long Branch paper.

"The Captain would invite his friends over for cigars and coffee and politics occasionally, and that year, since my new best friend's father was now a senator, I also became interested. My mother believed one was just as bad as the other and that since Abraham Lincoln, God rest his soul, they were all crooks. Except for General Grant, of course. He was a fine man, despite what some of the newspapers said. 'It's a pity his friends couldn't keep their fingers out of the till,' Mother said. I, of course, loved the old general as much as The Captain. After all, he had kissed MY hand.

"Nobody seemed to know who the candidate would be. I'll bet you never even heard of them, Kate! Let's see, there was John Sherman — a Republican. No," Gran said quickly, anticipating my question, "it wasn't *General* Sherman. It was General Sherman's *brother*, who happened to be Secretary of Something at that time. Then there was Senator Blaine. Blaine of Maine. The Plumed Knight. He was a Republican candidate once — but it wasn't that year. There were others, but the really important one was General Grant.

"Grant had already been president for two terms," Gran continued, "then he spent a couple of years traveling around the world. When he came back, he was even more popular than before. All the old problems and scandals were forgiven. He was still and always the Hero of Appomattox and a lot of people wanted to elect him again—for a third term. My father was a Grant man first, last and always.

"The Democrats? I hate to mention them at all, since my father was an ardent Republican, strange enough for an Irishman—even a Protestant Irishman. Anyway there was nobody of consequence running," she said. "General McClellan, ran for President way back in '64 against Lincoln, before I was born. He was a Democrat and Governor of New Jersey. A mighty poor one at that, according to The Captain. He was the last Democratic candidate anybody ever heard of. There were a few others supposedly in the running, but for all intents and purposes, the election in 1880 was going to have yet another Democrat nobody ever heard of.

"Since my father was mayor, and had been for six years, he was right in the thick of things—at least in the New Jersey thick of it. When he wasn't busy in the store or doing his mayor-duties, he wrote all the important Jersey Republicans to support General Grant at the Convention. And he would walk down to the telegraph office two or three times a day to get the political news as it came off the wire.

"Uncle Cork and The Captain fought continually for three months over the upcoming elections, even though neither of them knew who the candidates would be. They were, of course, the best of friends when they weren't arguing politics, but this year, it seemed they were *always* arguing politics. Many a Saturday night Aunt Phee and Miss Peg would have tea in the front parlor and the two men would begin a friendly game of gin rummy in the back parlor—till they started in on politics. Then my mother would come in to tell them both to hush up or go elsewhere.

"The Captain was convinced that General Grant would be nominated easily since Senator Conkling was so active on his behalf." I shrugged. It was an unfamiliar name.

"Roscoe Conkling was senator from New York," Gran went

on, "and one of the most powerful men in the country. Uncle Cork hated Conkling with a passion and said he was 'as crooked as a corkscrew in a windin' lane.' He personally knew a half-dozen New York policemen who were assessed a week's wages or more every time there was an election, like it or not. And he was still fuming that his friend from Staten Island was passed over for promotion even though he was on the force longer and had a finer record than the fellow who got to be lieutenant.

'Them New York politicians are all alike,' he said bitterly. 'They gave it to some blasted Republican, Johnny. And they gave it to 'im because his brother was an alderman or somethin'! That's Conkling's finger in the pie!'

"The Captain agreed Senator Conkling was no prize, but as he was one of the general's closest supporters, he couldn't be all bad. 'Pompous ass, Johnny,' Uncle Cork said. 'That stuffed shirt couldn't walk down the street without lookin' like a peacock with his feathers a-fannin',' Then he jumped up from his chair, jutted his chin, puffed out his chest, and strutted around the parlor in imitation.

"Oh, I remember that scene very well, Kate, since I couldn't stop giggling," Gran laughed. "I knew who Senator Conkling was. He came to Long Branch every so often and would usually stay at the Grant cottage. Even in the heat of the day, he'd be dressed in a shirt and vest and jacket, his tie neatly knotted, and his fedora perched jauntily on his head. And he always had his gold-knobbed walking stick. He was hard to overlook, since he was a particularly large man—six-foot-two or -three with a barrel chest. He had to weigh more than two hundred and thirty pounds. And he really did strut. Uncle Cork's imitation was dead on center! Sometimes he'd walk with General Grant, but mostly they'd drive. I guess Grant didn't want to look so dwarfed by that giant dandy!"

Gran laughed and laughed just thinking of that long-ago big shot whose name has been lost to history. I found myself laughing too, and made a mental note to look up the name

"Roscoe Conkling" in the college library. He might be a good character piece for a journalism class. I had a vague recollection of hearing that name mentioned in school once, but it had to be at least ten years ago, and I'm sure I was thinking of something more important at the time—like lunch.

Gran went on with her tale. "'And that funny business with Mrs. Sprague don't set well with a good many decent people, either, Johnny,' Uncle Cork continued. I was close to the doorway and was curious about exactly what funny business the senator could have with a Mrs. Sprague. Then my father saw me, shushed Uncle Cork, and they moved to the front porch. They didn't see me when I slipped quietly near the door to continue eavesdropping. For some reason, to a twelve-year-old, this conversation seemed extremely promising.

"'And him a married man and her a married woman carryin' on like that,' my uncle said. 'If he were from Jersey City, he'd be run out o' town! It's a wonder they keep re-electin' him, but I suppose most o' New York's in his pocket.'"

According to my grandmother, the New York senator had been involved in an illicit affair with Kate Sprague for several years. She was the beautiful and socially prominent daughter of one of Lincoln's old Cabinet members, and had married former Rhode Island Governor Sprague years before, during the Civil War. He was a homely man of slight build, but he was worth a fortune, and talk was that Kate had married him to help finance her father's presidential ambitions that never materialized. They said the marriage was very unhappy from the start and the governor drank to excess. Anyway, the affaire d'amour became well-known in Washington, and grist for all the rumor mills, and finally Sprague had had enough. Coming home unexpectedly one day, he caught them by surprise "in delicato," and buoyed by a copious amount of whiskey, he literally threw Conkling out of the house—a man twice his size! Then Kate was packed off to Europe to let things quiet down. That was a few years prior to 1880, but there were still many people who could never speak of Senator Conkling without a snicker.

"Naturally," Gran added, "I didn't learn the sordid details till Mollie told me and some of my friends about it during the summer. I don't know how she managed to find out all these tidbits, but she certainly knew a lot about what went on in Washington!"

Gran went on, imitating her father and uncle's conversation. "'I don't say Conkling isn't a pompous ass,' said The Captain, 'but he's a lot better than that lyin' thief from Maine.' Uncle Cork finally found something to agree with. 'Jim Blaine is indeed a lyin' thief, but,' he said dragging out the 'but,' 'James Gillespie Blaine comes from good Irish stock, and blood is thicker than water.' There was no blood involved, claimed my father. A fellow Irishman is as good as blood, insisted Uncle Cork, and besides, Blaine's wife was Catholic, which was a bonus for anyone named Corcoran. But it really didn't matter, since Uncle Cork insisted he would vote Democrat, even if they ran Blaine's horse.

"Uncle Cork would raise the Catholic issue when it suited him. Like my mother, he was from a Catholic family, but he gave up on religion by the time he came to America. I think the only times I saw him in any church were weddings and funerals. But oddly enough, every time Uncle Cork passed St. Mary's or any other Roman Catholic Church, he would cross himself. Just to be on the safe side, I suppose.

"Now, Kate," she continued, "don't ask me about the ins and outs of politics back then. I was a child. I was twelve the summer of 1880. I wouldn't be thirteen until October. But believe you me, those were heated conversations between The Captain and Uncle Cork. Once they were so loud, Aunt Phee and my mother packed them off to Uncle Walter's hotel to continue their fight.

"Uncle Walter, of course, was just as strong a Grant supporter as The Captain. His hotel had one of the best reputations in town for its food, and the general stopped by at least once every season to sample some of Aunt Elizabeth's good cooking. Grant said Aunt Elizabeth was the only one in Long Branch who knew how to cook a steak to his liking: burnt. Not a trace of red or pink showing. Uncle Cork could claim Blaine and the auld sod, but we were from the Branch, and claimed Grant.

'"It has to be the general,' insisted my father, during one of his ongoing political fights with my uncle. 'They'll vote for him because he's the only one they know.'

"'Not for a third term,' insisted Uncle Cork right back. 'We've never had a president for three terms, and with God's Grace, we never will! Two terms was good enough for Washington, and would ha' been good enough for Lincoln, God rest his soul, and they were both better men than Grant.' They had that conversation almost every weekend that spring.

"The Republican convention in June was a free-for-all," said Gran. "And, to make matters more interesting, if there were two people who hated each other intensely, they were Blaine and Conkling. Both men had enormous egos — what man doesn't? — and Blaine enjoyed poking fun at Conkling, which riled the pompous senator into a fury. It was a duel to the death. That's what all the papers said: A duel to the death. General Grant stayed above politics, befitting his station. I'm not sure he even wanted the third term, but he was too young to retire. Besides, he needed the income. He was not a rich man. They also said that *Mrs.* Grant wanted very much to be back in the White House.

"Blaine and Conkling, (who was campaigning very actively on Grant's behalf), went at it back and forth at the convention, and nobody was getting anywhere. The third fellow, Sherman's brother, wasn't getting anywhere either. He was pretty bland. Every day they'd vote three, four, maybe more times, and nobody got enough votes to win. The Captain finally paid a boy to run down to the telegraph office five times a day to bring back the results of the latest ballot."

For someone who claimed not to know the ins or outs of politics, my grandmother had an extremely fine conception as well as memory of those events.

"It seemed the key to the impasse centered around

Conkling's own state," she said. "The New York contingent was divided. A delegate named Robertson refused to vote for a third-term for Grant, and he and a bunch of other New York delegates steadfastly clung to that position, and succeeded in blocking the nomination for the old general. This, of course, also incurred Conkling's—and Grant's—bitter and unyielding enmity. If nothing else, Roscoe Conkling never forgot or forgave an enemy. They say his venom increased every year.

"Finally, after thirty-some ballots, they made their choice. My father left the store early and was waiting for me when I came home from school. 'Well, Louise,' he said, waving telegraph paper in his hand, 'it seems your friend's father is going to be the Republican candidate this year.'"

Gran paused, expecting my immediate reaction. I stared hard at her. "Wait a minute," I said incredulously, "Are you saying that Mollie's father ran for President?"

"Actually, dear," said my grandmother coyly, "Mollie's father *was* president. Her name was Garfield. Brown is her married name."

I was in shock. All my life I had heard about "Mollie Brown" and never thought she had any other name. When I met "the uncles," they never used a last name, and I had no particular reason to ask. This put an entirely new face on Gran's story.

"Does Mother know this?" I asked sharply.

"Of course she does, Kate, but we don't usually mention it. Mollie never talked about it either. She didn't want people to know she was President Garfield's daughter, so she always used her married name—and even used the initial 'R' for her maiden name on occasion. It was her mother's maiden name. Rudolph. My godson, your friend Hal's father, was named Rudolph."

I was trying to soak in all this new and unexpected information, wondering how much—or even if—Hal knew about his great-grandfather.

"This is fascinating, Gran," I said. "You should write it all down."

"You're the journalism student, Kate," she said, looking at me sideways under half-closed eyes. "You write it."

It would be a lie if I said I couldn't wait to write the tale. I waited more than fifty years. But when I returned to college a few weeks after our trip, I did spend several hours in the library researching whatever was available about the Garfields. There wasn't much. Besides, in 1947, nobody was the slightest bit interested in things that had happened seventy years before. We had just fought a long and terrible war where millions of people had died. The atomic bomb had been dropped. People were starving in Europe—literally. All my generation wanted to do was to get on with their own lives. Find jobs. Have children. Look forward. Build a future. Nobody would have been interested in my grandmother and her childhood friend—even if she *was* the President's daughter. Not even my sisters.

But I did make some notes and I did write a few character studies based on Gran's story. I got an "A" on a piece I did on Uncle Cork and The Captain. I wish I had known them.

Once my amazement at Gran's revelation had subsided, she continued her story. "Of course I sent Mollie a telegram with the congratulations of our family. My poor father was indignant," she laughed. "Once again, his political career had been eclipsed by his little daughter. First Grant had kissed my hand, and now my best friend's father was the nominee for President. It wasn't easy for a proud man like The Captain to be teased by his friends saying, 'So, Cap'n, do you think you'll be invited when your daughter goes to play at the White House?'

"A few days after the nomination, I got a letter from Mollie saying that everything was helter and skelter. Their house was overrun with reporters and well-wishers — plus the carpenters and painters and drapers her mother had engaged months before to do needed repairs on their house, long before her father had even been named senator. She said wherever she went she kept bumping into total strangers.

"During those first months of our correspondence, we wrote each other twice a month. After Senator Garfield was nominated, Mollie's letters began coming two and three times a week. She was lost and neglected in the bustle. Her father was busier than ever. Her mother was busier than ever. Mollie's bedroom was needed for the stream of guests, so she was ousted and moved in with her grandmother, a wheezing old woman who snored loudly, did not bathe often and complained constantly. Hal and Jim found plenty to do helping the farm manager with daily chores. They enjoyed working out of doors since it kept them far away from their books. Irv and Abe amused themselves and the flood of well-wishers by just being little boys.

"When Mrs. Garfield wasn't supervising the building contractors and the added housekeeping staff, she was answering mail, helping the senator with obligatory appearances, or being fitted for a new wardrobe. She wanted Mollie to get some new clothes too, but Mollie was at a very awkward age. She was a big girl, but still too young to wear grown-up clothes. Children's dresses looked foolish on her. She was obviously miserable.

"'The only person who is nice to me is my father's private secretary,' she wrote. 'He lets me address envelopes and sort mail.' When Mollie mentioned she would even be grateful for Lulu Rockwell's company, I knew my friend was in serious trouble.

"I usually read Mollie's letters aloud to my mother, who had become as fond of her as I was. Miss Peg was thoughtful for a few minutes, and then mentioned that we might invite Mollie to stay with us for a few weeks.

'Senator and Mrs. Garfield are obviously extremely busy,

and we would be doing them a favor.' she murmured.

"I was thrilled, but Miss Peg cautioned me not to say anything to Mollie until she could write to Mrs. Garfield for permission. Mrs. G. was very quick to respond in the affirmative, since indeed, they were very busy, and this way Mollie would be in good hands and kept occupied. She thanked *Mrs. Dunbar* profusely, and arrangements were made at once. I counted the days.

"Mollie came on the train all by herself. She was a bright and resourceful girl and only needed to change trains once, in Philadelphia. Miss Peg and I met her at the Long Branch station. We sat up chattering till three in the morning.

"Naturally when word got out the candidate's daughter was our guest, everyone wanted to invite her places, so we kept a very busy social calendar. A few of my school friends met her the previous summer, and I had talked about her often to my other classmates. At thirteen, or nearly so, we were at the age where we wanted to imitate adults rather than play. No more paper dolls for us. We gave tea parties and girls' luncheons and got all dressed up for the occasion. We were becoming very self-conscious of our hair and our complexions and our clothes. You know how it is.

"We were also approaching a romantic age, Kate. Oh, we were not permitted to go out with young men of course, but we were definitely aware of the boys. We read a lot of poetry and memorized dozens of lines from Shakespeare. Many a rainy afternoon was spent drinking cocoa and reading 'Annabel Lee' or Elizabeth Browning's sonnets."

I knew very little poetry in 1947. I know very little poetry now. I had enjoyed reading Dorothy Parker's clever verses, but I had had my fill by seventh grade when we had to read the entire works of Longfellow. It was hard for me to imagine 13-year-old girls actually enjoying themselves reading "Evangeline" aloud. It is nearly impossible to imagine it now.

"Of course we spent a good deal of time at the beach," Gran

continued. "Mollie's parents had given her a generous allowance and suggested she buy a bathing costume or even two. Miss Peg and Aunt Phee were delighted to take her shopping, and within an hour, she was the height of fashion. She looked very good in those old-fashioned swimming clothes, Kate. She was big, but she wasn't fat, and she could wear a lady's size. The styles were very much the same for children and adults in bathing costumes. She turned a lot of heads on the beach, too, since she looked more like sixteen than thirteen.

"But when I think of that wonderful summer Mollie stayed with us, I think mostly of those wonderful weekends when Uncle Cork would be visiting and fighting politics with my father. Mollie and I would sit in the back parlor with them and refused be chased away. Neither of them had met Mollie's father, and I had only met him once, very briefly. The Captain was eager to learn everything he could about the senator from Ohio who stole the thunder from our beloved General Grant. But Uncle Cork was delighted at the turn of events, since such an unknown quantity would make it all the easier to elect a Democrat, who, it would turn out, would be equally unknown."

Gran went on to say that Mollie's father may have been relatively obscure, but he had a solid resume of accomplishments. He had enlisted in the war at the outset, and became the youngest major general in the Union Army. Then too, he had been elected to Congress nine times, and had distinguished himself as an authority on finance and appropriations. A little boring perhaps, but suitable enough for 1880.

The one thing The Captain seemed pleased about was the Vice Presidential nominee: Chester Alan Arthur of New York City. Arthur had never held an elective office in his life, and had been ignominiously discharged as chief collector of the Port of New York because of a scandal a few years earlier. But Arthur had also been a quartermaster general during the Civil War, and The Captain had enormous respect for that position, believing that any quartermaster general had to be a first-rate administrator. 'Besides,' The Captain went on, 'Nobody found him guilty of anything in the New York ports. Everybody knows it he was the scapegoat because he's Conkling's friend.'

"As soon as my father mentioned Roscoe Conkling, Uncle Cork would spring out of his chair, puff himself up and prance around the room like a strutting rooster, and Mollie and I would shriek with laughter. My uncle was a wonderful mimic, Kate. He had the Conkling-walk down pat. 'All the more reason to vote Democratic,' he said.

"It turned out the Democratic candidate was also a Civil War General: Winfield Scott Hancock, with a voice that could out-boom a chorus of Garfields, so they said. He was a West Point graduate, and a bona-fide hero of Gettysburg. He had even been military governor of Louisiana for a while. Everyone said he did an admirable job, all things considered. The contest was going to be between two second or third-tier generals with very little national exposure."

My grandmother was enjoying herself, talking about her dear friend and those old days still so sharp in her memory. She had a gift for mimicry as well, and loved imitating Uncle Cork's Irish brogue, and her father's gruff humor, and even Miss Peg's soft decisiveness, which, according to Gran, usually put an end to all horseplay that was getting out of hand.

If the train trip to Pasadena was interesting, the return trip was a revelation. The memories of an old lady had become a litany of a specific time and event. It did not seem important in 1947. It may not seem important now. But in my own golden years, I think these little details of history, no matter how obscure and seemingly trivial, provide future generations with glimpses of the people who made the events. They become human and real, not merely data in the almanac or history books. And, in my particular case, they become very human ancestors, not merely faded photographs in the family albums. And it is the long-ago events and the people who participated in them that have made us what we are now.

Chapter 5

I liked the northern route better. The scenery was spectacular, and, for certain, it was not as hot. Each morning, Gran and I would wash up and change into clean, albeit badly wrinkled clothes, and breakfast in silence. A muffin and coffee were sufficient. Then we would take our second — or possibly third — cup of coffee into the parlor car, and she would resume her story. It was cathartic for her, I suppose. She wasn't telling me to pass the time; she wanted another living soul to know these things.

"Mollie and I spent a lot of time that summer talking and talking," she said. "We were that peculiar age, Kate. Not women yet, but almost finished being little girls. Mollie was beginning to develop and I, being nearly a year younger and smaller, would have to wait another year or so to catch up. But my head and Mollie's were always alike: more mature for our ages than most.

"We talked a lot about politics that summer, a strange subject for children, but natural, I suppose, since her father was running for president. She said everyone in the family was completely amazed at the sudden turn of events. They were happy enough just having him as senator. Mollie worried whether he could still be senator if he lost the election. She loved living in Washington and wanted to continue school there. Their house in Ohio was nice, she said, but it was more like a summer place.

"She told me she had had several political discussions with her father during the past winter. They were very close. 'I think Papa was surprised at my interest,' she told me, 'but he was pleased. My older brothers have no interest in anything other than sports.' By the way, Kate, all the uncles were superb athletes.

"Anyway, Mollie told me she had asked her father what a politician actually did. A good question, I thought. She said he explained that the main job of a politician is to help people.

"I was quick to ask, 'But isn't that the job of a minister?'

"Mollie grinned from ear to ear and squeezed my arm. 'That's why we're such great friends, Louise! We think alike! That was exactly what I said to Papa!'

"'What did he say?' I asked.

"'Well,' she said, thinking hard, 'first he said it was an excellent question and it showed great insight. Then he said the job of a good pastor and a good politician are very similar. He said a pastor's job is to help a person live with himself and with other people. A good politician helps a person to live with other people in a community.' I thought hard about that.

"Mollie continued, 'Papa said a pastor will tell you it's important to be honest with your neighbors and the people you do business with.'

"I nodded. Our minister often referred to honesty in his sermons.

"She went on, 'But a pastor doesn't make the laws that say where the boundaries of your property are. Or where Indiana ends and Illinois begins. Or how many pounds of potatoes should be in a bushel. A pastor says it's wrong to sell someone spoiled potatoes, but the politician is the one who makes the law that says if you receive spoiled potatoes you're entitled to press suit in a court of law. And the politician makes the law to hold the person who sold spoiled potatoes responsible. He must make restitution or pay a fine.' I nodded again. 'Papa also said it's the politician who makes the laws that allow Ohio and Kentucky to work together to dam a river or build a road. Or allow people from New Jersey like you to come and visit me in Cleveland and buy a picture postcard with the same New Jersey money and send it through the mail,' she explained.

"I developed a good understanding of the concept of politics that summer. Mollie and I listened intently to The Captain and Uncle Cork every weekend when they would light their cigars, sip their whiskey, start to play gin rummy and invariably argue the merits and liabilities of the two second-class generals who wanted to be President. Because of Mollie's intimate knowledge of at least one candidate, we were permitted to remain in the back parlor—and speak only if spoken to. But at the dinner table, we were allowed to say whatever we liked.

"So I mentioned one evening, 'Did you know Mollie's father studied to be a minister?'

"Uncle Cork looked at The Captain quizzically, and Aunt Phee smiled at Mollie. 'Really, dear? What denomination are you?' Mollie replied they had all been formally baptized Disciples of Christ.

"There was a big silence. The Captain looked at Mollie suspiciously under half-closed eyelids, and asked directly, 'That's not like the Mormons, is it?'

"She laughed and said, no, they weren't anything like the Mormons, and added that her mother was the only wife her father had. 'The Disciples are a small sect that began in the Midwest around 1840, when my parents were growing up,' she explained. 'Grandfather Rudolph, my mother's father, was one of the founding members, and Papa joined their church when he was in his teens. His own father had died when he was a baby, and the elders thought he was a smart lad, so they took an interest and sent him to school. That's where he met Mother. They were in the same class.'

"This was the kind of information The Captain loved to hear, Kate; the details few other people in town would know. Now he'd have all sorts of interesting tidbits to talk about at the next Republican meeting. So he asked Mollie why her father left the ministry. She took a deep breath, being well aware that she needed to provide the information correctly.

"'I believe Papa was ordained as a pastor before he was twenty, and actually preached a couple of services. But,' she continued slowly, 'back then, or at least where they lived, ministers also taught at the colleges.'

"My parents nodded. That was common at the time when higher education was rare. Ministers were usually the only ones with a broad education and they taught to augment their meager salaries. Mollie, as usual, seemed to read everybody's mind, and added, 'Not every preacher can be rich and famous like Henry Ward Beecher.'

"Uncle Cork and Aunt Phee laughed because my uncle was always saying what a hypocrite the Reverend Doctor Beecher was, especially with that funny business a few years back with a married woman in his parish. It took me a few years to understand what kind of funny business my uncle was referring to, but I imagine you know what I mean." I nodded. I knew exactly what kind of funny business she was talking about.

"Anyway, since her father was such a good student at their little Ohio college, Mollie said the elders thought he should continue at Williams College in Massachusetts. There was another silence. We had never heard of Williams College any more than we had heard about the Disciples of Christ.

"'It's a small school with an excellent reputation. There was also a community of Disciples nearby, so the elders knew he would be among friends and not tempted to stray,' Mollie explained. She also told us that her father was undecided then, whether he wanted to preach or teach or do public service."

I suppose that's a common problem for most young people—even some not-quite-so-young people. My own feelings about journalism were ambivalent, and Hal Brown had mentioned that even though he was studying law, he didn't really feel strongly about it. He added that his namesake, the Uncle Hal who had died a few years before, had also studied and practiced law, but his heart wasn't in it either, and he wound up being an educator. He eventually became the president of that same Williams College for many years and loved it. Perhaps there is an "indecision" gene that runs in families, too.

My grandmother continued her narrative. "Mollie went on to say that after her father graduated Williams, he returned to teach at his old Ohio college, and was even its president, but then he was elected to the state legislature.

"'My goodness,' commented my mother, 'he must have made quite an impression on people to be elected at such a young age.'

"'Oh he does make an impression, Miss Peg,' Mollie said very proudly, 'especially when he speaks in public.'

"The Captain was impressed. Oratory was an extremely important asset to a politician. My father would practice his speeches for hours in the back room of the store. Then he'd come home, plunk my mother and me down on the parlor divan and try them out on us. He was a fair speaker, but not an orator.

"'When Papa was in the legislature,' Mollie continued, 'he had a little extra time, so he read law with one of the other legislators, and was admitted to the bar. But he never really practiced law.'

"'My, my, my,' said Uncle Cork, 'a preacher, a teacher and a lawyer—and not makin' a livin' at any of 'em.'

"Uncle Cork didn't mean to offend Mollie. He was as fond of her as the rest of our family. It was just that he was a proud Democrat who swore up and down that if he had lived in Long Branch, he would even vote against The Captain, just on principle. 'Nothin' personal, Johnny,' he'd always add with a twinkle in his eye.

"Mollie was very quick to defend her father. 'I think he might have practiced the law, Mr. Cork, but the war had started and he felt it his duty to enlist.'

"Well that put a cork in Uncle Cork. *Everybody* enlisted during the Civil War, Kate. My father did and so did Uncle Cork, for that matter. And so did Uncle Daniel Defoe and Uncle Homer. Uncle Walter was a little too old and had four children by then, and Uncle Doomis was still too young. Uncle Alexander Pope?" She paused to think. "I don't quite remember what they said. Maybe it was his poor eyesight. I believe he wore glasses.

"Anyway, according to Mollie, Senator Garfield's war record was superb, particularly for a volunteer soldier, and the Republicans were quick to circulate copies and proclaim him the hero of Chickamauga. 'Papa said he always hated to fight, but once committed, he was determined to win,' she said, adding that her father had been elected to Congress in absentia, but declined.

"'He wrote that he was deeply honored, but it would be cowardly to leave the field of battle and his comrades-in-arms for the comforts of Congress. But President Lincoln wrote Papa personally, saying that he had plenty of major generals, and could really use a good Republican Congressman from Ohio. So Papa went to Washington.'

"We learned a lot about the Garfields that summer, and I got to know a lot about Mollie. For all her quick mind and fine insights, she must have inherited the Garfield trait of indecision as well. She had no idea what she wanted to do with her life, although it's perfectly understandable when you are only thirteen. I wanted to be a teacher, Kate. I knew it early on, and I remember mentioning it to Mollie. She thought I'd be very good at it, but she herself had no interest in teaching. She said she really didn't like being around little children, except for her brothers.

———

"At dinner one evening, The Captain asked Mollie if she was acquainted with President and Mrs. Hayes," my grandmother continued. "Mollie said she was in the same class as their daughter Fanny, and they were fairly good friends.

"'I've been to the White House to play a few times. The President stopped in to say good afternoon once. He's a lot shorter than you'd think. A *lot* shorter than my father. More like General Grant. Mrs. Hayes is very sweet. Not too tall either. About like you, Miss Peg, but plump. You would like her. She always makes us feel welcome when we come for a party. She even joined us for lemonade and cake one time.'

"My father loved hearing things about Rutherford and Lucy Hayes that made them seem more human. And, of course, it gave him insights nobody else in Long Branch would have. At least not the year-round residents.

"'It just so happens that the Hayeses are coming to Long Branch in a few weeks. They'll be staying at the new Elberon Hotel,' my father announced. That was exciting news. We had become accustomed to General Grant as a summer resident, and it had been a long time since we pulled out all the pomp and ceremony to host a President.

"My mother was on the decorations committee to make bunting and banners, so she recruited Mollie and me to help. She taught us how to cut and stitch red-white-and-blue rosettes and string them together in festoons. They don't do that anymore, I know. You can buy them easily enough for a dollar. The Captain organized a large welcoming committee, and he practiced his speech so much we *all* had it memorized. Governor McClellan was coming, plus our senator and local congressman and people from the state legislature. Three ministers were scheduled to speak, and a colonel from the Grand Army of the Republic would present the President—another former Union general, by the way—with a special engraved silver tray.

"Ladies Auxiliaries of every group in town were cooking and fixing all week. They hoped to sell cakes and pies and cold drinks, the proceeds to go to the Soldiers Aid Society, I think. The whole town was abuzz, Kate. Everyone was going to the station for the Great Arrival Ceremonies and the parade escort to the Elberon Hotel.

"The big casinos and the Monmouth Racetrack owners agreed to issue President Hayes special passes as a courtesy, but they also expected him to decline. Rutherford and Lucy Hayes were devout Methodists, and the President was not inclined to anything other than very high-moral activity. Racing and gambling was not something he espoused. After the Grand Welcome, everyone conceded it would be a very dull week, socially.

"It was also common knowledge that Mrs. Hayes did not serve spirits in the President's mansion. Mollie was quick to comment how a lot of congressmen brought their own flasks to a soiree at the White House and sneaked off to a cloak room to refresh themselves if the party got too boring.

"'Of course I'm not supposed to know about those things,' she admitted, 'but my parents always talk about politics at dinner. They believe their children should get a broad education. Including me. My father is a very religious man, too,' she added, 'but he enjoys a brandy or whiskey after supper.'

"Then there was the gossip about how the Hayes family spent Sundays. After church services and a family dinner, they would invite friends over to sing hymns and have coffee and cake. My father looked at Miss Peg. We could think of many more interesting things to do on Sundays. That was usually our outing day. After church, we'd go to the beach or out to Pleasure Bay for a clambake. If it was *very* hot, we would take the steamboat all the way to New York City and then turn around and come back again—for a whole day out on the water.

"And as far as singing goes, we had a piano and my mother could play. But she didn't play hymns. My father and Uncle Cork (who had a fine baritone voice by the way), loved the old war songs like 'Tenting Tonight' or 'The Battle Cry of Freedom,' so that's what she played. Mollie played piano too—sort of. Every letter she received from her mother that summer reminded her to practice an hour every day. I don't think Mollie liked the piano much and I don't remember her practicing too often. Certainly not an hour a day. I also don't think she was very good, but who am I to say? I have the Dunbar tin ear. Mollie kept playing *Fur Elise* over and over until we were all thoroughly sick of it. Even today, I absolutely hate that tune."

I could sympathize. I think I inherited the Dunbar tin ear, too. I had a fair sense of rhythm and I could dance well enough, but I never could carry a tune. After a half-dozen piano lessons when I was eight, my teachers gave up on me. And I gave up too. Gladly.

Gran continued her story. "Finally the big day came, and we all went down to the station to welcome President and Mrs. Hayes. Since my father was mayor, it was only fitting we have a few privileges, so Mother and Mollie and I had seats close to the platform for a good view. It was decorated with flags and bunting and rosette festoons and a huge sign that said 'Long Branch Welcomes President Hayes.'

"Mollie was right. The President was short with a beard like General Grant, only longer, and Mrs. Hayes was plump. Not as plump as Mrs. Grant, but pleasantly plump, with a sweet face under her wide-brimmed summer hat. As far as I could tell, they had to be the most ordinary looking couple I'd ever seen. Hardly what I expected a President to look like. Even General Grant had more, how could I put it? More oomph about him. And Grant didn't look like a President either—let alone a great general. But the high school band played 'Hail to the Chief' and the band from one of the hotels played 'Hail Columbia' and the Methodist choir sang 'Faith of Our Fathers' or something like it, and the soldiers' band and the fife and drum corps played something rousing, and all the big shots made speeches and presentations. It was a grand show!

"Finally my father got to make his welcoming speech. Since Hayes had been a general, The Captain, ever mindful, came to attention and gave the President a snappy salute—with his left hand. Hayes was confused by the left hand business, so my father simply said, 'Fourth New Jersey, sir. Harper's Ferry,' and glanced over at his useless right arm.

"Well, President Hayes was so considerate! He grabbed The Captain's left hand with both of his, and pumped it up and down, and announced for all to hear, how delighted he was that our town mayor was another old soldier who had given so much to save the Union. Hayes had been wounded four times himself, once seriously.

"But it was amazing, Kate. The entire week the Hayeses stayed at the Elberon Hotel, which was gaining a reputation as a haven for the 'fast' set, they hardly left their rooms."

Gran went on to explain that Elberon was a little pocket borough at the southern end of Long Branch. A wealthy man named L.B. Brown (no relation to Mollie's in-laws) had owned several hundred acres, and offered it up for subdivision some years before, provided they name the little borough for him, hence Elberon. The hotel, the newest one along the bluff, was a smaller affair than the huge 300-room hotels like the Ocean House, but it included many new amenities. There were bell-pulls and speaking tubes in every room. And the dining room was said to be the finest in town, with a grand view of the ocean from every table.

And, according to Gran, President Hayes kindly thanked the casino and the track owners for their invitations, but declined to participate, just as they expected,. He declined all invitations and accepted few callers, explaining that he and Mrs. Hayes were there to rest and relax, and that was exactly what they planned to do. It was a very dull week, socially.

"But The Captain and Miss Peg took tea with them one afternoon," said Gran. "Miss Peg was surprised when a messenger came with the President's invitation, and of course Uncle Cork had a good laugh when he heard about it.

"'A lotta good it'll do you, Johnny. A has-been president who never should ha' been in the first place, drinkin' tea with you. Did he ask you to sing "Onward Christian Soldiers"?'

"Of course my father ignored Uncle Cork's ribbing. The Hayeses were very nice indeed, according to my mother, especially Mrs. Hayes. Miss Peg liked her a lot better than she ever liked Mrs. Garfield."

As our train rumbled across the country that summer of 1947, my grandmother relished every memory that came flooding back about her "wonderful summer," as she called it.

"Mollie wrote her family every other day," Gran said, continuing her tale, "and we were pleasantly surprised that despite how busy and preoccupied the Garfields were, one of them took the time to write to her almost daily. Her mother usually reminded her to practice the piano or work on her Latin and French—which Mollie liked as much she liked the piano—and to be sure to thank *Mr. and Mrs.* Dunbar for their kindness. I'm not sure why Mrs. Garfield never referred to my parents as Captain or Miss Peg like just about everybody else in the world. To her, they would *always* be Mr. and Mrs. Dunbar. I suppose she just wanted to maintain a distance.

"Mollie's father, however, wrote interesting letters, and treated Mollie more like an adult rather than as his little girl. She was happy to read his letters aloud to us at dinner. I think she considered us part of her family."

Gran laughed, obviously remembering a particular incident. Her eyes squinted a little when she laughed, and the sound she made was a merry one. "Anyway, the senator said in one letter, that he finally got rid of the fourteenth glee club that came to serenade him that day, and if he never heard 'When Johnny Comes Marching Home Again' *again* it would be too soon! (The same way I felt about *Fur Elise*.)

"The senator also said nearly every hour of his day was filled meeting and greeting hundreds of people who flocked to their home in Mentor. Nobody had ever heard of that little town outside Cleveland before, but now it was famous. The senator's secretary set up office in an adjoining building for the reporters who were driving him to distraction. And then he said something my father found very interesting. He said Chet Arthur was finally making himself useful by arranging for General Grant and Roscoe Conkling to come to Mentor in a few days. 'We'll never win without New York's electoral votes,' Garfield had written, 'and we'll never get New York's bloc without Senator Conkling.'

"Oh, Kate, The Captain was in his glory that summer! Tea with President Hayes and his wife. Hosting the candidate's daughter. Hearing inside information about the political scene. I don't think I ever saw him so happy!

"One evening at dinner, my father asked Mollie if she knew Senator Conkling. 'I've seen him, Captain," she replied, 'and I would know him on the street.' (Well, who wouldn't, Kate? He was unbelievably conspicuous!)

"At the mention of Roscoe Conkling's name, Uncle Cork jumped up, twisted his hair into a Lord Byron curl, and started prancing around the room, clutching my mother's brass candlestick like the senator's gold-tipped cane. We were beside ourselves laughing, and insisted it was a perfect imitation. Mollie said her father would laugh heartily, but then scold him for being unkind. 'Pooh, pooh,' said Uncle Cork.

"Mollie continued, 'I think Senator Conkling and Papa get along amicably, but I don't believe they are social. He's never been to our house like the Blaines.'

"Uncle Cork summed up the entire election situation. 'It'll be very interestin', Johnny. Everybody hates each other. Grant and Conkling can't abide Blaine and don't care much for Garfield, and nobody has a good word for Chester Arthur. Don't be surprised if Win Hancock don't sneak up and swipe the whole pot.'"

Chapter 6

Among the photo albums and boxes of Mollie-letters that I inherited when Gran died in 1954, was a spiral notebook from October 1947 in my handwriting. They were the notes I had made in the college library when I first thought to write down the events our trip.

From Kate's notes:

Largely because of the Grant scandals and the disputed election of Rutherford Hayes in 1876, a strong reform faction had arisen in the GOP. The reformers wanted government appointees to be qualified for their positions, and once proven satisfactory, should not be dismissed for purely political motives. This is taken for granted today, but it was a novelty after the Civil War. Naturally it did not sit well with many congressional leaders in both parties, who were expected to reward their own in times of victory. This had been a practice dating back to Andrew Jackson, some half-century prior.

In the four presidential elections after Grant, less than 10,000 popular votes separated the candidates; the mid-term elections for Congress and local offices changed hands regularly between the Republicans and Democrats. But the Democrats were so weakened by twenty years of Republican rule and Civil War bitterness, the fact they came so close to victory in both 1876 and 1880 was astounding—particularly since their candidates were unknown and uninspiring. If the Republicans hadn't been splintered by their in-fighting, the Democrats would have been trounced.

In 1880, the population of the United States was 50 million, a 10% increase over 1870, and more than 25% more than in 1860, the half-million casualties of the Civil War notwithstanding. There were 38 states. Six more would join the Union by the end of the decade. Federal patronage neared 100,000 positions in 1880, the number growing at a rate to equal the population. The post office accounted for the majority of those jobs, but customs officials, Indian Affairs agents, tax collectors and similar positions were on the rise, and with western territories applying for and being granted statehood, patronage jobs were at a record high. And this did not include state, local and territorial patronage!

About Roscoe Conkling:

Roscoe Conkling of Utica, New York, was a political boss of the first magnitude. He began his career as a district attorney in upstate New York, and served a few terms in Congress during the Civil War. By 1867, when he was elected senator, he was a staunch Radical Republican, with a gift for making trusted cohorts and viciously bitter enemies. New York was the country's most populous state and Conkling ran it with an iron·fist and a pompous, condescending manner in keeping with the power he wielded. He was more than six feet two inches tall, wore foppish, almost Oscar Wilde-ish clothing, and dominated any room he entered, adding an urbane and sophisticated charm, if you could overlook the foppishness. He also had a suspicious and tyrannical nature, and twice declined an appointment to the Supreme Court rather than relinquish his power base. At one time, there was serious talk of him being a presidential candidate. As legislator, Conkling accomplished little; as party wheeler and dealer, he was unsurpassed.

The Grant Administration saw Roscoe Conkling at his pinnacle, but by 1880, Conkling's star was on the wane for a variety of reasons, not the least of which was the "funny business" with Mrs. Sprague. However, after four years of festering hatred of Rutherford Hayes and the "reform" wing of the Republican party, he endeavored to elect Ulysses S. Grant to an unprecedented third term. With Grant in office again, Conkling would be in a position of renewed strength. A Cabinet office would be assured; perhaps even the Presidency in 1884.

About James Gillespie Blaine:

James Gillespie Blaine was born in 1830 in Pennsylvania, and as a young man, relocated near his wife's family in Maine, where he became the influential editor of the "Kennebec Journal." His genial charm, oratorical gifts and a knack for remembering names and faces led him into the Maine legislature, where he was twice elected speaker. First sent to Congress in 1863, he became Speaker of the House of Representatives before he was forty. Although a strong supporter of Negro rights, including suffrage, he was never considered one of the diehard "Radical" Republicans during the Reconstruction decade. Almost by default, he became the nominal leader of the liberal wing — the "Half-Breeds," as they were called. And as expected, part of his leadership emerged because of the enemies he made. Conkling was high on that list. The men had loathed each other for years.

More than anything, it was a personality clash between two men with enormous egos. Conkling was bluff and bluster; Blaine exuded charm and the urge to stick pins in the Conkling balloon. Early in their careers, Blaine compared Conkling to a "strutting turkey gobbler" — the slap in the face for a political duel to the death.

This longstanding enmity with Roscoe Conkling did not preclude Blaine from his own scandals, however. The Credit Mobilier was chartered at the end of the Civil War as a holding company for railroad stock. Its complicated financial transactions, while technically legal, embroiled several congressmen, senators and other public officials during the Grant administration. Blaine was one of the foremost legislators involved in receiving gifts of stock, eventually worth many thousands of dollars. (Garfield was peripherally involved as well, but it was minuscule and generally overlooked. Garfield didn't even remember receiving the stock, never sold it, and it was only valued around $300.) Blaine's attitude, common for the day, was that a man's private business should remain his private business, but Credit Mobilier allegations followed him to his dying day and into history.

Elected senator in 1876, Blaine managed to quell criticism to a point that most Liberal Republicans could be satisfied of his integrity. Then too, the Grand Army of the Republic, the biggest lobby in the country, was strong in its support. Blaine did not serve in the Civil War, but he was a staunch supporter of veteran's issues, and was first in line to "wave the bloody shirt."

The 1880 rivalry between Blaine and Conkling would be mortal combat. Each would sacrifice his own ambitions to prevent the other's advancement. As candidates jockeyed for position in Chicago, Conkling, on Grant's behalf, would battle Blaine to a standstill. Neither they nor their followers were willing to give an inch.

About John Sherman: (Not much available on him!)

The wild card in the bunch was Hayes' Secretary of the Treasury, John Sherman, of Ohio, the brother of General William Tecumseh Sherman of the "March to the Sea." General Sherman, non-political by nature and desire, would be torn between supporting his brother and his old friend and comrade, General Grant.

John Sherman was a prominent attorney and senator whose political activities had stretched back a dozen years prior to the Civil War. He looked very much like his illustrious brother physically, but was a colorless, albeit capable man. He had few devoted followers and inspired no one. However several months before the nominating convention, Garfield secured Sherman's endorsement for the Senate, and in return, pledged to support Sherman's presidential hopes. He even agreed to place Sherman's name in nomination.

But one of the major considerations in 1880 was still sectionalism. "Being from Ohio" was critical; it was an industrial, populous state. It was Midwestern, perceived to be neither North nor South. There was no chance of a "traitorous" Southerner being nominated, and Southern Republicans (a small maverick group) were vehemently opposed to traditional Northern domination. States in the far west were not populous enough to provide a viable voting bloc, so the Buckeye State became the Second Mother of Presidents for fifty years after the Civil War.

The Republican Convention of 1880:

Grant's supporters came to the Chicago convention with 300 "sure" votes out of the 379 needed for the nomination. The Southern

States were certain to give him their 176 combined votes. Illinois, Pennsylvania and New York could give him another 170—making him virtually unbeatable. Blaine also came with nearly 300 "sure" votes and if they were combined with Sherman's, he could win. New York, with the greatest number of votes, was key to the nomination, and Conkling controlled New York. But did he? There were nineteen New York delegates who steadfastly opposed a third term for Grant. Those nineteen were prepared to put their own political futures on the line by defying Conkling—a man known to take no prisoners.

Conkling's strategy was to promote the "unit" rule, whereby each state would vote as a unanimous entity: majority rule. In New York, Conkling had the majority. Garfield, pledged to support Sherman (although personally preferring Blaine and against a third term for Grant), realized the key to Conkling's defeat would be the unit rule. "Each man's vote should count" was his policy, and he worked tirelessly behind the scenes to see that the unit rule was defeated. Conkling glowered.

Grant's name was put in nomination to raucous cheers and pockets of hisses. Blaine, the "Plumed Knight," a sobriquet he was given at the 1876 convention, drew thunderous applause when his name was placed in nomination—along with pockets of silence.

Garfield nominated John Sherman, giving a powerful oration. He spoke for more than a half hour, waved the "bloody shirt"—that emotional appeal to the passions of the Civil War, still fresh in everyone's memory—and stressed party unity, something nobody could fault. But John Sherman's name wasn't mentioned until the very end, causing Garfield's detractors to suspect he might be nominating himself. Indeed, Conkling, unquestionably a shrewd politician, declared Garfield to be the "real dark horse" from Ohio.

For two days and 32 ballots, the vote swayed back and forth among the three candidates with little change. The nineteen disaffected New Yorkers, led by its Assembly Speaker, Judge William Robertson, were determined to stand their ground and vote for Blaine, despite Conkling's scorn, rage, threats, coercion and maneuvering.

On the 33rd ballot, a Pennsylvania delegate cast a lone vote for

Garfield. It was becoming increasingly apparent that neither Grant nor Blaine nor Sherman had enough strength to be nominated. It was just as apparent that none would give way, either.

On the 34th ballot, Wisconsin, in a surprise move, gave its 16 votes to Garfield. After a momentary silence, there was thunderous applause. Perhaps the stalemate could be resolved. On the next ballot, Indiana cast 35 votes for Garfield. By the 36th ballot, over Garfield's attempt to demur (quickly overruled by the convention chairman), and after the usual political maneuvering amongst Blaine and Sherman supporters (who could legitimately support a Garfield candidacy), he was over the top. Conkling's Old Guard remained true to Grant till the bitter end. They refused to turn over their 300-odd votes to make the nomination unanimous. It was their turn to be the disaffected "Stalwarts."

However, there was also the matter of choosing a Vice President. Garfield was deeply involved. He owed his nomination to his friend Blaine, who he knew would campaign actively in his behalf. But he also knew New York's 38 electoral votes were crucial to his election. Besides, James Garfield was, by nature, a conciliatory man. While he had never been a close friend or even an admirer of Roscoe Conkling, he never harbored any deep resentment nor had he incurred the New York senator's personal antipathy. They could get along. Traditionally, the Vice Presidency went to the defeated faction; the inconsequential office was a geopolitical accommodation of honor.

Unbeknownst to both Conkling and Garfield, some of the Stalwart New Yorkers approached Chester Alan Arthur with the idea of the Vice Presidency. It was a position of great prestige and little effort—a higher office than Arthur would have ever achieved elsewise. It would also allow him to remain active in New York politics. Arthur, just 50 years old and a recent widower with half-grown children, relished the opportunity for new activities. While his loyalty and personal friendship were unwavering to Conkling, he was by nature more moderate. He believed he might actually do some good for his party, bridging the gap between factions, while protecting New York patronage. To the unspoken dismay of both Garfield (who wanted someone else), and Conkling (who had no preference other than being the spoiler), Arthur accepted the bid, and was nominated on the first ballot.

So who was happy at the outcome?

James Garfield, while deeply honored by his nomination, immediately realized his chances were razor-thin. He was overcome with grave responsibilities and self-doubt. His body rebelled. He developed acute indigestion and insomnia.

Blaine, while sincerely happy for his friend, and equally happy that his worst enemy had been beaten, at least to a standoff, was keenly disappointed that his second attempt for the White House had failed. (A third effort four years later would win him the nomination, but he would never become President.)

John Sherman was also deeply disappointed. He had truly believed he would emerge victorious in a standoff between Blaine and Grant. Sherman would never be completely satisfied Garfield hadn't been treacherous, but the friendship would hold. And Sherman would continue actively and honorably as Ohio's senior senator for many years.

Ulysses S. Grant seethed. The long standoff and his ultimate rejection at the Convention embarrassed him. Grant was the Victor of Appomattox. He was a two-term President. He was not prepared to lose, especially within his own party. The only reason he had even consented to run was the assurance from his supporters that he would be unbeatable. And too, it was in Grant's nature to want to maintain his stature as the Republican leader. It was also in his nature to hold grudges. The lukewarm cordiality between Grant and Garfield chilled considerably.

Roscoe Conkling was in a venomous rage. His great friend General Grant was angry with him. He had been humiliated; his hold on the Republican party was badly weakened—a situation not likely to improve. His party's hopes in November were equally weak, which would result in further erosion of any political preferment. If Winfield Scott Hancock were elected President and carried New York, Conkling's influence would be minimal. There would be no Cabinet position; no chance for his own nomination in 1884. Adding insult to injury, his oldest and closest friend, Chet Arthur, had accepted the second spot on the ticket—against his advice. So New York's senior senator decided to lay low, sit out the 1880 election, and concentrate on New York politics only. He would rebuild his faction and then he would decimate Judge Robertson and the 18 others who had dared defy him in Chicago.

Chester Alan Arthur, however, was happy. The nomination for Vice President was a bolt from the blue, a higher honor than he had ever dreamed. He was also named chairman of the New York State Republican Committee, a position of substance and action. He would have ample opportunity to demonstrate his considerable administrative and political talent in the weeks ahead. Perhaps for the first time since President Hayes had dismissed him as collector of the Port of New York a few years back, he felt vindicated. Possibly even avenged. He had never been accused of personal malfeasance in office. His dismissal was a political effort to clean up some of Conkling's corruption in the Port of New York. But then again, Conkling had never been (nor would he ever be) specifically accused of personal corruption either.

Chapter 7

It occurs to me in the wisdom of old age and the expertise of hindsight, that the years following the Civil War were generally devoid of a "big issue." We were at peace with ourselves and the world — a wonderful state of affairs that I pray should only happen today. The country was prospering, despite the huge influx of immigrants knocking at our doors. Social issues like women's suffrage and prohibition and labor unions were fringe issues that few people took seriously. Political processes and mechanics were the subjects dear to the hearts of the politicians, and patronage was as important then as election and campaign spending is to the current generation. And it was just as difficult to control.

Gran remarked that after the turmoil of the Civil War, where a half-million men lost their lives or were armless, legless or otherwise wounded; and after the turmoil of reconstruction, and freeing the slaves and giving them the vote, people just wanted to relax and go about the business of making decent lives for themselves and their families. So if politicians had little else to do except worry about who was going to sort mail in Ja-bibb, who really cared? That sounded a lot like how we felt in 1947.

"Did Mollie ever talk about her father and Conkling or Grant?" I asked Gran.

"Not a lot that I recall, dear. Mollie was always instinctively closed-mouthed when it came to how other people felt about each other. She didn't like gossiping. But I remember her telling me that her father always tried to get people to compromise and get along together. He hated acrimony," she said. "Maybe it was the preaching part of his nature."

———

The night after Gran began telling me of her friendship with Mollie *Garfield*, I lay awake in the upper berth. Gran's gentle light snoring from below made me marvel how the elderly woman could sleep so soundly. She claimed the clackety-clack was lulling and comforting. To me it was just one more thing keeping me up. I felt completely boxed in, not only on four sides, but on top as well. It was like sleeping in a coffin. It was also brutally hot, even for August! But mostly, I was thinking about Hal Brown, and reliving the wonderful week we enjoyed together.

I had stayed up late in the lounge car writing to him. What did he actually know about his grandmother? He was the President's great-grandson. He must've known she was the President's daughter. But my thoughts rambled, and I found myself preferring to relive those moonlight kisses, and think about how blue his eyes were. I had never met anyone like him before—nor had a kiss affected me that way before either.

As we crossed the over the northern Great Plains, I learned more and more about Mollie. Gran was deriving great pleasure or comfort (or both) in talking about her dear friend who had just died. Closure, I suppose.

"You know, Kate, I've never talked much about Mollie to anyone. Charlie was fond of her, but wasn't interested in my olden-days talk. His early years were full of poverty and misery and I think he found it hard to listen to anyone talk about a happy childhood. Your mother, of course, was never interested in anything requiring serious thought, and Uncle Henry only liked mechanical things. And your Uncle Walter wasn't especially interested in a woman he met once or twice, and who paid little attention to him. But you, Kate. You're the one to pass it along. It may not seem like much to pass along, but it's a part of our family, and it should be treasured—like the old photographs.

"Anyway, dear, Mollie and I had one of the most delightful summers you could imagine! We went to the beach when it was hot. And we went to the parks, played croquet and hopscotch, and The Captain and Uncle Cork would take us to Pleasure Bay on Sunday afternoons. Something was always going on there. Games, contests, church fairs and picnics. There was a restaurant there with the best clam chowder! And we took the horse car down Ocean Avenue to Broadway to look in Steinbach's window once every week. That was our department store—almost as nice as Wanamaker's. We were at that age when window-shopping was much more fun than dolls.

"The Pach brothers had a photographic studio on Broadway. They were pretty famous—at least in New Jersey. All the important and wealthy people were photographed by Pach. The photo of The Captain and General Grant was by Pach. Mollie and I had our pictures taken too. You didn't smile for the camera. Taking a photograph was a serious matter then, and everybody had to look very pompous. Of course Mollie and I giggled constantly throughout the session, and poor Mr. Pach would ask in his thick German accent, 'Vy can't ve just sit still?' I still have a couple of those photos somewhere. Mollie kept hers as well.

"Sometimes we'd meet some of my school friends downtown for ice cream. Or maybe go to one of their houses for a tea party. If it rained, we made fudge. Every day was filled with something delightful!

"Then Mollie's mother wrote they would be coming to the Elberon Hotel for a fortnight. They were exhausted from the campaign traffic at their home, which had been nicknamed

'Lawnfield' by the press, and they both needed a rest. My mother wrote back suggesting that Mollie remain with us. She had settled in so comfortably, she added, why should she crowd their rooms? And she also invited the entire family for dinner any night they would find convenient.

"That was very much like Miss Peg, Kate. Always willing to extend herself for someone else. Mrs. Garfield responded quickly and thanked *Mr. and Mrs. Dunbar* for their kind invitation. She said Mollie could stay with us if she liked, but she wouldn't know the senator's plans until after they arrived. I suppose that was true enough."

"Did you have a big hoopla at the train station when Senator Garfield arrived?" I asked.

"No, as a matter of fact, we didn't," Gran frowned, "and I don't recall why we didn't either. Perhaps the senator preferred it that way. But I do know that his good friend Col. Rockwell—Lulu's father—arrived a few days in advance. He showed up at our house one afternoon, and Mollie was delighted to see 'Uncle Jarvis.' He stayed for a cold drink and to meet Mollie's hosts. I always liked Col. Rockwell. He was a jolly man! I can't understand how Lulu got to be such a pill with him as a father. Anyway, he arranged for rooms at the Elberon to be set aside as Garfield's office, and I think for Joe Stanley Brown to receive the newspaper reporters, who were becoming a nuisance."

"I assume this is the same Joe Brown who married Mollie," I remarked.

I didn't need to ask Gran what she thought of Brown. She attacked the subject with vigor. "It is indeed, Kate. That summer was the first time I met him. I knew Joe Brown almost as long as I knew Mollie, and of course I would never have said this up until a few days ago, but I never could warm to him. Neither could Henry Cobbs—or Charlie. I don't know what it was exactly. He stifled Mollie so badly. There was no doubt he cared for her and was devoted to all the Garfields, but it occurs to me he was a lot like Mrs. Garfield. Cool and formal. Very straitlaced. No fun in him. Mrs. G. adored her only son-in-law, and he treated her like a goddess.

"Joe was ten years older than Mollie, and Charlie and I came to the opinion long ago that he married her to stay in the Garfield family. I'm almost positive that if he were ten years older and Lucretia Garfield were ten years younger, he would have married her instead. Joe and Mollie had little in common, and I don't mean just their interests. Their whole personalities and characters were opposite. I don't think I'll ever know why Mollie married him. I never pried, and she never volunteered that type of information. She was so young—only eighteen when they married. And she had wanted to do so many things! I supposed she married to get away from her mother. That's usually why girls marry young. But I think she wound up marrying her mother—at least in disposition. But I digress.

"Anyway, once the Garfields arrived in Long Branch en famille, we received an invitation for luncheon—en famille. My father took the afternoon off that day. I can still picture him in his pearl-gray summer suit and straw hat. Most of the time he wore a black business suit—summer and winter. But today was special. Mother wore a white lawn dress. She usually wore white lawn dresses in the summer. And a straw hat with blue ribbons. And I wore a white dress with a pale blue sash, and a straw hat with blue ribbons. I think every twelve-year-old girl had a dress like that. And straw hats with ribbons. The style really didn't change till after World War I. And Miss Peg, being so handy with a needle, made me pink sashes and yellow sashes and matching hat ribbons, so it looked like I had more outfits than I really had.

"Senator and Mrs. Garfield were as cordial as could be, after all, we had been host to their daughter for six weeks. The senator called my father 'Mr. Mayor,' which pleased The Captain no end, as it signified that he was considered a political associate. He and my father talked about their wartime experiences. The senator had fought at Chickamauga, and, as I think I mentioned, my father was wounded near Harper's Ferry just three days before Antietam.

"Then The Captain discussed politics with Candidate Garfield, who declared it would be a hard-fought and hard-won canvass. I don't remember what my mother talked about with Lucretia Garfield — Crete, as her husband called her. It was probably just polite chitchat. I was too busy eavesdropping on The Captain's conversation (it was more interesting) — and realizing how handsome Jim was. He was fifteen then, and the best looking one in the family.

"The upshot was the Garfields would be extremely busy during their stay. The senator had received dozens of invitations, and needed to spend a couple of days in New York to woo and placate the Conkling crowd. But when my mother asked if the Garfield *boys* could come for dinner, Mrs. G. was quick to accept, 'If it wasn't too much trouble for *Mrs. Dunbar*.'

"It was the first and perhaps the only time my parents had a table full of young boys in their house, and what a delight! One of the Marys outdid herself with a delicious dinner, and chocolate cake for dessert. Mother used her best white tablecloth — for *my* friends. I was so proud! Mollie insisted the dinner be at a time when Uncle Cork and Aunt Phee were there, as if they would miss it! She adored them as much as I did, and had written pages and pages about 'Mr. and Mrs. Cork' to her brothers all summer. Everybody wanted to meet them.

"What a grand time we had, Kate! The stories we told! Of course Mollie mentioned Roscoe Conkling, since she knew Uncle Cork would be up in an instant, prancing around the room with his imitation. We were not disappointed. Irv and Abe immediately jumped up and pranced around with him. Uncle Cork looked like the Pied Piper with the two younger Garfield boys trailing him. We shrieked with laughter!"

"Can you do it?" I asked her. Gran thought for a few seconds, then rose, steadied herself against the parlor chair of the rumbling train, and proceeded to mimic the long-forgotten conceited politician. "You must remember he was a great deal larger than I am, Kate, with a big barrel chest. And he wasn't nearly eighty, either," she said as she tilted her head at an angle, and wrinkled her nose as if she were smelling something offensive. "He always carried a stick," she added, extending her hand in pantomime, "and he would walk—no, he really would strut. He always paraded like he wanted everyone to watch him. He was a very snappy dresser, too. If all the men wore gray or white summer suits, Conkling would wear yellow."

Gran began sauntering through the parlor car, swaggering and staggering as the train rumbled, pitching her forward. She grabbed the hand bar on one of the seats to steady herself, and I jumped up to help her. "I'm fine, dear, I'm fine," she said re-seating herself, and staring down a dozen other passengers who were looking on in amazement at this elderly woman clowning around. "I haven't done the Conkling strut in sixty-five years," she said, looking a stunned passenger right in the eye. I have no doubt nobody had the slightest idea what she was doing.

I walked to the bar car and brought back Cokes. We needed a little refreshment. Gran took a long sip and a deep breath and continued her story.

"After dinner we went into the front parlor and my mother played the piano and we sang the old war songs my family loved so much. Only Uncle Cork and my mother could carry a tune. The Garfields all sang as badly as I do, but lusty we were, as well as off-key! Nobody cared. We were having a grand time. Then Aunt Phee politely asked Mollie to play something, and I could see Harry glancing around, shaking his head vigorously at his brothers, who winced and groaned at the thought of Mollie's lack of virtuosity, which they knew as well as we did.

"So Mollie sat at our spinet and started in on poor *Fur Elise*. No sooner did she plunk out the first few notes, than Jim began singing 'Dixie,' except he sang, 'Oh I wish I had a wad of cotton...' Of course we were all rolling with hysterics, since we all concurred about Mollie's noticeable lack of talent. She blushed a little, and Aunt Phee scolded all of us — including Miss Peg — for being rude and unkind to our dear guest, and insisted she continue, and we should mind our manners. Thus chastened, we kept still the best we could while Mollie tortured *Elise*, and then, as the last chord finally crashed down, Abe began singing *Glory, Glory Hallelujah!* Well, needless to say, the hysterics began all over again. It was one of the most joyous evenings I remember from my childhood."

Tears of laughter rolled down my own cheeks when Gran finished her tale of Mollie's piano playing that night. I could picture it in my mind, and it dawned on me that when I was sitting in the hospital solarium shortly before Mollie died, the five of them were obviously reliving that joyous evening as well. It is good to die with wonderful memories in your mind.

—◆—

"When the summer finally ended and Mollie went back to Ohio with her parents, there was no talk of our writing to each other," Gran continued. "Our friendship was so firm by then, it was a foregone conclusion that the correspondence would be maintained.

"'If we win the election, you'll come visit us at the White House,' Mollie said, 'and if we lose, you can come to the farm for Christmas.' I had never been to the White House nor had I ever been on a real farm. I couldn't decide which I would prefer.

"About three weeks later, a large package arrived from A.T. Stewart's. It was an exquisite Minton tea set from the Garfields, to thank us for our hospitality. Do you remember the blue and gold teapot and cream and sugar in my breakfront, Kate?" Gran asked. I didn't recall. "It's magnificent. There are a dozen cups and saucers as well, but they're packed away for special occasions. I can only imagine what it's worth today. Back then, it cost around $100." Since I had no expression on my face, she explained, "Put it this way, dear. In 1880, my father paid his best clerk $10 a week. That set would have been nearly three months of his salary."

I was impressed. The Minton set is now in my possession, with eight of the cups and saucers. In Gran's will, my sisters each got one, as did Uncle Walter's sons. I have no idea if they still have them. I had the tea set appraised six or seven years ago, and produced a small card wrapped in tissue paper and put in a baggie (by me) that said, "To Mr. and Mrs. J.M. Dunbar, with sincere thanks for their affectionate hospitality," and signed Senator and Mrs. James A. Garfield. The appraiser said it would be worth several thousand dollars today.

"Not long before the election, I got a cryptic letter from Mollie," continued Gran. "She said she had a great secret to tell me, but it must be in person. It couldn't be put in a letter. I suggested we devise a code, but she said no, it would have to wait. So I waited.

"Meanwhile, election day grew closer and the campaign became extremely acrimonious. Both candidates were alternately praised and vilified as they usually are. The Captain and the town Republicans went all out, spreading the good word about Senator Garfield. They had their usual torchlight parade. The Democrats in Long Branch did the same about General Hancock. Then they borrowed the torches and had their own parade. Uncle Cork insisted he would write 'Blaine's horse' on his ballot.

"Garfield won. Barely. He won the electoral vote—including the New York block (just barely)—but less than 10,000 popular votes separated the two of them. My friend's father was now going to be President of the United States.

"Of course we were thrilled with the results. My father let out a Rebel yell in his excitement." She paused for a moment. "I am not sure of this, Kate, we never discussed it, but I think The Captain may have had thoughts of running for the state legislature or perhaps even Congress. Uncle Cork insisted he marked "Blaine's horse" on his ballot, but he later admitted that he voted the straight Democratic ticket—for Jersey City—but he marked James Garfield for President. He said any man with five such excellent children had to be a fine man himself.

"Naturally I wrote that news to Mollie as soon as I could, and she eagerly passed it along to her parents. She replied that her father said he was grateful to every man who voted for him, but the vote he received because of his children was the one he'd treasure most. Our new President was a devoted family man."

From Kate's notes, 2002:
The books I researched in 1947-48 were universally laudatory of Garfield's exemplary family life. Unless there were well-known tragedies or major scandals (like Senator Conkling, Mrs. Sprague and the "funny business"), a man's family life was private. Then, in the 1970s, a few fine historians re-examined James Garfield in earnest, and discovered that he did not walk on water, as previously inferred.

In brief: Garfield had been a classmate of Lucretia Rudolph at the Geoga Eclectic Institute in Ohio, which appears to have been similar to a high school. They also continued at Western Reserve College, where "Crete" was one of several female students in Garfield's circle of friends. He was a big, muscular, handsome man, with steel blue eyes and a cheerful outgoing disposition, which, not surprisingly, attracted many of the opposite sex. One of his classmates, a woman a few years his senior, found him particularly attractive and they became fast friends. Whether anything other than platonic friendship transpired is unknown, although the friendship continued for many years until her death.

He became engaged to Crete—I will never know why—before he left for Williams College in Massachusetts. At twenty-two, he was one of the oldest students in his class. While at Williams, he became intimately (what did 1850s people consider intimate?) involved with three or four women—all the while carrying on his engagement-by-

lukewarm-correspondence with his patient fiancée, who, more than once, expected the engagement to be broken. And strange as it seems, Crete not only visited Garfield at Williams, but she was warmly welcomed into his ménage-a-trois—or ménage-a-four or five—by his lady-friends, and she seems to have thought nothing peculiar about it. (Like I said, what was considered intimate in 1850?) Perhaps the Disciples of Christ and the Mormons had more in common than they thought.

Current historians agree with Gran that Crete was a cool, introverted woman, reluctant to express her emotions. She apparently kept a diary of her inner thoughts, however and, when pressed, allowed her fiancé to read some selected pages. Thus satisfied as to her feelings (supposedly), the Garfield wedding took place—five years after the engagement. They were both nearly twenty-seven.

They took a room in a boarding house, common enough in those days, which also housed some of his old friends from Western Reserve, where he had become a teacher and then its president after graduating Williams. His old female classmate (the one with the crush on him) also boarded there. Garfield's shabby treatment of his fiancée carried over to shabby treatment of his wife, since it seems he spent far more time with his pals than his bride. But he must have spent some time with her, since she immediately became pregnant with a little girl they named Eliza, nicknamed "Trot" after a Dickens character. The child died two or three years later.

Meanwhile, Garfield went off to serve in the Ohio State Legislature and shortly thereafter when the Civil War started, left Crete, pregnant again, to serve in the Army.

When he was elected to Congress (in absentia), he again left Crete at home and went to Washington, supposedly at Lincoln's expressed request. He stayed with the Chases. Secretary of the Treasury Salmon P. Chase had been Governor of Ohio and was thus acquainted with former State Legislator Garfield. The housing arrangement served several purposes. The ambitious Chase needed support wherever he could find it, and an up-and-coming Republican Congressman from his pivotal home state was important. Garfield, for his part, was ambitious as well, and the powerful Chase would be a strong ally. It also saved rent money, and Garfield was not wealthy. Finally, they both enjoyed a good game of chess.

Chase's daughter Kate (prior to being Mrs. Sprague of the "funny business") also found Garfield pleasant company despite his marital status. He was seen escorting her to various social and political functions in town, and gossip ensued. Ditto even more rumors about a lady friend Garfield had made when he visited New York.

When word of this reached Crete (as of course it would), she finally spoke up and offered him a separation if he chose, remarking that in five years of marriage, they had only spent five months living together as man and wife. For whatever reasons (not the least of which might have been his political career), Garfield was immediately chastened. He brought her and the baby to Washington, and it is said, the marriage actually began at that point. He was completely devoted to her from then on, and they became the truly loving couple the old reference books claim, and my grandmother knew first hand.

I doubt that Mollie or the uncles ever knew this part of their family history. It is unlikely that such a reserved woman would have bared her soul to her children, particularly about their martyred father, whom they had been brought up to idolize. For certain my grandmother never know those details. To her, the Garfields would always be a close, loving family, including the cool Crete.

Chapter 8

"As it turned out, we never did get to stay at the White House," Gran said about an hour before our train was scheduled to reach Chicago. "We were invited to the inauguration of course. I still have the formal engraved invitation tucked away with the birth announcements and obituaries. But The Captain decided it would be too expensive for one thing, and for another, with the crush of people attending the ceremonies, Mollie and her family would have no time for us. But the real problem, I believe, was that it would be far too strenuous for Miss Peg.

"I was keenly disappointed we wouldn't be there, but Mollie quickly replied that it didn't matter. The Captain was right about the demands on their time. She said I mustn't fret, and perhaps in the spring, once things were settled, we could all come and stay at the White House for a few days. We decided May would be a fine time.

"Shortly after the inauguration, she wrote that the day had been exhausting for all of them, including her elderly grandmother, who had come for the great honor, and was now sharing her incredibly small White House bedroom. Eliza Garfield was the first mother-of-a-president to attend inaugural ceremonies, so a big fuss had been made over her, and she was in her glory. But all the activity was a strain on everyone and the First Family was too tired to enjoy the huge Inaugural Ball. They left early.

"A month later, she wrote that her mother was ill. A bad chill, the doctor said, and ordered her to bed. I sent best wishes from all the Dunbars including Uncle Cork and Aunt Phee. Her next letter said her mother was worse. She had a high fever and a doctor and nurse were in constant attendance. They said Mrs. Garfield had a severe case of malaria and might not survive. The children weren't allowed to see her, although they would write notes to her every day. Little Abe would make drawings—he was always a fine artist—and slip them under her door.

"She added that her father was under enormous political pressure, since there was an equal number of Republicans and Democrats in the Senate, and they couldn't get anything accomplished. They couldn't even decide who would be majority or minority. And if that weren't enough, the Republicans were hopelessly divided between the Grant faction and the Blaine faction, who hated each other more than they hated the Democrats.

"Then, too, her father was inundated with office-seekers lining up in droves in the White House halls every day looking for positions from diplomatic posts to street sweepers. And understandably, the President was seriously concerned about Mrs. G. He sat with her every evening, holding her hand, reading to her, and keeping a cool, wet cloth on her forehead.

"Mollie said she missed me a lot and needed a good friend to talk to. I remember writing back, enclosing a little code I had concocted, in case she wanted to share something private. She said my code was too complicated, and anyway she couldn't concentrate. The whole family was worried.

"Of course I could understand how everyone was irritable and worried. I didn't understand the political maneuvering since I was still a child, and when I got older, it no longer mattered. But I did understand what it would mean if Mollie's mother died.

Note from Kate, 2002:

When I decided to write Gran's story a few years ago, I spent a good deal of time at the local library, and thanks to my granddaughter-in-law, "on line," even at my advanced age. The gist of the complication lay in the fact that Garfield, immediately after election, named Senator Blaine as his Secretary of State, thereby re-infuriating the already infuriated Conkling, Grant, Chester Arthur and their friends. Garfield took great care to balance his Cabinet, a practice common in those times (perhaps even today), to include representation from all areas of the country. New York needed a Cabinet post because of its obvious importance logistically and commercially, but doubly so because Conkling (and Grant) eventually had made some effort in Garfield's campaign, delivered the state's essential electoral votes (just barely), and deemed themselves owed big-time. The Vice Presidency for Arthur was nice, but it didn't count.

Garfield had promised to give "consideration" to New York, but was growing more and more irritated at Conkling, indeed the entire Stalwart bunch, for meddling too much in appointments. There were more than 100,000 federal jobs up for grabs, a large number of them requiring the president's personal approval. Even Grant got into the act requesting consideration — or non-consideration — of somebody he favored or opposed. The office-seekers my grandmother mentioned were indeed a serious, time-consuming problem. Twenty years before, Lincoln had complained bitterly about the same thing. It took up an inordinate amount of time, and nothing was accomplished. Fortunately for the country, there were very few pressing issues of real consequence in 1881.

◄━━◄

"The whole country was concerned about Mrs. Garfield," continued Gran. "The Captain, as mayor, issued a proclamation for her recovery, and every church and synagogue in Long Branch offered special prayers for her renewed health. Perhaps the prayers were heard. By mid-May, Mrs. Garfield began to recover—very, very slowly. The children were finally permitted to see her for five or ten minutes twice a day. She had lost a great deal of weight—and she was small to begin with.

"By early June, it was decided Mrs. G. would recuperate faster and better at the seashore, since Washington summers are always oppressive and bad for everyone's health. Malaria is a recurring disease, Kate. It's not like smallpox—once you get it you're immune. Malaria can flare up again all your life. The doctors didn't want her to relapse. Mollie wired she was coming with her mother and younger brothers, and they would all stay at The Elberon.

"The Elberon Hotel was only twenty minutes by horse-car. I could still see her almost every day, and I did. Irv and Abe had their tutor with them, so he kept the boys occupied. Mrs. Garfield's friend Mrs. Childs lived down the street and organized card games and book clubs and other non-strenuous activities to amuse the first lady. And of course the Rockwells-plus-Lulu were on hand. I don't think the Garfields went anywhere without them. Mollie and Lulu and I spent a lot of time together. I began to like Lulu a little better—but not much. She was still a whiner, and you can ask your mother, Kate, how much I can't abide whining! But Mollie kept hinting that she needed to talk to me 'in private,' so one afternoon, when Lulu had the sniffles or something, Mollie took the horse-car to our house."

Gran shifted in her seat and complained of being stiff as a board. It was the first time I had heard her complain during the whole trip. Traveling on a train for three or four days is definitely not comfortable, no matter what the advertisements say. I don't know how the pioneers of olden days traveled in covered wagons for months on end! My own young bones were aching, and each morning when I would pry myself from the upper berth, I could swear my joints made noise. But Gran never said a word.

We got up and walked through the cars to stretch our legs,

and then sat in the lounge car and had a Coke. It seemed to rejuvenate her, and she continued her story.

"We went upstairs to my room, closed the door, and Mollie started telling me her great secret. 'Shortly before Papa was elected last November,' she began, 'my parents were obliged to attend some political dinners out of town, so I accepted an invitation from an old friend of theirs to spend a few days in Cleveland. Their daughter Jane is two years ahead of me, but we've always gotten on well, and the invitation was welcome. Jane had tickets for a lecture. Some of her school friends were going, chaperoned by one of their mothers. It seemed innocent enough. But you'll never guess who the lecturer was! It was Miss Anthony! Miss Susan B. Anthony!'

"Now Kate, of course I had heard of Susan B. Anthony. Everyone had heard of her. She was probably the most famous woman in the country. The Captain and Uncle Cork made jokes about her, and my mother and Aunt Phee would glance at each other and laugh nervously when Uncle Cork remarked it was 'a shame the old battleaxe wasn't pretty so's she would ha' married and had a family instead of stirrin' up trouble.'

"'I was never so enthralled by anyone!' Mollie told me. 'She is a wonderful speaker, Louise. As good as any man I ever heard. Everybody in the room could hear her, and there must have been more than three hundred people! Everything she said made perfect sense. She talked about how our grandmothers and great-grandmothers had worked hard and had overcome terrible obstacles to come to this country or had gone West with the pioneers. How they worked the fields, ran the house, spun and wove, cooked and sewed, doctored the sick, bore and buried children and sometimes fought alongside their husbands against hostile Indians. She said our ancestresses did not suffer these trials so their granddaughters and great-granddaughters could be shoved into the background like puppets on strings, bullied by their fathers and husbands.

"'She said more and more women were being educated

today. The war had turned orphaned and widowed women into wage-earners. More and more were becoming doctors and lawyers and teachers. More and more were working in shops and factories and offices right alongside men. Meanwhile former slaves and ignorant or illiterate men, immigrant men who could barely even speak English were all allowed to vote, while these educated, competent and self-supporting women were treated like inferior beings! Oh Louise, I wish you could have heard her!' Mollie said.

"'Last summer I had no idea what I wanted to do with my life, but that has changed! I want to work with Miss Anthony! I told Jane I should like very much to meet her, and she mentioned it to her friend's mother, and can you believe it? I was invited backstage afterwards. I'm sure it was because my of father, but I didn't care! I was thrilled just being in her presence. It's funny, Louise,' she continued after a pause, 'she's fairly small—smaller than I am, but a little bigger than Mama. Maybe like your Aunt Cork, only a little stouter. And older. Old enough to be my grandmother. And she is certainly not pretty. But when she looks at you, her eyes have a warmth and shine to them, and in a way, she becomes very beautiful. When I told her I wanted to work with her, she smiled and asked my age. She was surprised when I said I'd be fourteen in January, and guessed I might have been sixteen or more.

"'Then she asked how my parents felt about women's suffrage. I told her Papa believed an intelligent woman would always have considerable influence on her husband—and that included politics. Mama and Papa always exchange views on current events. But Papa doesn't believe a woman has the ability to comprehend a large number of issues at the same time and weigh them in good balance so as to cast a well-considered vote. Besides, he says our church frowns on it. My mother is bright and well read, and she enjoys political discussions. But Mama....well, Mama always thinks what Papa tells her to think.'

"Now, Kate, I just sat there amazed at what Mollie was telling me. I had never given any thought to voting—men or women. But then again, I was only thirteen.

"Mollie went on. 'That's not all, Louise! Miss Anthony smiled and patted my hand, and said I was still a little girl and must not disobey my parents, and especially since Papa might be President, I must always behave properly. She said when I got a little older, if I still felt the same way, perhaps I might become more involved. I said I was old enough and wanted to help. She smiled again. She has a radiant smile, Louise. It lights up her face! She said in that case, I should read two or three newspapers cover to cover every day in order to keep abreast with what is going on. And of course, I should always listen attentively whenever my parents discuss political issues, and ask questions, if they permit it. Then I asked if I might write to her. She was delighted, and gave me her general delivery address, which forwards her mail since she travels so much. And I gave her two dollars—to help with her expenses. She hugged me and thanked me and said she looked forward to hearing from me.'"

I watched Gran's face closely while she was talking about Mollie and Susan B. Anthony. I would be eligible to cast my first vote in the '48 election, thanks I suppose, to Miss Anthony. She had devoted most of her life to women's suffrage, and I think she died of old age several years before it was actually passed. I had always known Gran was very active in the suffrage movement. For sure she voted in every election. I think my mother voted too, but I wasn't as sure. What interested me most was that when Gran talked about Susan B. Anthony, I swear she looked twenty years younger.

"Mollie said there was still more to the story!" Gran continued. "She said shortly after the election, she mentioned women's suffrage (but not meeting Miss Anthony) to her father, who reiterated his position that an intelligent woman exerts great influence on her husband, and that included political influence. 'But when I said perhaps I should start reading the newspapers every day,' Mollie said, 'Papa positively beamed, and said what a fine idea! My parents always took several papers while they were in Washington, and once in the White House, would receive dozens from all over the country. He said I could clip out articles of interest and leave them on his desk if I liked. So I did.

"'I wrote Miss Anthony about it, and shortly before Christmas, I got a letter from her saying I was doing splendidly, and might consider slipping in an item or two about women's suffrage along with other clippings. I wrote back and said I had already been doing that, and I enclosed another $2 for her expenses.

"'Then,' she paused very ominously and said, 'after Papa was inaugurated and we moved to the White House, I got into a scrape. All the mail for the family goes through Joe Stanley Brown, Papa's secretary. I am fond of Mr. Brown,' she said, 'but he is very thorough. He saw a letter addressed to Miss Mollie Garfield, with a return address from Susan B. Anthony, and he immediately sent it on to my father, who sent for me. He handed me the letter, unopened, and said he suspected that I favored women's suffrage, since I kept sending him so many clippings on the subject.

"'Then he got very serious. He reminded me what our pastor said, adding that I was entitled to my opinions, of course. He also said if he were plain Mr. Garfield, or even Congressman Garfield, he would not object to my corresponding with the infamous Miss Anthony. But since he was President, such a correspondence could be very embarrassing. Miss Anthony might use my name improperly and cause a scandal, and she and her supporters liked nothing better than to cause a great commotion. He said our whole family was now in a position of public trust, and we must never do or say anything even slightly improper to draw unnecessary attention to ourselves. He said I must never correspond with Miss Anthony again as long as he was President. He made me give him my solemn promise.'

"Now, Kate," Gran said, "my mouth fell open while Mollie was telling me all this. She was absolutely right about it being too secret even for a cipher code. Then she went on. There was more! 'I was devastated,' Mollie told me. 'I didn't want to disobey my father—the President of the United States. But I didn't want to lose touch with Miss Anthony either. If I didn't respond to her letter, she would write again, wondering why she hadn't heard from me. If I sent her letter back unopened, it would be unconscionably rude. So I wrote her and told her exactly what Papa had said, adding that I had a wonderful idea. I told her to use the name Sarah Allen, and I would concoct a story about her being a school teacher friend—of your Aunt Cork, by the way, who traveled a lot. I suggested she send me picture postal cards from time to time. They are popular and innocent enough. This way, when she sends a letter occasionally, no one would think anything of it. And if I write to a Mrs. Sarah Allen, I wouldn't be breaking my promise to Papa. At least not technically.'

"I was astounded, Kate!" Gran exclaimed. "I hardly knew how to respond. I never thought Mollie could be so devious, or clever, for that matter. It was very clever. Mollie casually mentioned at dinner one evening that her friend Louise (whom they all knew) wanted to be a teacher. Very commendable. Both the President and Mrs. Garfield had been teachers. Then she added that Louise's Aunt Cork (whom they all had heard about dozens of times) had a friend who taught school, and now that she was a widow, went to all sorts of interesting places. She had asked Louise if her aunt's friend might send her a picture postal card to the White House. She had decided to start a collection.

"Mollie wasn't exactly telling a lie. It was a sort-of lie. 'Sure enough,' Mollie continued, 'a few weeks later I received a card from Denver, Colorado, from Mrs. Sarah Allen. By then, Mama had taken ill and people were sending their good wishes from all over the country. Nobody was bothering about my mail. I've gotten post cards from Salt Lake City, San Francisco, Fort

123

Worth, Texas, and New Orleans. And two real letters.' Mollie was obviously very proud of her friendship with Miss Anthony. 'And she promised she wouldn't use my name or do anything to embarrass my father. I am still a child, according to her, and she has strict rules about children honoring their parents. A little deviousness notwithstanding. She said when I got older, I might help her embarrass another president, if I wanted.'"

"'And nobody knows about this?' I asked her, with my eyes wide open in wonderment.

"'Just you, Louise. I can't trust anyone else. When I write her, I sneak my letter out in one of my school books and mail it in a public mailbox, but I'm afraid I might drop it and the letter would slip out, or someone might pick up my book accidentally. So I need to ask a great favor of you.' Mollie hesitated and then continued. 'Everybody knows we write long letters to each other almost every week. If I send my letter to Miss Anthony along with yours in the same envelope you could mail it for me. I would put postage on it of course. That is, if you would.'"

Gran took a deep breath and looked directly at me. "That's how I became involved in the suffrage movement. I became a secret postmistress between Mollie and Susan B. Anthony. We never told this to anyone. Not ever. She never told Joe or her brothers. Or her grandchildren. Now that she's gone, you are the first to know.'"

I was dumbfounded. There was so much I didn't know about my grandmother. It seemed to me that she was deriving great pleasure and perhaps a form of release by finally divulging a secret she and her friend had kept between them for more than sixty-five years.

———

We switched trains in Chicago for the last leg home to Pittsburgh, and as our train rattled through Indiana, Gran had an idea. "We stop in Indianapolis in an hour, Kate. Suppose we wire Uncle Henry and tell him we're taking a few extra days. We'll go on to Philadelphia, and then take the train to Long Branch for a couple of days. My treat." When I didn't respond, she tempted, "You've never seen the Atlantic Ocean."

Large water is large water, I supposed, and hesitated further. I desperately needed a good night's sleep — in my own bed. I needed clean clothes. Everything I had with me had been jammed into suitcases and if nothing else, was horribly wrinkled. I needed a hot, luxuriating bubble bath. Most of all, I knew there would be a letter from Hal waiting for me and I was counting the hours.

"I would so love to see my old home town again," Gran sighed, "I'm old now, and Lord only knows what time I have left. I know it won't be the same, but it's where I grew up." Then she added softly, "I want to visit my parents' graves again. And Uncle Cork's and Aunt Phee's. And Henry Cobbs'. I've paid every year for them to be maintained, and it would be nice to see that my money hasn't been wasted."

Gran knew exactly what she was doing. Her mention of graves reminded me how my own father was in his grave, and I went every year around his birthday to place a wreath and have a chat. Of course it would mean a lot to her. If I didn't go, she would never go by herself or have the chance again. It would be another good deed to put on my credit side. I said okay.

I wired Uncle Henry, adding that when we reached Long Branch, I would wire again. Then I sent a wire to the Scarboro Hotel, per Gran's instructions, reserving a room overlooking the ocean. My grandmother was very happy.

—◦—

"Mrs. Garfield recovered steadily at The Elberon, thanks to her basically strong constitution and refreshing cool ocean breezes," Gran continued, as the train pulled out from the Indianapolis station. "The hotel put a carriage at her disposal, and she would go to the Iron Pier and sit in the shade under the pavilion for a while. Mrs. Rockwell or Mrs. Childs usually went with her, and sometimes Lulu and Mollie went along. There were dozens of little stalls so they could window-shop. Sometimes I met them there, and we'd walk out all the way to the end to watch the New York steamboats dock, and hundreds—and I mean hundreds—of people would get off!

"Mrs. Garfield was even well enough to spend a day at Mr. Hoey's gardens, which had become quite an attraction in town. Miss Peg and Aunt Phee loved going!"

Mr. John Hoey, I came to learn, had been president of a large freight shipping company, and was consumed—truly consumed—by his passion for gardening. A couple of dozen gardeners and stone masons and their families had been brought over from Italy at enormous expense, expressly for the purpose of turning Mr. Hoey's property into a showplace, which they did. His home was magnificent, with palatial gardens, and neo-classical statues everywhere you looked. They said one of the flower beds was designed to duplicate an ornate Oriental carpet he had purchased. Thousands and thousands of flowers planted in precise order to match the colors as exactly as possible. Mr. Hoey could look out his window and actually think he was looking down on a huge carpet. It was definitely a showplace. Hoey spent millions, and, as it turned out a dozen years later, he was also helping himself to the company's treasury to pay for his avocation. He ended up in prison for fraud or embezzlement or both. It is a fact: the more things change, the more they stay the same.

"Anyway," Gran said, "one morning a messenger came with formal invitation for Mrs. John M. Dunbar and Miss Louise Dunbar. Mrs. Garfield was giving a tea at The Elberon in a few days. There was a handwritten P.S. saying if Mrs. Corcoran were available, she would be welcome. We immediately wired Aunt Phee, who took the train from Jersey City by herself, sporting a new hat. It wasn't every day she was asked to tea with the

President's wife. Uncle Cork was understandably miffed. Everyone else was getting presidential attention except him — the one who provided the 'most treasured vote.'

"It had to be the largest and grandest tea party my mother and Aunt Phee ever attended. There were at least a hundred women in The Elberon's ballroom, and a half dozen of Mrs. G's friends poured for her. The hotel outdid itself with cucumber and watercress sandwiches, and twenty or thirty types of pastry, each prettier than the next. They used their finest linen and china and elegant samovars and tea services. Even the sugar was fashioned into little cubes. Oh, it was such a fancy party! Aunt Phee talked about it for the rest of her long life!

"Mollie helped pour for a while, too. She was looking very grown up lately. She was maturing rapidly and was always what you would call 'well endowed.' Shortly before the election, her mother insisted she start wearing a corset. I was growing up too, but I still looked more like a child. People seeing us together usually thought she was my elder by three or maybe even four years. She wasn't even fifteen, and looked eighteen. I was a little shy of fourteen, and looked it.

"Then Mollie announced her father was coming the following week. His first four months in office had been extremely trying, and he was looking forward to a pleasant holiday.

From Kate's notes, 1947:

Once the excitement of the election victory subsided, Garfield faced the task of choosing a Cabinet. It was a monumental exercise in diplomacy; he owed rewards to both the "Stalwarts" and the "Half-Breeds."

In appointing Blaine Secretary of State, Garfield opened a can of worms. The Secretary of State was the most important — and visible — Cabinet position, tantamount to a prime ministership. The Stalwarts fumed. They felt Garfield would be in Blaine's thrall; that Blaine, not Garfield, would be running the show. After all, Garfield was unknown. Blaine had been in positions of leadership for years.

The new President asked New York industrialist Levi P. Morton to serve as either Secretary of the Treasury or Minister to France. They had known each other for years, and while Morton was nominally connected to the Stalwarts and thus to Conkling, he was also an honest man whom Garfield could trust and endorse. But Morton consulted Conkling, who was seething over Blaine's appointment. Conkling insisted Morton would be pitted against Blaine in constant political battle, and the business giant was a political novice; Morton would be no match for the Plumed Knight. Morton declined.

But if Morton would not take Treasury, Garfield would not give Treasury to New York. Treasury had entirely too many important patronage positions, and the President would be inviting not only scandal and corruption, but inferences of being under Conkling's thumb. Garfield was no novice. He fully intended to be his own man. He would be glad to meet and consult with all interested parties, but in the end, he would make his own decisions.

Garfield labored for weeks choosing his official family. Stalwarts like Pennsylvania's Don Cameron and Illinois' John Logan needed to be rewarded with acceptable Cabinet seats. Likewise the West and the South. And of course, the Half-Breeds who supported Blaine—and who eventually espoused his cause. Everyone needed to be included.

After sleepless nights, bouts of indigestion and dozens of letters and telegrams, only a Cabinet position for New York remained. Postmaster General was traditionally deemed the most "political" place of all. While it was of low consequence vis-à-vis governmental affairs, it had the distinction of offering the greatest number of patronage assignments. Thomas James, a Stalwart and close associate of Conkling, after considerable political wheeling and dealing, and again, over Conkling's advice to decline, accepted. To make matters even worse, Thomas Platt, New York's junior senator, was cajoled into supporting the Cabinet nomination.

At a special session the day after the inauguration, the Senate heard

Garfield's carefully chosen Cabinet nominees. He had plotted it with the precision of a quadrille. But Postmaster General was a paltry reward for all New York had done for Garfield, and Garfield had promised to take care of New York in return for Conkling's half-hearted efforts. The senior senator was livid. But despite his wrath, the cautiously selected Cabinet was approved by Congress with little fanfare.

Then came four months of intense in-fighting, during which time the country nearly ground to a halt. The Senate was equally divided: 37 Democrats and 37 Republicans. According to the Constitution, the Vice President, as president of the Senate, has a vote ONLY in the event of a tie. He has no vote whatsoever in political caucuses. Which party would be majority and which minority? The Senate could not organize itself. No one would give an inch. And since the Republicans were squabbling amongst themselves, it remained sensible strategy for the Democrats to chuckle and allow them the proverbial "sufficient rope."

For three months, Garfield and the Senate, led by Conkling, fought over everything—but mostly appointments. There were 100,000 federal positions for the President to bestow, and a half-million applicants. In 1881, the White House, as well as all government buildings, was open to the public. Anyone wishing to see the President or a Cabinet Secretary merely had to show up and wait his turn. The lines were long. Garfield, like his predecessors, was inundated by office seekers, waving letters of recommendation for post offices, embassies, customs inspectors, and the like. Joe Stanley Brown's office was besieged daily by people requesting appointments with the President.

If squabbling and office-seeking weren't enough of a headache for the new President, Garfield had an outspoken traitor in his "official family": Vice President Chester Alan Arthur. Arthur had no national experience or exposure. The new Vice President and Conkling had a twenty-year friendship so his loyalties lay with his friend—and with New York. Vote after vote culminated in a tie and when Arthur cast the deciding vote, it was a Stalwart vote.

James Garfield was an accommodating man by nature. He tried his best to please the Stalwarts. *He approved a long list of New York appointments suggested by Conkling, and in doing so he believed he had fulfilled his so-called "promise" to consider and consult with the New York Republicans. Conkling might be livid about the paltry Postmaster Generalship going to his state, but thousands of jobs were at the disposal of that office.*

Finally, Garfield needed to reward William Robertson, the leader of the renegade New York Republicans whose disaffection had led to the President's eventual nomination. It had to be a job of substance. He appointed him Collector of the Port of New York, the position held by Chester Alan Arthur—until President Hayes removed him in a cleansing initiative against a corrupt department full of Conkling's spoilsmen.

Now it was insult added to injury. If Conkling was furious about the insignificant Cabinet post, he positively lost complete control when he learned that his arch-enemy, William Robertson, was to be given the highest federal appointment in New York, if not the country. He exercised the long-practiced tactic of "senatorial privilege," by which a senator of the President's party can deny any appointment made in his state—without the need to justify his refusal. This unwritten policy had been upheld since the early days of the Republic, and the senators guarded their purview zealously. No one was more zealous than Conkling.

He raged and fumed, wheedled, cajoled and bullied his fellow senators to support his denial of Robertson, employing every political maneuver in his extensive stable of parliamentary procedure, of which he was an acknowledged expert. No senator was willing to forgo his right to "senatorial privilege."

But Garfield was fully sick and tired of the Machine Boss and the openly traitorous Arthur, who by now, was completely loathed by the entire Cabinet. If the President were truly to be President, it must be on his own terms, and not dictated to by Roscoe Conkling—or the Senate. Through some shrewd political maneuvering of his own, albeit with some tactical suggestions from Blaine, another parliamentary expert, he forced Conkling's hand. Now it was personal. It would be winner-

take-all. He announced in no uncertain terms that it was not the job of the President of the United States to be the recording clerk of the Senate.

The country was electrified! It had had its fill of Conkling, too. Telegrams poured in congratulating the President for his courageous stand in tackling the Boss system. Newspaper editors across the country were unanimous in their praise. According to one of them, "With the overthrow of machine control as it has existed in New York and Pennsylvania, and the old would-be dictators remanded to their proper place, a great advance has been made toward that purer condition of political and public affairs that all honest men favor."

At last, in a desperate attempt to win back the cause of senatorial privilege, Conkling persuaded his fellow New York Senator Thomas C. Platt to play their "ace." They decided to resign their seats, certain the New York State Legislature would immediately re-elect them and return them to the Senate in triumph. They would be exonerated. Senatorial privilege would remain intact. The Senate would be the supreme branch of government. Garfield would be humbled. And above all, William Robertson would not receive the plum appointment.

To the astonishment of Conkling and Platt, their resignations were accepted, and the automatic re-election by the New York Legislature was not forthcoming. Indeed, even after weeks of bickering, bargaining, humiliating campaigning, and a personal extra-marital scandal concerning Platt, the senators from New York were replaced. Conkling would retire from public life entirely. Platt, the more affable of the two, would rise again as Party Boss during the next decade.

Garfield had earned his vacation.

"I don't remember much about the President's visit that week, except for two things," Gran continued. "First, Uncle Cork finally got to meet President Garfield. The Elberon Hotel had hung a big silk flag out front to signify the President was in residence, but Garfield had asked Col. Rockwell and Admiral

Porter and a couple of his other friends to greet his well wishers and take cards, but to turn everyone away—politely. He needed a rest and wanted to spend private time with his family.

"He didn't want his wife under a strain greeting people either, now that she was beginning to feel better. He just wanted to listen to the quiet lapping of the sea upon the shore, he claimed, and other than going to Church on Sunday, he seldom left his rooms. Late in the evening when the hordes had gone, he and Mrs. Garfield would walk along the bluff for a while. The summer cottage residents—the wealthy ones, and even Garfield's personal friends—all respected the President's wish for privacy, and stayed away. As a matter of fact, the social scene was very dull that week, according to the people who ran the casinos and clubs and the track and the caterers and florists. Nobody gave parties, since they couldn't have one without inviting the President. It was just as dull as when the Hayeses came.

"The Captain received a personal note, however, inviting him to stop by any time it would be convenient. It was just a courtesy, but it was very important and welcome to my father. He brought me along—and Uncle Cork. Col. Rockwell had gotten to know me quite well by then, so when we all showed up, he personally escorted us to the President's rooms, where we were greeted with warmth and enthusiasm. It was true what people said: Garfield was an outgoing, friendly man. He hugged me and told me I had grown since he last saw me, and that I was getting to be a real beauty.

"Then he shook hands with The Captain who presented his brother-in-law, 'Sergeant Daniel Corcoran of the Jersey City Police Force.' Garfield grinned broadly when he was finally introduced to the provider of 'the most treasured vote,' and pumped his hand up and down and clapped him on the shoulder.

"'So you're the Mr. Cork I've been hearing so much about,' the President said. 'My children have praised you to the skies!'

"You can tell when a politician is glad-handing, or when he is sincere, Kate. Garfield was one-hundred percent genuine in his greeting. When Uncle Cork replied that he was honored to meet a man with five of the finest children he had the privilege to know, the President beamed from ear to ear, and remarked that perhaps he should send them to have dinner with members of the Senate so they might be more co-operative. Then he winked at The Captain.

"Ah, Kate, Uncle Cork lived to be sixty-six years old, and to his last breath insisted he was a diehard Democrat, except for Garfield. He said he could take a man's measure by looking him straight in the eye, and Garfield's clear blue eyes held no subterfuge. He had nothing to gain from my uncle. Garfield's charm was not political, it was personal, and it was a mighty charm. Uncle Cork would have voted Garfield for King.

"I expected to get to know President Garfield a lot better, especially since I had been invited to spend a fortnight at their farm in late August, and was looking forward to it more than anything else—even more than going to the White House, which they said I might do at Christmas. Hal and Jim (who was getting better looking every day) offered to teach me to milk a cow. Of course, as things turned out, I never got there that summer, and I still don't know how to milk a cow, not that it matters.

"The other thing I remember about the President's visit was all the talk about the deliberate snubbing by Grant. General Grant, for all that we loved him, was a peculiar man in his own way. Complicated. Full of contradictions. Part of him was warm and affectionate, like he was with me and all children, I think. Sympathetic to his old comrades in arms. Gentle with animals. But a part of him was ice-blue steel. Unforgiving. Cold to the core. Maybe that's why he won the battles. But the rancor of the past year's politics had been festering. Grant valued loyalty above all else, and gave it in return. He stood with Conkling, and wanted nothing to do with Garfield.

"Grant had made a couple of appearances on behalf of the

party ticket and expected certain courtesies as a former president. He recommended some of his friends for patronage offices, and while Garfield was happy to oblige where he could, he had finally had his fill of Grant's meddling, too. The new President was polite, but firm.

"Meanwhile, politicians from all over had come to Long Branch the week President Garfield was in town, even knowing they'd be turned away. But they came anyway, shook hands with Admiral Porter or Colonel Rockwell or General Swaim, another of Garfield's old friends, left their cards and signed the book as a gesture of respect. But Grant fumed and stayed away, even though his cottage was only a few doors down.

"The general was very conspicuous by his absence. I'm not sure why he didn't arrange to be out of town if he didn't want to call on Garfield. Had he come, he would have been ushered in immediately, out of courtesy from one President to another. But the acrimony of the past year was smoldering. Senator Conkling had resigned by then." Gran shook her head slowly, trying to remember the once bold headlines that had now become fine-print footnotes. "People said the resignation was a ploy and Conkling fully expected to be returned to the Senate when the New York legislature met. Only it didn't work out that way. The New York legislature named someone else. Conkling never came back to the Senate. Or to Long Branch.

"The talk about Grant not paying his respects to Garfield eventually became so loud it made the general uncomfortable, so he finally showed up at The Elberon at the last minute—an hour before Garfield and his four sons were to depart. They shook hands, made some strained small talk according to Colonel Rockwell, and Grant left in five minutes.

"Mrs. Garfield, Mollie and the Rockwell women were to planning to remain for another week. The President had been invited to be commencement speaker at his old alma mater. Since it also coincided with his 25th class reunion, he was looking forward to seeing many old Williams College friends.

Hal and Jim were set to attend Williams in the fall, and were coming along to register early. Then the family would tour New England for a week. Secretary Blaine had invited them to his home in Maine. The whole Cabinet was going, Mollie had said, so a huge entourage would pick them up at the train station on July 2 and go directly to New England."

Gran stopped. It was getting late. The following day we would arrive in Philadelphia and then go on to her birthplace, the town where she grew up and lived until she married for the second time. "I'm tired, Kate," she said. "I will finish the story tomorrow."

She had been telling me about Mollie and her family for three days. Of course she was tired. I sat up a while longer, writing my diary-letter to Hal, asking him dozens of questions about his family, and suspecting I knew far more about them than he did. I wished he could have been with me to hear Gran's story. He is like me that way: a keeper of the family flame.

<hr>

"The following week, we were getting set for the 4th of July," Gran said as we took our third cup of coffee to our now-familiar seats in the parlor car. "We always did it big in Long Branch. There was a parade down Ocean Avenue to Broadway, and then up Broadway for another half mile or more. All the hotel bands marched and played. All the school bands and town bands marched and played. All the old soldiers marched. General Sheridan would lead the GAR contingent and General Grant had agreed to review the parade. We had a dozen floats, each pulled by two horses. High-school girls dressed up in white dresses with red, white and blue sashes, and rode on the platforms depicting 'Columbia' or 'Liberty' or the 'Spirit of Union.' Some tall man in town was always Abraham Lincoln on one of the floats—a tableau with the theme, 'He still lives.' Vendors sold peanuts and ice cream. We pulled out all the flags and bunting and rosettes and decorated the gas lamps on the streets. Everyone in town participated. If they weren't marching, they were lining the street to watch.

"All the churches and clubs had outings. The Captain and Uncle Cork planned to march with the GAR, of course, and then as Mister Mayor, my father would speak at the Town Hall where they always laid a wreath to their fallen comrades. Then we were all going to our church's picnic. My father would stay a while, then go on to the Republican Club picnic. And later that evening, The Captain and Uncle Cork would stop at Daly's Casino for a whiskey and some camaraderie with their old army buddies.

"Neither my father nor uncle gambled except for a small wager at the racetrack once in a while. They worked too hard to throw their money away on the spin of a wheel or turn of a card. But the Long Branch casinos were famous for their opulence and glamour. I never went there myself. Ladies weren't welcome, and besides, they closed it down by the time I was twenty-one. The Captain only went for official business and the 4th of July party with the Grand Army of the Republic.

"July 2 was a Saturday that year. Saturdays were always busy at the dry goods store. But at 9:30 that morning, my father drove the store wagon in front of our house, bounded up the steps and looked straight at Mother and me. He was pale and obviously agitated.

"'The President has been shot!' he said as we gasped, trying to comprehend the unthinkable. 'I don't know much more. It just came over the wires. I'm going to see if Mrs. Garfield needs any assistance, and then I'll be at the town hall.' With that, he ran back down the stairs and took off in the wagon, leaving Mother and me stunned.

"I wasn't even fourteen years old, Kate. I didn't quite grasp the seriousness of the situation for the country. I wasn't even born when Lincoln had been assassinated in '65. But, unlike the rest of the country, my best friend's father had been shot—a man I was very fond of, and whom I expected to get to know much better than most. I was in a flood of tears, and begged Miss Peg to take me to The Elberon to see Mollie right away. She said firmly that Mollie needed to be with her mother and we would be in the way.

"So instead we went to church, which was filling up with our fellow Lutherans, said a prayer for the President's swift recovery, and then took a horse car to the town hall, where dozens of people were milling about. There was a telegraph office inside, and a clerk nailed bulletins to a board as soon as the news came over the wire. The big hotels had telegraph wires direct to their lobbies and were doing the same, as was the newspaper office and the railroad stations. People gathered at the closest telegraph office. I think everyone in town had heard the news by 10:30.

"The Captain showed up ten minutes after we arrived at the town hall, spied us, and motioned to follow him upstairs. He said he had seen Mrs. Garfield and Mollie and they were bearing up admirably. Mr. Childs had sent his carriage and driver to take them to the station and the Pennsylvania Railroad was sending a special train to rush them back to Washington.

"He said Mrs. Garfield was uncharacteristically warm as she thanked him for coming, and mentioned that General Grant had just stopped by to pay his respects. He told her he had seen thousands of wounded soldiers similarly injured during the war and who survived to this day.

"'Do you think that's true, Captain?' she asked my father, using his familiar nickname for the first and only time.

"'Of course the general is right,' my father told her, patting his own useless arm. 'I hardly notice my right arm anymore, and feel no pain. There must be thousands more who've had worse,' he added.

"He said it seemed to give her comfort. And he added that my friend Mollie was behaving with uncommon bravery.

"The basic story, as it began to emerge, was that Garfield had been at the train station when he was shot — twice. His condition

137

was serious, but he was conscious. There were conflicting stories with every telegraph message, but at least two doctors had been summoned to the station within fifteen minutes, and confirmed the urgency. After an agonizing hour lying on the floor of the station on a mattress pulled from a Pullman car, they finally brought the stricken President back to the White House.

"As bulletin after bulletin was nailed to boards all across the country, people began mumbling less about the President and more about the assassin, who turned out to be a strange little fellow named Guiteau. He was supposedly a staunch Stalwart, who expected to be rewarded handsomely when Chester Arthur became President. They said he wanted to be Minister to France or Austria, or some inconceivable position like that. There was ominous talk about a conspiracy. Every adult in town could vividly remember when Lincoln was shot and the conspiracies that subsequently unfolded.

"After two hours standing around the town hall waiting for updated bulletins, Miss Peg was getting very tired, so we went home. By then Aunt Phee and Uncle Cork had arrived for the 4th of July festivities. I took one look at their sad faces and immediately started crying again. Miss Peg brought out the Bible and some paper and pens, and said we would each read a passage, and then write to Mrs. Garfield and Mollie to let them know our prayers were with them.

"Needless to say all the 4th of July plans were cancelled, and every church in Long Branch was packed to the rafters for special services. I suppose it was like that everywhere. The bulletins were coming every half hour. Garfield was critical, but he had survived the night. Specialists from New York and Philadelphia had been summoned, and while they tried be optimistic, they said he was very seriously injured and the prognosis was uncertain. Meanwhile, Guiteau, safely behind bars, still proclaimed to be the 'Stalwart of the Stalwarts,' and expected General Sherman to free him and Chester Arthur to reward him handsomely for his ultimate act of loyalty.

"Three days later, I received a long letter from Mollie. She said their special train had derailed en route to Washington, frightening them all to death, and they were lucky nobody was hurt. The Pennsylvania Railroad had to send another train, and what should have been a five hour journey wound up taking seven hours. They were all tired, hungry, cross and desperately worried by the time they arrived at the White House. Lulu was whinier than usual, but Mrs. G. was a tower of strength. Mollie wasn't permitted to see her father, but her mother did, and managed to get him to rest. Jim and Hal had been waiting for Mollie all day to fill her in on the terrible day's events.

"Irv and Abe had left first thing that morning to stay with their Aunt and Uncle Rudolph at the Mentor farm," Gran recounted. "Jim and Hal had gone to the station with Col. Rockwell, and had boarded. The President had arrived with Secretary Blaine just five minutes before the train was to depart. They had been walking through the ladies' waiting room en route to the platform when a funny-looking fellow brandished a gun and 'shot Papa twice' — once in the arm, a slight wound, and again in the side, which was extremely serious. He fell bleeding to the ground. The policeman at the station managed to apprehend the assassin, and dozens of people ran to the wounded president. By the time Jim and Hal reached him, the matron of the ladies' waiting room was sitting on the ground, cradling the President's head in her lap. Blaine had summoned a doctor, and the other Cabinet members, who had already been seated in their train compartments, rushed out to send telegrams.

"Mollie went on to say that Mr. Brown had a telegraph wire in his White House office, and received the horrible news by accident. He just happened to be walking by as it was being tapped out. With excellent presence of mind, he ordered the gates closed to all but family and officials, had the President's room prepared and then asked the War Department to send soldiers to guard the White House.

"Mollie's father was very badly injured and in great pain, even though he was conscious and tried to comfort his sons by telling them that 'the upper story is all right, it's only the hull that's a little damaged.'

"But we all knew differently. Mollie and I wrote to each other two or three times a week that summer. Mollie needed a friend. She was always close to her brothers, but she needed a girlfriend and Lulu Rockwell didn't count. Her mother, barely recovered herself, sat with the President, who was kept in isolation. Now it was her turn to read to him, fan him with palmetto leaves and change the cold compresses on his forehead—as he had done for her only a few short weeks before. He was losing a lot of weight, Mollie said, because he could not hold anything down. 'They give him oatmeal,' she wrote, 'and he hates it. He's always hated oatmeal.'

"Vice President Arthur had taken the night train from New York and arrived at the White House the morning after the President had been shot, Mollie said. He was very kind and paid his respects to her mother, spent a few minutes with the ailing President, and then went to a Cabinet meeting, where, according to gossip, he was deliberately and rudely ignored. The Vice President had made himself totally obnoxious to Garfield and his Cabinet during the patronage squabbles that spring, invariably taking Conkling's part against the President. Even The Captain, who admired Arthur because he had been a fine quartermaster general, was disgusted with him. 'A President's Cabinet is like his family,' my father said. 'They should stick together. The Vice President was behaving treacherously.' No wonder the Cabinet found him odious.

"I wrote back giving her all the news I had heard. We had become good observers of the political scene—especially for two young girls, who were expected to be oblivious to such unseemly subjects, as well as being incapable of understanding them. I repeated the story Uncle Cork told of how Vice President Arthur had gone to his New York townhouse as soon as he heard about the shooting, bolted the doors and windows and drew all the curtains. And Conkling, according to my uncle, positively refused to leave his hotel rooms and admitted no one. Even when they were assured there was no conspiracy, they were still afraid they'd be lynched by the crowds. The entire country was turning on the Stalwarts. After all, they figured, the assassin was a self-proclaimed 'Stalwart of the Stalwarts.'

"Now, Kate," Gran went on, "neither Conkling nor Arthur and certainly not General Grant had anything to do with the assassination, and I doubt they even knew this Guiteau fellow, who turned out to be crazy as a loon. They may not have liked Garfield, but they certainly weren't about to sanction murder. But it had only been fifteen years since Lincoln, and everyone was alarmed.

"I read Mollie's letters aloud to my parents, and The Captain remarked more than once how astute she was in her observations and comments, and how well she expressed herself. 'It's hard to believe she's only fourteen,' he said. My father loved when I read those letters. He was receiving first-hand personal information about the President that sometimes even the newspapers didn't even know. Like about how he hated oatmeal."

We arrived in Pittsburgh at lunchtime, but since we were going on to Philadelphia, we went into the dining car for one last meal on the Broadway Limited. I always got a kick out of the fancy names the railroad companies gave their modern streamliners. Gran insisted we have a glass of sherry to celebrate our trip.

"You don't know what it means to me to have seen Mollie this last time," she said softly. "When you get to be my age, almost everything is in the loss column. Lost friends. Lost family. Lost vitality. But my memory is still sharp, and I need to pass these things along to you while I can. I can give you the family albums, Kate, and I can give you the Minton and some other things, but they are meaningless unless you know what they signify. True stories are just as important as photographs. You'll be telling your grandchildren about when Roosevelt died or V-E Day. I need to tell you about when Garfield died so you can pass that along to them as well."

She was silent for a long time, and I didn't press her with questions. For one thing, my head was reeling from all the information she had been pouring into me for the past three-and-a-half-days. For another thing, my mind was still full of Hal Brown and how much I missed him. I kept reliving those long goodnight kisses in the moonlight with the Pacific Ocean lapping on the shores in the distance. Garfield wasn't important, I thought. A third-rate general, a no-rate-by-default President nobody remembers. All it really meant to me was that his daughter was my grandmother's best friend.

"It was terribly hot that summer of '81," Gran said, waking me out of my reverie. "And Washington was always a pit of murky humidity. They didn't have air-cooling like they do in the movie houses today. I imagine they'll have it sooner or later in our own houses. We could certainly use it. That's why they had sent Mrs. Garfield to the seashore to recuperate. To get her away from the heat. Most of official Washington always left town before mid-June anyway. The government went on summer holiday for three or four months every year.

"The poor President was cooped up in the White House in ninety-degree temperatures. Mollie said 'Dr. Susan,' (who had treated Mrs. Garfield through her malaria), and Mrs. G. took turns fanning him and applying cool compresses trying to keep him as comfortable as they could. Dr. Susan served as a nurse, since a woman doctor couldn't examine the patient. Mollie also mentioned the ordeal turning him over, which they needed to do several times a day. Of course she hadn't been in the room when it was done, but she said six strong men lifted him up by the bed sheets to roll him over. That must've been something!

"A couple of weeks later, Mollie wrote that her father was beginning to feel a little better, and would spend ten minutes with his children, or see Blaine or another Cabinet member. Occasionally he even felt well enough to play a hand of gin rummy with Col. Rockwell or General Swaim, but he couldn't work. He had no concentration. Besides, the doctors were giving him strong opiates to relieve his pain. The only letter he wrote during this whole time was a short note to his aged mother, so she wouldn't worry too much.

"Then somebody came up with the idea of using an electric fan to circulate the air over strips of cloth soaked in ice water. It was reported in all the papers. They even made drawings of it. The idea seemed to have merit and was simple enough for army engineers to rig up in a day. It helped. They said it lowered the room temperature nearly fifteen degrees.

"Mollie spent most of her time helping Joe Brown, since she couldn't go anywhere, and was sick to death practicing *Minuet in G*. (*Fur Elise* had been retired.) Joe was busy issuing reports on the President's condition two or three times a day, as well as trying to respond to the mail. Thousands of letters poured in with good wishes and prayers from people all over the country. Mollie helped Joe open and sort the mail, and they devised a nice form letter to thank people for their concern."

Then Gran laughed. "But the big problem the doctors had — and there was a pile of them parading in and out of the White House — was they couldn't find the bullet. They hadn't invented the x-ray machine yet, so the doctors would poke their fingers," she paused deliberately, "their *unwashed* fingers directly into the wound to try to find it."

My jaw dropped as I winced at the thought. "That must have been excruciating," I said with a grimace.

"Indeed," she replied. "I can only imagine how that poor man must've suffered with all those men poking fingers and probes into his body. Anyway, since the President's condition was reported blow-by-blow in all the papers, day after day, everyone knew the doctors were unsuccessful in finding the elusive bullet. It was also widely reported that Alexander Graham Bell had come to the White House with a metal detecting machine he had invented. It was supposed to locate the bullet, but it proved to be futile.

"Meanwhile, the mailbags were also filled with suggestions for finding the bullet. Mollie said one man wrote they should hold the President upside down and shake him hard and the bullet would fall out of his mouth. I read that letter to my family, and after we all had a good laugh over it, The Captain and Uncle Cork grinned maliciously at each other. Then they grabbed me, turned me upside down and each took a leg and shook. And oh, how we laughed, Kate! But Miss Peg quickly announced I was getting a little too old for such horseplay, so they stopped. I wrote Mollie about it. She read my letters to Jim and Harry and they told the President about shaking Louise upside down one afternoon when they were allowed in for a five minute visit. They liked telling funny stories to cheer him up. She said he sent his regards."

Then Gran became serious. "I don't think Garfield was doing very well at all. Oh, he had good days and bad days that summer. But he was losing a lot of weight. He couldn't keep food down. I suppose now you can be fed through a tube, but that hadn't been invented then, either.

"Mollie was also enclosing some letters along with mine, by the way, and I was forwarding them to Miss Anthony for her. She said 'Mrs. Sarah Allen' had sent sincere wishes for her father's recovery. Mollie also said she was the one sorting most of the daily mail and could intercept her own personal letters easily enough, but she was still concerned about mailing them."

Note from Kate, 2002:
It is incomprehensible today that the entire government would or could shut itself down for three or four months, but that is basically what happened until, perhaps, Woodrow Wilson's time. The weather

in Washington was so sultry and unhealthy that everyone sought respite elsewhere if they could possibly afford it. This included Garfield, who had planned to spend two months at his farm near Lake Erie after their New England trip. Congress had adjourned. Senators and Representatives, judges and administrators departed for their home districts or summer places. What business there was could either be done elsewhere via telegraph and the newly-invented telephone, done by someone else, or wait until fall. The government was literally closed for vacation.

It is equally inconceivable, since Garfield never arose from his sickbed, that the Vice President was neither asked nor expected to assume any responsibilities. Technically, Congress would have had to pass legislation to permit Arthur to take charge, and Congress was off for the summer. And, taking it a step further, Vice President Arthur not only categorically refused to assume any presidential functions as long as Garfield was alive, but was widely commended for his restraint. According to every historian of the era, the public's estimation of Chester Alan Arthur rose steadily that summer due to his impeccable behavior (despite the rumor he was hiding in his townhouse with the curtains drawn). It was true that half the Cabinet detested him (the other half merely loathed him), but even they had to admit the Vice President was doing everything right by keeping a concerned, but low and silent profile.

Furthermore, despite the fact it quickly became obvious that the assassin Guiteau was insane, and there was absolutely no plot or conspiracy whatsoever, the mood of the country had shifted noticeably away from the Stalwarts. Although Grant remained and always would remain beloved, Conkling and his minions became conspicuously unpopular. While bossism would always be a fact of political life in various cities around the country, it was on the wane.

When Gran and I arrived in Philadelphia, we wired Uncle Henry of our plans to stay at the Scarboro Hotel in Long Branch.

The connecting train took an hour or so, and Gran grew more and more nostalgic as we drew closer to the town of her youth.

"I haven't been here for twenty years, Kate. Aunt Phee died in '27, and she wanted to be buried with Uncle Cork and my parents, so Charlie and I brought her coffin back for burial. That was the last time I was here. 1927."

"I thought they lived in Jersey City," I ventured.

"They did, dear," Gran said. "But after Charlie and I married and moved to Pittsburgh, The Captain was all alone in our big house. When a notice was posted that Long Branch needed a new constable, Uncle Cork fit the bill and knew most everyone in town, so he left Jersey City and joined the force in Long Branch. It was softer police work than in Jersey City, and he was getting older. He and Aunt Phee moved in with my father. It was a wonderful arrangement. It spared me from worry, since The Captain had aged a great deal and became very melancholy after Miss Peg died, and even more so after Henry Cobbs died. After The Captain died, Uncle Cork and Aunt Phee kept the house till Uncle Cork died. Then we sold it, and Aunt Phee moved to Pittsburgh near me."

Gran anticipated my next question, adding, "Our house was torn down right after the First War. The whole block was torn down for smaller homes," she sighed. "I have no idea what's left in Long Branch, although I believe it's run down hill. I'm not sure I'd even know anyone except Alice Ann. She's still there. We've exchanged Christmas cards for fifty years."

Alice Ann Marsden Langer had lived down the street from my grandmother when they were children. She was a few years younger, but as Gran had said, "they got on well," and Alice Ann had been to both of Gran's weddings. And Gran had gone to hers. Her husband died in the 1919 flu epidemic and she never remarried.

We arrived at four in the afternoon and took a taxi to the Scarboro, only a block from the Atlantic Ocean. Two oceans in one week! But Gran was right; Long Branch was definitely shabby. It was hard to imagine it had once been the glamorous playground for the robber barons and celebrities of the 1880s. Pasadena was a lot nicer. A *lot* nicer. But the salty air penetrated everything and I liked it, despite its shoddiness.

Gran took a good deep breath of the salt air as we climbed the steps of the hotel, and I swear she dropped ten years. It's amazing how good thoughts can change the expression on one's face and make a person look younger or even prettier. I find myself being acutely aware of that phenomenon since the years are gathering rapidly on my own face. Whenever I have my picture taken now, I never say "cheese." I just think of my most delightful memories and hope the camera "which never lies," will see the truth through all my wrinkles.

"Oh, how good it is to be home," Gran sighed as we entered the lobby of a sorry-looking hotel, obviously fallen on hard times and in need of complete overhaul. "I never liked Pittsburgh. Don't misunderstand, Kate. I've always enjoyed our home and our friends and all the fine things Pittsburgh has to offer, but it's an ugly city — and it smells bad."

The Scarboro Hotel was an old relic my grandmother remembered with far fonder memories than realities. I'm sure she couldn't have known how dingy it would be when she asked me to make the reservation. It was a light year away from the sunny, elegant Ritz Carlton in Pasadena, with its Rose Bowl photos and flowers everywhere. This lobby was decorated in genteel poverty, if one were to pick a fashion style. I assumed there were better hotels in town, certainly newer ones, but Gran had specifically chosen this one. "Charlie and I stayed here in '27 when we laid Aunt Phee to rest," she said.

The lobby probably hadn't been painted since 1927, and the carpet was badly worn. The odd assortment of tables, chairs and writing desks looked as if they had been picked up randomly as leftovers from other hotels. I have a feeling I wasn't far off the mark. When a hotel closes, the scavengers come to feed. Even the lighting was poor. I suppose dim lights hid its obvious condition, but the dimness only enhanced the depressed atmosphere.

A bored-looking, fairly elderly man at the desk assigned us to our rooms, which were little improvement. I doubted they had been painted since 1927 either, and the bedding smelled musty and damp. The bathroom fixtures were from a bygone era, the only concession being a flush-toilet. I could still make out the outline of the high-mounted tank and chain that preceded it.

I tipped the bellhop and told him to return in an hour for our laundry, which they promised would be ready the next day without fail. I pulled out just enough clothes for the evening and the next morning, and everything else I owned except my shoes was going to be cleaned! Then I helped Gran do likewise. And finally, while she took an hour's nap in a real bed, I took a half-hour's soak in a real tub.

My mind was a muddle of a million thoughts, not the least of which was Major Brown. I'd send him a postcard to let him know where I was, so he wouldn't wonder why I hadn't answered his letter, which I imagined was sitting in the pile of mail at home.

Gran had put the bee in my bonnet about "writing her story" or writing Mollie's story, or writing whatever story she claimed should be written. I didn't know if I was up to it, or indeed, if I even wanted to write it. I still hadn't made up my mind about a profession, although since meeting Hal, my thoughts had become decidedly domestic. But my mind was filled with movie-like images of Gran as a young girl, the formidable Mollie Brown (who I found difficult to believe had *ever* been a young girl), The Captain and Miss Peg, Uncle Cork and Aunt Phee, plus a cast of supporting players like General Grant and Sherman and Roscoe Conkling and the Garfields. I saw them in my mind's eye, parading up and down in glorious Technicolor, with brightly colored bustle-gowns and parasols and great houses with domes and turrets. It was hard to believe that scene had become loose shutters, broken shingles, a rash of tiny cheap-looking bungalows, and faded paint everywhere one looked.

Gran and I had supper at our hotel, since we were still exhausted from our long train trip and needed a good night's sleep without being all cramped up. The food was indifferent; not even as good as the meals on the Broadway Limited. Certainly not served as well. The place left me cold. I could no longer see things through Gran's eyes. Reality claimed another victim.

Gran telephoned Alice Ann Marsden Langer, whose number was in the book, and who was thrilled to hear from her old friend. She invited us to dinner the following night, refusing to take no for an answer.

"Let's go for a walk on your famous bluff," I suggested, looking out the lobby window wondering where it was.

"It no longer exists," Gran said simply. "Mother Nature is fickle. She provides a beautiful seacoast and a cool breeze, then turns around in winter—we have bad ones here—and storms wash away the beaches. The bad storm, when my Henry died, did terrible damage to the bluff. Washed away half of it. There were gaping gouges in the sand up and down the shore for five miles or more. Another two or three winters later, nothing was left. A ten or fifteen-foot high five-mile-long bluff completely washed away. I suspect the sand is sitting somewhere in Cape May."

So my grandmother and I put on light sweaters and sat on rockers on the sprawling porch of the dilapidated Scarboro Hotel overlooking the ocean, and listened to the slapping surf and breathed in the briny, fish-smelling, clean and healthy salt air—so different from the sooty, oily, grimy smell of Pittsburgh.

"The Scarboro was one of the newer hotels," Gran said. "It was built around the time I married Charlie. We stayed here when we sold my father's house. Then we stayed here with Mollie and Joe in '18, I think. It was when Mrs. Garfield died. They brought her back to Ohio to lie in the Garfield Memorial. Cleveland isn't far from Pittsburgh so we all went for the ceremony. Charlie and I, your parents, Henry and Rose. Walter, too.

"They were unveiling a statue of President Garfield in Long Branch about that same time, and as long as Mollie and Joe had come East, they decided to attend. So Charlie and I came with them. We had a grand time, although Mollie noticed how Long Branch had changed. More 'middle class,' I think. Not the vacation spot for the wealthy anymore. Just about all the big hotels were gone. Fire mostly. They were made of wood. And rot and disrepair. And weather, too."

We sat quietly for ten or fifteen minutes. Then she added, "We had bad storms in summer, too. I remember one—I must've been seven or eight. The Captain had just been elected mayor that year. It was hurricane season, probably. Anyway, the wind was so bad, it blew the windows out of the Ocean House Hotel. So The Captain went to inspect the damage, and he told us the wind not only blew out the windows, but a gust had come through the broken glass, slipped under the big oriental carpet in the dining room, and billowed the carpet up like a lady's petticoat, tossing the tables and chairs all over. Luckily nobody was in the room, and the tables hadn't been set." She paused. "We get some dreadful weather all up and down the shore."

I don't know where the silly old memories are stored in people's brains, but there is something about being older that makes them pop up at the oddest times.

Chapter 9

At breakfast the next morning, I asked Gran what was on her agenda. "Walk," she said, obviously invigorated by a decent night's sleep. "Walk all over town. I want to walk down Chelsea Avenue where I was born, and over to Fourth where Henry and I lived. And I want to walk down Ocean Avenue. The Elberon Hotel is long gone, but I think Grant's old house is still there. And I want to walk down Broadway where our store was, and where the Pach brothers had their photography studio. Oh, the memories, Kate!" You could have heard her sigh all the way to Pittsburgh!

The only item on my agenda was to buy a postcard for Hal. The only ones around were reproductions of Long Branch in its heyday, or at least a good thirty years ago. Gran was seeing the town through the same lens as the postcards: a playground for the upper-middle class, if not the robber barons of her youth. The town's better days were long gone. It was now a playground for a seedier crowd.

"I think the demise of Long Branch had a lot to do with Atlantic City," Gran had admitted the previous night as we rocked on the porch, sipping our ritual coffee night-cap. "Atlantic City had put in its grand boardwalk and Steel Pier, and had built tall hotels with elevators. When I was little, the elevator had just been invented and none of our hotels had them. None of them were more than three stories, the top one for servants—and children. And our old Iron Pier had been splintered like a toothpick during one of nature's rages. Then of course," she added, "there was the Depression. That didn't help."

"Nothing is as I remember," Gran sighed as we walked up Chelsea Avenue where The Captain and Miss Peg had lived. She shook her head. "Gone forever. Not even an old tree remains."

The neighborhood had been completely razed shortly after World War I and a dozen or more non-descript two-story houses stood where once had been five or six graceful Victorian homes with sprawling verandas and great expanses of lawn. Now there were small patches of grass and long stretches of cement leading to a garage in back. Nice enough, I suppose, if people keep them up. A few houses had window boxes or flower pots with geraniums on the porch to give a modicum of color.

"I think it was here," Gran said, pausing in front of a grayish-blue house with white shutters in need of repair and paint. There was a red wagon and a tricycle in front, and some hanging baskets of the ubiquitous geraniums on the porch. Gran smiled wistfully. "Life goes on. I hope the people here are as happy as I was."

But Long Branch was not a happy place. It had fallen precipitously over the past four decades. It was no longer a vacation paradise. Oh, people still came in summer, but they usually drove over to Asbury Park or Belmar or Seaside Heights for entertainment. The big hotels and casinos were gone long before Prohibition. The year-round residents were not the rising middle class of Gran's era. They were the descending middle class, fighting back from the Depression.

Broadway was little better. "Of course I don't expect the same stores to still be here," Gran said with a wry smile. "I'm nearly eighty, and few businesses are in the same place for seventy years!" Indeed, there was very little remaining on Gran's Broadway except the street itself, and the way it curved to the southwest. But it still remained Long Branch's shopping district, with dozens of small seashore-town stores.

"Here's where Dunbar's was," she said, pointing to a luncheonette situated next to a Buster Brown shoe store. "Our store would have been where both these places are. The Captain started in one building, but when he became mayor, he bought the place next door and expanded. She pointed down the street. "And here's Steinbachs! My, my, it hasn't changed much since I was here last," she exclaimed. The old department store was still in its original spot, although it had been renovated and modernized on several occasions.

Then she pointed in the other direction and said, "And here's where our first real ice cream parlor was. It wasn't there when Mollie was here. They sold ice cream at the drug store then. Ice cream parlors came later. But I remember going there with Henry Cobbs and later when Charlie courted me. Aunt Phee and Uncle Cork loved to go on Sundays for an ice-cream soda. They said it kept them young."

I wondered what Mollie and the uncles would have thought of this shabby, depressed town. Mollie had spent more than forty years in California, where it was clean and clear and elegant—echoing what she would have remembered about the Long Branch of her childhood. I decided it was a good thing they never came back. Perhaps we should have gone directly home too.

But my grandmother found a perverse pleasure in the nondescript buildings that had replaced those of her youth.

"Everything changes in time," she said philosophically, "sometimes for better and sometimes for worse. What doesn't change is what we remember. And I remember gas lamps on the curb, and people on horseback or in carriages. I remember little boys in sailor suits riding bicycles—the old kind, with the huge wheel in front. And I remember ladies walking up and down these streets wearing white summer dresses, carrying pink and yellow and blue parasols.

"And I remember men in their pearl gray or buff-colored summer suits wearing straw hats and carrying walking sticks, like in those Fred Astaire movies. That's what I see, Kate. I'm seeing past all this…this…" she shook her head and sighed, "all this reality. And I'm seeing myself wearing a navy and white middy-blouse with ribbons in my hair." She sighed again. "I don't look like that any more, either."

Gran was a pretty fair philosopher. I hope I inherited that gene.

The smell of something delicious greeted us as we walked up the path to a simple beige house with green shutters. Alice Ann Marsden Langer was overjoyed and embraced Gran with a bear hug, which extended to me as well. Alice Ann was five-foot-one, no more, and while not fat, was definitely on the stout side—a reflection of her excellent cooking skills, I suppose, since she had prepared a sauerbraten to die for.

After all the greeting and hugging, we settled in her comfortable chintz and pillowed living room, with framed photographs on every table. She was one of six, and she had six of her own, and now was grandmother to twenty, and still counting. As far as nieces and nephews and "greats," she said she lost count after thirty. If anyone looked like she should be a grandmother to a large clan, it was Alice Ann.

"You must be disappointed in our old town, Louise," she said, pouring us each a glass of some icky-tasting sweet wine that I sipped very slowly. "It's fallen on hard times. It was slipping when Atlantic City became the rage in the '20s, and then the Depression delivered a deathblow. We don't get much summer traffic anymore—and the kind we do get, we'd prefer not to have. A lot of riffraff. Not like the old days."

"Actually I find myself seeing it through my old eyes," said Gran. "I've been dredging up memories I can hardly believe I still remember. Like the flags at the hotels—each one had their own colors. The first thing I looked for on Ocean Avenue was flags, but of course they aren't there. Do you remember how the wagons were painted in the hotel's colors, and coachmen wore liveries? We could tell who was going where just by the colors of the station wagons. Where is all this coming from?" She shook her head in amazement.

"I remember your old house, Louise. On the top floor there was a round window just under the eave. I don't know whose room it was..."

"Aggie. It was our maid Aggie's room."

"Anyway, she must've had a lamp table under that window, because every evening there would be a light."

"And you, Alice Ann. You couldn't have been more than ten, marching up and down the street, pushing a baby buggy, with a couple of children in tow. Always the little mother."

"I was the eldest of six," Alice Ann said to me, by way of explanation. "I taught your grandmother how to take care of babies—and she taught me to cook."

"It's true, Kate," Gran said as she laughed. "I never had brothers or sisters and we didn't engage Miss Cray until Henry was born. When your mother was born, my mother had already died and Aunt Phee never had children. Henry's mother, was way off in Yonkers, so Alice Ann came and taught me how to change diapers and bathe a baby. And you were what? Eighteen? Nineteen?"

"I was engaged when I was eighteen, and you were a few years older and already married. I knew everything about babies since my mother had a pile of them, but I didn't know the first thing about cooking, since we always had a cook. So I'd come over and you would show me how to roll dough and season a roast."

"I learned to cook when I married Henry Cobbs," Gran explained. "We had a small house, and a day-girl was all we could afford. It was wasteful to hire someone just to cook supper for the two of us, so I bought a cookbook, spent several afternoons with Aunt Elizabeth, one of the best cooks in town, and became pretty fair myself."

That was an understatement. My grandmother was a superb cook and baker. Christmas dinners at her house were better than the ones our cook ever prepared—and Mother and Daddy paid handsomely for a good cook. I'm afraid I never inherited the cooking gene.

"And it's not hard to season a roast, Alice Ann...." Gran added.

"Of course not, Louise. But if you don't know how, you still need to learn. My husband George was nearly ten years older than I was—and I was petrified of his mother. She was very cool to me, but once I proved I could find my way around a kitchen very handily, she treated me with much more respect. We became good friends, and she even shared some of her 'old country' recipes. Tonight's dinner is one of hers."

To this day, it was the most delicious sauerbraten I have ever eaten.

"Did your grandmother tell you that I used to baby-sit for the Princess?" Alice Ann asked me.

Gran and I looked at each other in puzzlement.

"Princess Canticuzene," she explained. I still drew a complete blank. "She was one of the Grant grand-daughters. One of the little Julia Grants. There were a few little Julia Grants, I think, but this one was Buck's daughter. Anyway, she married a Prince a long time ago. She may still be living, but I'm not sure."

I was convinced my mother would have known. Like about the Potted Palm woman.

Alice Ann explained that her mother was a Sloane, and one of her cousins was part of Mrs. Grant's intimate social set, so Alice Ann's mother would occasionally be invited for tea or something at Grant's cottage. Once, when the Grants' grandchildren were staying with them (which was often), Mrs. Grant gave a children's party, and the Marsden crew were invited. "Little Julia and I hit it off so well, that every time she was there, I was usually asked to come over," Alice Ann continued. "She was really my sister Edith's friend. They were close in age. I was the chaperone, I suppose."

"Did you meet Grant?" I asked, taking another small sip of the godawful wine I had to drink out of courtesy.

"Several times, dear. But he was old then. And sick. He didn't talk much because of the throat cancer. But I remember the house very well. Were you ever it in, Louise?"

"No. I just passed by."

"It was a very ordinary house. Not much more than my house—my *old* house. But what I remember most was the cookies. Mrs. Grant always had a plate of cookies on the parlor table for her grandchildren and their little friends. The house itself was modest. I think they had sold most of their personal things when the general went bankrupt. But there were always cookies." Alice Ann paused, and then asked quite suddenly, "But, Louise, you never said what brought you back home!"

Gran smiled faintly. "Do you remember my old friend Mollie Brown?"

"The Garfield daughter?"

"Yes. You knew her, didn't you?"

"I met her at your wedding to Charlie Stanfield. And again when The Captain died."

"That's right. When I married Henry Cobbs, she had either just given birth or was about to. She couldn't travel. But she stood up for me when Charlie and I married. Anyway, she died last week."

"Oh, I'm sorry."

"She was eighty and her heart had been bad for a while," Gran said matter-of-factly. "Anyway, Kate and I went for a final farewell and her funeral." She paused. "It got me remembering a lot of things. A lot of old times. I suppose it's like that when we get to be our age."

Alice Ann nodded. "I think that's why I've stayed here all

these years. My kids are all nearby. Not Long Branch, but in Belmar and Freehold. One in Lakewood. Fred is the only one out of state. He went to Washington with the New Deal," she explained proudly. "He's a lawyer."

"But this isn't the house..." Gran began.

"Oh Lord no," Alice Ann said and laughed. "What would I do with a fifteen-room house all by myself? I sold it in '22, a couple of years after George passed. Influenza," she added, nodding my way. "The children were practically all grown. My youngest was fifteen or sixteen. So I moved here. This was one of the first batch of houses put up after the First War. It had good indoor plumbing and a big kitchen, which appealed to me."

So far, Alice Ann Marsden Langer had done most of the talking. On our way into the dining room for the sauerbraten (the tantalizing aroma had me practically drooling), I noticed several framed photographs hanging in the hallway. One was inscribed to Alice Ann by Carrie Chapman Catt, a name I recognized. There were at least a half-dozen framed citations and certificates. "I see you were active in the League of Women Voters...." I said as I sat down at the table.

"Still am," she replied proudly. "It was a logical step after suffrage. I've been president of the Long Branch Chapter twice, and served as vice chairwoman for the state for six years." She looked over at Gran, who nodded and smiled. "Your grandmother is responsible for that, too, dear," she said. "She was always so active and has done so much. I always admired Louise Dunbar. I still do."

Gran concentrated on the sauerbraten, which she insisted was the best she had ever eaten.

"Your grandmother is being coy, Kate. She is a wonderful writer, you know."

I didn't know. Gran had never so much as written me a letter.

"She wrote wonderful articles for the suffrage newspapers. Eloquent, moving articles. So well thought out. And letters to the editors of papers across the country! Oh, your grandmother was quite a celebrity — at least in suffrage circles. My dear friend Alice Paul thinks the world of her." Another person I assume I was supposed to have heard of, and hadn't.

I had never heard my grandmother talk about writing articles or letters to editors either. My mother, on occasion, had mentioned Gran "had been active," but I assumed she meant that Gran went to meetings or marched in parades or gave money.

"You must give me this recipe, Alice Ann," Gran said in a deliberate attempt to change the subject. "I don't think I've ever made it, and it's so delicious!"

"It's just a mix of vinegar and sugar, Louise. And cooking slowly for a long time. And of course I throw in a cup of wine..." Alice Ann beamed with pleasure that her old cooking teacher though so well of her pupil.

"Are you still active in the League, Louise?" she asked, bringing Gran back to the original subject.

"I don't go to meetings anymore, but I pay my dues every year."

"What about you, dear? Have you joined? What about your mother? Is Clara active in the League?" She looked directly at me.

"I think Mother pays dues, but I never remember her going to meetings or anything," I answered. Then, since I had a vague feeling an apology was required for my mother's indifference, I added, "Mother has a bunch of charities. She's raised tons of money for diabetes and she's been on the board of the Pittsburgh Symphony for years. It's one of her pets."

This was true. Daddy's sister Katherine (my namesake) had been a diabetic, and the whole Atcheson family contributed heavily for research into the disease that claimed her life when she was only thirty. Lord only knew why my mother fancied the orchestra. She had the Dunbar tin ear, but she always said she was an "appreciator." I personally thought she supported the symphony because people got all dressed up for their concerts and fund-raisers, and Mother loved to dress up. Her closet was full of evening clothes.

"Hmmmpf. The League isn't a charity, Kate. It's a civic obligation. Now that we have the right to vote, we need to make sure every woman has the information she needs to cast a considered ballot. You said so yourself, Louise."

"I didn't say anything, Alice Ann."

"Well, you wrote it, dear."

"No. Actually, I didn't. And now that Mollie is dead, I suppose I can tell the truth."

There was a long pause as Gran looked at me, and then at her old friend, and then back at me. "I am not a writer. I am much better as a bookkeeper. The letters and articles were not mine. Mollie Brown wrote them. She asked me to sign them and assume authorship, which I did as a favor to my friend. But they were hers."

Alice Ann and I were equally taken aback at this unexpected confession. For more than fifty years, it had been common knowledge that L. D. Stanfield was one of the pillars of women's suffrage.

My grandmother took a deep breath and a sip of the terrible sweet wine, and explained. "Very shortly after Garfield died—the family had not yet gone back to Ohio—Mrs. Garfield called the children together. Robert Lincoln was there. He and Mrs. Garfield had had several long talks during the President's illness and had become good friends—a relationship that would last till Mrs. Garfield died. Sometimes it's like that between two remote people. They instinctively understand how to form their own close bonds.

"Robert Lincoln told the children, from his own unique perspective, how they had a very special place in history as the orphaned children of a martyred president. Much would be expected of them—more so than ordinary children, or even children of a former president. He delicately explained how his mother's mental instability, while unfortunate, was now open to public criticism and speculation. He, personally, could never take any action without thinking first how it might reflect on his late father's reputation. He added very sadly, how deeply he regretted the need for so much inhibition; it was not at all to his liking. But he had no control over that part. The only part he could control was how he dealt with it. Then Mrs. Garfield told the children they must behave far better than other children, and bring credit to their dear departed Papa, who would be forever watching over them. She said they must never do anything to attract public attention, unless it was something very wonderful and admirable to bring pride to the family and "dear Papa's memory." She made them solemnly pledge on their dead father's soul that they would always behave modestly and with great care to avoid scandal or gossip."

Gran took another deep breath and another sip of wine. Alice Ann was staring at her with her mouth open. For some strange reason, I was not nearly as surprised as I ought to have been at this confession of fifty years of deceit.

She went on to explain that a month after Garfield died, Mollie invited her to spend Christmas at their farm. This was immediately followed by a letter from Mrs. Garfield to *Mrs. Dunbar* urging that Louise be permitted to go. The boys had each other, she said, and Mrs. Garfield had her own family nearby, but Mollie seemed to be adrift. My parents, who loved her dearly, decided since I was fourteen and quite level-headed, I might travel alone to Cleveland.

"All five children met me at the station," Gran said. "Harry drove their buckboard. I hadn't seen them since before the shooting—at least not the boys. Mollie had grown. She was almost fifteen, and had reached her full height. She had also changed somewhat. More mature. More reserved in a way, like her mother."

"During the Christmas visit, Mollie told me of the solemn vow she made not to do or say anything to cause scandal and sully their dear dead father's memory. She said she received a sweet letter of sympathy from Miss Anthony, but hadn't responded.

"Mollie was terribly depressed—not only about her father's death, which was understandable, but because she believed she would never be able to do things she truly wanted to do—a fact known only to me," Gran said. "So I volunteered to continue as secret conduit for her correspondence. She would enclose a letter for me to mail, and I would receive letters back, which I would send to her—unopened. I never knew—and I don't to this day—what was contained in those letters.

"I never told my parents, and casually fibbed that 'Mrs. Sarah Allen' who occasionally wrote to me was a lady I met in Cleveland. No one ever questioned me. The letters would be exchanged every two or three months, so it never aroused any suspicion.

"Meanwhile," she continued, "Joseph Stanley Brown remained in close touch with the Garfields, and, co-incidentally, with Robert Lincoln as well, who encouraged his career, and generously supplied good business advice. As time went on, Joe began to court Mollie. They had always been good friends, but quite honestly, I had a feeling she was self-conscious about being a big woman, without the delicate features men find attractive. Her choices were extremely limited, and I don't mean just in the way of suitors. She would either marry or wind up an old maid. A career for a woman was frowned on. It was merely something one did while waiting for a husband. Most of all," Gran added, "Mollie didn't want to live with her mother. It wasn't that they didn't get on. I think for the most part they did. But Mollie wanted a life of her own, and it was impossible for her to leave her mother's house under any circumstances other than marriage. So I suppose Joe was her way out. She was only eighteen. I stood up for her, and our whole family went to Ohio for the wedding—including Uncle Cork and Aunt Phee. They wouldn't have missed it for the world!"

What Mollie never realized, at least not then, in Gran's

opinion, was that by marrying Joe Brown, she was in essence, marrying her mother. The two were incredibly alike. Joe was more devoted to the Garfield memory than any of the Garfield children—although every one of them brought credit and honor to their family. And it was Charlie's opinion that since the Garfield family was the recipient of nearly a half million dollar trust fund, it might have encouraged Joe Brown's courtship. Cyrus Field had established the fund for them after the President died, and people across the country contributed their nickels, dimes and dollars to the family nest egg. The Garfields would never worry about money. Charlie also said (according to my grandmother) he believed the country was ashamed they had neglected to provide for Mrs. Lincoln, so they overdid it with the Garfields. He may have had a point.

Anyway, it was Joe Brown who organized and hosted the periodic reunions of Garfield's friends and associates, and stayed in close touch with the Rockwells and the Swaims and the old Cabinet members—and worked tirelessly for Blaine's losing presidential effort in 1884. I think he may have wanted to be Presidential Secretary again.

Mollie was no fool, Gran insisted. She knew Joe was a controlling man, deeply set in his ways, however benign, and expected his wife to obey a conventional code of conduct. She also knew Joe truly cared for her and was a devoted husband and father. She would work around him.

"After Henry Cobbs and I were married, Mollie and Joe and their children moved to New York City," Gran continued. "She wired asking if I could visit for a couple of days. Henry liked Mollie and was amenable, and Aunt Phee was happy to watch Clara, so I went. Mollie announced she was taking me to a lecture at her Woman's Club—one of the activities Joe Brown approved, since it was a charitable organization.

"As it turned out, it was a suffrage meeting and Susan B. Anthony was the featured speaker. Mollie wanted us to finally meet, after all our deceptions. By this time, Miss Anthony was around seventy, but she still had the power to compel an audience. We went backstage for tea, which was the first and only time we met. She embraced Mollie like a mother to a daughter, or even a grandmother to a granddaughter, and she smiled and shook hands with me, their secret postmistress. It seems Mollie had gotten her wish to play a more active role. Without my knowing it (since I never opened the envelopes between them), Mollie had been writing very well stated explanations of policy and action for the suffrage movement's higher councils. Miss Anthony praised Mollie to the skies, complimenting her rare talent to see a situation clearly, and find the precise words to make it understood—even to the least educated.

"Now Mollie needed to go a step further. Miss Anthony admitted her age had caught up, and her health compelled her to curtail travel. Carrie Chapman Catt, who had been on the platform with her, would take up the reins. I expect Mollie was heartbroken, since traveling and speaking out for suffrage was exactly what she had longed to do. Public speaking was in her blood. Her father had been a fine orator, and her brothers—even Abe, the architect—were all excellent speakers. Of course, Mollie's tongue would remain silent. But not her pen.

"Miss Anthony suggested she start writing articles, not for the hierarchy, but for the rank and file and the new converts to the movement who were joining in droves. 'It's only a matter of time until we reach our objective,' she said. 'Put the complex issues into the simplest of words.' Those were the instructions. But Mollie couldn't use her own name. She had given her solemn word.

"I had joined a suffrage society in Long Branch, as you know Alice Ann. You joined as well. I had joined out of respect to Mollie, although I truly believed in the cause. I wasn't very active, since I was busy with the babies and had other things to do, but I paid my dues each year. Henry Cobbs had no objection, and I was used to clucking by The Captain and Uncle Cork, who insisted I was much too pretty to be one of those 'old biddies.'

"So I volunteered my name, along with my mail-forwarding services. The men in my life never read suffragette newspapers and magazines. My only proviso was that L.D. Cobbs and later L.D. Stanfield would never make any public appearances."

Gran smiled at the incredulous Alice Ann, and then looked at me. "Oh yes, dear. I have a box full of citations and awards from Suffrage, but I never hung them up, nor did I ever accept in person. Whenever they were to be presented, I insisted the president of the local chapter accept in my place. It was Mollie's work being awarded and appreciated, not mine. And if she couldn't accept on her own, I had no right to accept what wasn't mine. The movement could accept on her behalf. Mollie said it was a lovely gesture."

There was a long uncomfortable silence while Alice Ann Langer absorbed all this information from the old friend she hadn't seen in twenty years. Finally she excused herself, mumbling "I'll get the coffee," and disappeared into the kitchen.

"Does my mother know this?" I asked Gran.

"Of course not, Kate. Nobody knows. Well, now you and Alice Ann know. Charlie knew, of course. He thought it was very amusing. He didn't care for Joe Brown especially, except to play golf on occasion, and he was tickled pink at the way Mollie managed to get around his iron rule." She paused again, and said, "And I don't think I shall tell anyone else."

Alice Ann entered with the coffee pot and an apple cake to put professional bakeries to shame. The poor lady was shocked by the last half-hour's conversation, and didn't know how to respond.

Gran eased her discomfort. "Mollie and I talked about this before she died," she said. "I asked her specifically what she wanted me to do. I was perfectly willing to make a public statement, or write to the papers." There was another of those pauses Gran was so good at. "'I'm leaving the correspondence to you, Louise,' Mollie told me. 'Your letters to me, along with the enclosures. I trust your judgment to do with them as you see fit.'"

In 1947, my grandmother did not know what was fit. She made her confession to me, as her granddaughter and recent friend of the Garfield family, and to Alice Ann Marsden Langer, a woman who had been deeply committed to women's suffrage, and who had thought the world of L.D. Stanfield. Gran needed the closure on suffrage just as she needed to talk about her dearest friend. Once done, she never told another soul.

***

"You're probably very disappointed with our old town," repeated Alice Ann, sipping her coffee, deliberately changing the subject. Gran smiled weakly. The past two weeks of emotion and hard travel were finally catching up with her eighty-year-old body.

"I suppose a little," she remarked, "although even when I was here twenty years ago, it was falling into disrepair. I'm falling into disrepair myself."

"But it *had* been so beautiful," Alice Ann sighed. "So elegant. In my heart, I still see the grand old hotels and cottages in all their glory. And the ladies promenading up and down the bluff, wearing their summer dresses and carrying pretty parasols. Nobody uses a parasol today."

"Hmm," Gran nodded. "I was picturing the same thing earlier."

"There's talk of selling the Grant place, you know."

"Oh no! Never! It should be maintained and treasured. Like Mt. Vernon."

"Mt. Vernon was neglected for nearly a hundred years before it was made into a national memorial," said Alice Ann matter-of-factly. "Besides, there's Grant's Tomb in New York. And after all that's happened with the war, who has that kind of money? It's a very low priority. Our town council says it's a valuable piece of beach property. They want somebody to buy it and put up apartments."

We both considered the truth of her statement. Whatever funds, public or private, that were available for "charitable" expenditures were going toward veterans' benefits—and there were nearly a million of them. Then there was devastated Europe. Billions of dollars were spent helping it back from the rubble. Alice Ann Langer was right. Fixing up Grant's cottage was a very low priority on anybody's list.

"Do you remember when Garfield's train came in?" Gran suddenly smiled, looking up at her old friend. Another thing I knew nothing about.

"Do I? How could I ever forget? I was what? Ten? Eleven? It was the first time in my life I stayed up all night."

"I thought Kate and I would walk the old route tomorrow. I want to tell her about the night the whole town came together. The Captain used to call it Long Branch's proudest hour. Would you like to join us?"

Alice Ann Langer beamed her agreement.

Chapter 10

The next morning the hotel manager called a cab for us, and in ten minutes we were at the train station, another old relic on The Elberon side of Long Branch.

Like everything else in town, the station had fallen upon hard times. The paint was faded and peeling from many summers of neglect. One of the shutters (at least one that I could see—there were probably more) was hanging precariously. The steps leading to the platform were rotted in several places, and the banisters needed sanding. As we entered the waiting room, Gran remarked it was exactly as she remembered. The station master's window was in the same place, with the same shelves to hold the train schedules. It had been a fine, proud old building at one time, with beautiful woodwork and paneling. After seventy or eighty years, the basic structural integrity still held promise even its decaying state. It had been well built. Love, and a *lot* of money, was all it needed to return it to its old grandeur.

"They took out the benches," Gran said sadly, noticing a dozen odd chairs around the edge of the room. "They were beautiful benches, too. Pine or maple. Oh, I don't know. Some kind of highly polished wood, with wrought-iron railings. They don't make them like that any more."

That was sixty years ago, and my grandmother was right. They don't make them like that any more. Today community groups raise funds to restore old stations as a mark of civic pride. But after the war.... Alice Ann was right. Nobody had time, money or interest in such frivolous things as old buildings.

I'm told The Elberon train station is still in use, but it has been completely razed and rebuilt to modern design and specifications. It is totally lacking in character. Sad, but it's the way of life, at least in this country.

How many old buildings had been destroyed in Europe? Centuries' old buildings — with far more grandeur and art and history than a little train station in a little resort town in New Jersey that few people have ever heard of. What does it matter?

Ten minutes later, Alice Ann Langer arrived, also by taxi. She had given up driving some years before, when her eyesight began to fail. Cataracts, she said, although the doctors told her they were slow growing, and she'd probably die of old age before they robbed her completely of her sight. Not worth a complicated operation.

"I was telling Kate how badly President Garfield had been wounded," Gran said.

He had been up and down ever since July 2 when he was shot. Throughout the month, it appeared as if he might yet recover. Mollie's letters had been optimistic. But by early August, new developments were ominous. Various pus pockets on the President's body indicated infection had set in. Two or three times, the doctors drained the affected areas; once even administering chloroform to spare the poor man from excruciating pain while the hideous pustules were excised.

Through it all, Garfield had borne ordeal after ordeal with fortitude and indeed, bravery. He was never more admired than when he lay dying. Bulletins were issued three times a day, indicating his temperature, pulse rate and respiration. Some bulletins alerted the public as to his bowel movements. Nothing was sacred. The entire country was aware of every change in his condition. He was losing weight at an alarming rate, and as he became weaker and weaker, his usual good nature and optimism became a depressed resignation.

Mollie and her older brothers were permitted only infrequent short visits to the sick room. It was thought the sight of their rapidly failing father would upset them. Even worse, it would upset the President to have his children see him in that pitiable condition. But Mrs. Garfield sat with him for hours every day, nursing him, reading to him, and comforting him the best she could. She alone had hopes for his recovery, but whether it was naiveté, religion or a good act on her part remains open to conjecture.

Mollie had written Gran that her father longed to be home in Mentor. It would be cooler. His own bed would be more comfortable. He wanted to see his elderly mother again. He wanted to see his sisters and cousins—all "the old folks" who had meant so much to him over the years. He wanted desperately to see his "little" boys—Irvin and Abram—who were still with Lucretia's family. But his doctors adamantly refused. The stress of the long journey—more than 500 miles—would be extremely painful, if not fatal, they insisted.

It was Crete Garfield who suggested the sea air in Long Branch might restore his health. After all, it had helped her own recuperation, and she had been seriously ill. Besides, the President loved the place. Whether the doctors held any real hope for his recovery or whether they merely thought to make the patient more comfortable in his remaining days, they finally decided a lesser journey to Long Branch, only 250 miles, might be undertaken.

"The Captain received the first of I-don't-know-how-many dozens of wires about two days before the President came," Gran told us as we started walking the long stretch down Lincoln Avenue toward the ocean. "It might have been from Joe Brown or perhaps Blaine. They said arrangements were underway to bring the President to Long Branch to recuperate, and full cooperation with the railroad and other authorities would be appreciated. The next wire said Charles Francklyn had offered the President and his family the use of his cottage and adjoining buildings directly behind The Elberon Hotel, fronting on the ocean. He owned the entire property and was a major owner of the hotel. Keeping his private cottage was part of the deal when the hotel was built. Mrs. Garfield knew where it was, and approved.

"Henry Cobbs had gone back to college by this time, so The Captain left a clerk in charge of the store, put on his mayor's hat and went to The Elberon to make sure everything was in order. The hotel staff was a flurry preparing Francklyn's cottage for its pre-eminent guest, as well as preparing dozens of rooms for Garfield friends, doctors, servants, the politicians and the scores of newspaper and magazine writers who were descending upon the town. Additional telegraph wires were installed on the hotel premises. Additional staff was engaged and supplies ordered.

"Within the hour, everyone in town knew Garfield was coming. My father promised our local newspaper special consideration and exclusive stories providing they did not disturb the President's party. Then The Captain, *the mayor*, began receiving telegrams from the Pennsylvania Railroad. They were arranging a special train for his entourage, and several railroad executives and surveyors would be arriving shortly to manage the logistics.

"The Captain, along with our chief of police and a local newspaper reporter went to the station, met the railroad people, and drove to Francklyn's Cottage. It was about three-quarters of a mile over an unpaved street. This street." Gran looked directly at me, adding, "Remember, Kate, transportation was either trains, horses or on foot. There was no need to pave streets for horses." Alice Ann Langer smiled, recalling those old days before automobiles ruled.

"But the street was bumpy and full of stones," continued Gran. "The doctors insisted the slow pace of a wagon over that rutted path would be a dreadfully painful ordeal. The President would have to be moved from the train to a wagon, another ordeal, and it would take at least an hour, bumping up and down, feeling every pebble along the way. So the railroad men suggested that a spur track could be laid from the station right up to the front door of the cottage. Garfield would be spared an additional move, and the ride would be a hundred times smoother.

"Of course it required a lot of manpower. The land had to be surveyed and graded. Right-of-ways had to be given," Gran continued as we walked along the broad, tree-lined avenue. "Probably dozens of other problems as well. My father had promised our town's complete cooperation and everyone was eager to be of service. The proper right-of-way papers were drawn up, and The Captain sent veterans and members of the Republican Club around to all the residents on Lincoln Avenue for signatures so the spur line could be excavated. Everyone signed the waivers gladly.

"Of course time was of the essence. The home office started sending seasoned railroad workers and engineers to Long Branch. The Secretary of War sent army engineers to assist. We were told three doctors rode the train back and forth between Washington and somewhere in Maryland the day before, to calculate every possible bump and jolt. One doctor made the trip all the way to Long Branch to determine when and where stops would be made.

"Meanwhile the railroad people were sending in extra freight cars to bring in the rails and ties and rivets and whatever equipment would be needed. And you would be surprised at all the little things that were needed! It was a madhouse!"

As we walked down Lincoln Avenue that August day, nearly sixty-six years after the spur had been laid, it was hard to imagine the street bustling with two thousand people playing their tiny roles in history. It was now a quiet residential street, somewhat wider than the other ones in town. The houses were new in comparison to the event we were recreating in our minds, and in *much* better condition than the ones we had seen earlier. These homes were all built after the turn of the century, most of them after the First World War, when much of the town was torn down to make way for newer, smaller and cheaper houses with electricity and modern plumbing. Nobody on the street would remember the old event; for sure they didn't care about it. Half of them probably never heard of Garfield.

"Cracker boxes," Gran said disparagingly, looking at the houses on each side of Lincoln Avenue. I smiled. They looked beautiful to me. It was obviously the nicest part of town. The homes were set back with more property around each dwelling. The lawns were well cared for. Besides, if these were cracker boxes, I could only imagine what my grandmother thought of the tiny houses going up by the thousands in developments across the country where every house looked exactly the same as its neighbor.

"That day," Gran continued, "the day before the President came, was one I shall never forget."

"Nor I," agreed Alice Ann.

"Everyone in town was mobilized. The merchants, the police and firemen. The doctors and the Ladies Aid Society. The hotel people. Women and children. Everyone played a part. The Pennsylvania Railroad sent in 300 workers to lay the track. Plus the surveyors. Plus the engineers. Plus the big-shots. They sent picks and shovels and axes and all their special tools. Everybody who had a horse and wagon pitched in to carry off dirt from the digging.

"All afternoon, the railroad surveyors went door-to-door with the Republican Club or veterans, advising the residents that several feet of their front yard would be dug up."

"Do your remember old Mrs. Rodney?" asked Alice Ann. She didn't wait for an answer, but continued immediately. "It was in papers all over the country. When the railroad fellow said that her flowers requiring the labor of many summers would be ruined, she said proudly, 'I am willing you should ruin my house and all I have, if it would help to save him!'" Alice Ann gestured dramatically as she quoted what the old lady said. "They printed those words in the New York papers and in Chicago papers and even in the San Francisco papers. I think they even used it in a book. Mrs. Rodney was a celebrity for the rest of her life in Long Branch."

"Come on," I said, "People really didn't talk in all that flowery language, did they?"

"They certainly did for the most part," Alice Ann defended. "And for sure they wrote in very exalted tones." That part I knew from all my classes. Writers tend to develop a language all for themselves. And in Victorian times, they tended to write the most mundane things as if they were scenes from Shakespeare.

Gran smiled remembering the bustle of sixty-six years before. "Everybody pulled together that day, Kate. The same way they did for the war effort. Boys with bicycles became messengers, riding all over town at top speed. It was a huge task, laying that track in only one day. Most of the men in town closed their shops or left work early to help out. Every blacksmith was sharpening tools and keeping their fires hot—in ninety-degree weather, no less.

"The actual laying of the track didn't start till around suppertime. The surveying and paperwork took up the afternoon. Meanwhile, the President was due to arrive the next day. September fifth. They would have to work through the night."

"Everyone needed to be fed. The bakeries stayed open, and there was quite a run at the grocery stores, with everybody buying bread and cheese and ham and bushels of lemons for lemonade. The West End Hotel, which was close to Lincoln Avenue, prepared dozens of chickens and sausages. Other hotel kitchens made gallons of lemonade and orangeade and cold tea. The ice wagons worked non-stop. The brewer in town offered to send over kegs of beer, but the railroad people declined. They wanted the workers cold sober."

As we walked a leisurely pace toward the ocean, I could see through Gran's eyes again. A street filled with hot, sweaty workers, digging up lawns, carting away excess dirt in horse-drawn carts, grading the street, laying down rails, and hammering the wooden ties with red hot rivets. I could see young and old, male and female, rich, poor, black and white, all working together to create a minor miracle, in the hope that by coming to this little seashore town, the major miracle of restoring the President to health would occur.

"I don't think the Red Cross was founded yet," Gran said, "But our Ladies' Aid Society had been around for a while, so they set up two first aid stations along the way, with bandages and iodine and ice packs for minor cuts and injuries. Of course the town ambulance and doctors were on hand in case of anything serious, but thank goodness, all bruises were minor. I think the biggest problem was the heat. It was oppressive.

"I don't believe there was a hammer, rake or pickaxe left in a store," Gran continued. "And I don't think there was a sack of flour or sugar left on the shelves. Even though it was beastly hot that day, the women in town kept their kitchens going, baking and boiling. Children were sent around to collect cloths and towels to soak in cold water for the workers to mop their sweaty faces. By four o'clock in the afternoon, it was nearly a hundred outside.

"The ladies piled their sandwiches and cakes in buckboards and lined them up along both sides of Lincoln Avenue. The West End Hotel rigged up a special trolley wagon with food for anyone who wanted it. And we fetched out the rosettes and bunting and flags, and every house along that street was decorated for the President. Of course I doubt he saw them himself, but his family and those with him saw them. And the town saw them. And that's what counted."

"What did you do that night, Louise?" Alice Ann asked.

"I was one of the 'Molly Pitchers.' Miss Peg sat in a buckboard with a big keg of lemonade, filling cup after cup for anyone who wanted a cold drink, although it was hard to keep anything cold in that heat. I filled a pitcher with ice and lemonade, took a tin cup and walked among the workers offering drinks. Were you there?"

"I was there," nodded Alice Ann. "I came with my father. He had brought his wagon and was carrying away truckloads of dirt and rocks and whatever else needed carrying off. I was only ten, so I found a place with the Ladies' Aid, and rinsed out cool cloths for the men to refresh themselves. Then I fell asleep under a tree someplace."

"How could you have slept with all that racket?" Gran asked.

"I was ten," Alice Ann said, looking her straight in the eye. "*Midnight* was hours past my bedtime."

"I suppose you're right. But I don't think I had ever heard so much noise," said Gran. "The banging and clanging of the men hitting their hammers on the wooden ties! And the hollering and calling to each other, 'Heave on the count of three, lads!' and 'Over here, boy, another rivet.'" She gestured dramatically. "And the horses panting in the heat, bringing more heavy planks. Then there was the bell on the trolley from the West End Hotel. Every time it started ringing, we knew there was a fresh batch of ham and roast beef sandwiches and cold chicken coming down the street. Then there was the farmer with his watermelon cart. He set up a sawhorse and plank table, whacked those watermelons into chunks, free for the asking. I think I must have been his best customer. I love watermelon to this day!

"People were calling to each other all night long, giving directions for grading the road or carrying away rocks and dirt on the one end of Lincoln Avenue and foremen on the other end of the street calling out instructions to the workers, hammering away at the rails and ties on the other. Mothers wiping the brows of their sons, calling for Harry to replace Jack for a spell so he could rest and cool off. As if anyone could actually cool off in that heat! And then the calling out for lemonade and ice water and whatever else was available to drink. I couldn't begin to count the gallons of lemonade we must have gone through that night! It was so brutally hot!

"And, come to think of it, the stench was terrible, too, with all the horses and the sweat and the torches and the hot rivets and planks, and the night-blooming flowers with their sweet smell. And the smell of the different food. And the salt air from the ocean. It all mixed together and was definitely not a pleasant smell.

"My father was busy being mayor that night, and of course, with his bad arm, he couldn't do heavy work," Gran continued, "but he donated the store horse and wagon to carry away rocks. I think mostly he worked with the railroad people, making sure they had everything they needed."

Lincoln Avenue was the part of town that reminded her most of her youth, when Long Branch was a beautiful, thriving resort town. It was a lot like Gran herself: the years had taken their toll, but there were definitely traces of the beauty that had once been.

"Everybody worked together that night," she said softly. "Neighbor helping neighbor, stranger helping stranger. We were very proud of ourselves. If it hadn't been for the sorrowful reason we built that railroad spur, it would've been a great lark!"

We walked along quietly until we neared Ocean Avenue (which had been renamed Ocean *Boulevard*, when Gran turned suddenly to Alice Ann and asked, "Do you remember the torch boys?"

"Good Lord, Louise! What a memory! The torch boys!"

Gran noticed one more blank look on my face. "We didn't have electric lights then—at least not here, and I don't think there were too many gas lamps on Lincoln Avenue. I don't remember if the moon was out or not. But the men laying the track needed light, and a lot of it, so the Republican Club and the Democratic Club brought all their big torches—the ones they used for the political parades. The young boys in town became torch boys. They were around my age—thirteen or fourteen. Too small for hard physical labor, but too big to remain idle. So every ten feet along the road on both sides, there was a lad with a torch. Those poor boys were my best lemonade customers," she laughed. "With the weather, the heat from the torches, and the hot irons and rivets, it must have been dreadful for them. Sweat was pouring down their faces. The Ladies' Aid mopped them up, poor boys. They had to change off every fifteen or twenty minutes and bring in new boys, and send the hot sweaty ones to rest and try to cool off."

"One of them passed away a couple of months ago," said Alice Ann. "Past eighty, I imagine. I didn't know him, but I read his obituary in the Asbury Park papers. It said he was one of the torch boys when they built Garfield's railroad track. Every so often the newspaper resurrects the story. It's a nice feature."

Gran nodded. "It was quite a night. Miss Peg said it did her heart good to see people working together that way. It truly was our proudest hour. We were all exhausted, but that little track finally crossed Ocean Avenue, right past The Elberon and right up to the front door of the Francklyn cottage by six in the morning."

It occurs to me how little I, or for that matter, anyone knows about Garfield and his time. As I tried to put on paper all my memories of that trip in 1947, and the family lore my grandmother entrusted to my keeping, I found myself struggling to make sense out of a seemingly senseless assassination. Admittedly, Gran's recall on the subject was sketchy at best, and, as she said more than once, her memories were "little girl memories," hardly mature or well considered. By the time she was old enough for more serious reflection, she was a married woman with three children and Theodore Roosevelt was in the White House—enough to make anyone disregard those nobody-years after the Civil War.

I'm not exactly sure when I decided to write the story of my grandmother and the Garfields. I suppose it was when eighty-year-old World War II veterans began appearing on television telling their little pieces of history. I can easily place myself at FDR's death and Kennedy's assassination, but I didn't know them. They are just names in history books to me. A hundred million people can make the same claim. But Gran knew the Garfields. She had met the President and, as she said, had fully expected to know him much better. His daughter was her dearest friend. She had known Mrs. Garfield for forty years. She was close with the whole family until they died. Gran was the last survivor. Her story was not merely of the President's assassination; it was a personal story.

My granddaughter-in-law Sandra teaches high school history. Last year, when she was pregnant, her doctor insisted she leave work in her fourth month and stay off her feet as much as possible. So one afternoon, probably due to extreme boredom, she came to visit. Our retirement home is only a half-hour from where she and Dave live and it was the first time she and I had ever spent any appreciable time in conversation. A champion yard sale antique addict, Sandy made a beeline for the Minton set in my china cabinet and the silver service the Millses gave Gran and Henry Cobbs. Then she saw my collection of Mollie-cups on the shelf in the spare bedroom and demanded to know about my treasures—in detail. When I told her, she was fascinated and insisted on looking through Gran's old family albums, with a complete narration. The autographed Grant photo with my great-grandfather blew her away! She said it would probably be worth a thousand dollars. I nodded. It is not for sale.

With time on her hands, a sincere interest in my story (and she is the only one I've told about my writing project) and an ability to navigate the labyrinth they call the Internet, she volunteered to try to make some sense out of Garfield and his presidency. The next chapter—including the comments—is entirely hers.

Chapter 11

By Sandra Heller:

James Garfield was one of those bearded Presidents of the last half of the 19th century recognizable only to serious scholars. He served little more than six months, three of which were spent dying. Most historians give him a "bye" the same way they pass over William Henry Harrison, our president-for-a-month.

Grandma Kate was right on the money when she told me how her twice-great Uncle Cork remarked that Garfield was a "teacher, a preacher and a lawyer, and not makin' a livin' at any of 'em." What Garfield was, first and foremost, was an orator. He not only looked good (six feet tall, between two hundred and two hundred and ten pounds), he sounded good. He could spellbind an audience for an hour or two on assorted subjects, captivating them with his mellifluous voice, his classical references (a standard practice in speech-making back then) and the ability to say nothing, or at least very little, in flowing, flowery language, generously flavored with $10 words. In today's world of press conferences, radio, television, and instant messaging, Garfield would be laughed off the nearest stage.

In poring over books and articles on the man and his presidency, I was amazed at the wide swing of popular opinion. But then again, I stopped being amazed thinking of the wide swing of popular opinion on just about every president. Those who admired Garfield believed him to be fraught with potential, "too soon mowed down by a dastardly deed." Those opposed said he was a third-rate political conniver who never had and never would have an original idea.

True. Garfield was always ambitious. For a poor fatherless boy to succeed, ambition, usually accompanied by a belief in oneself, is essential, and not to be held against him.

True. Garfield believed in his destiny. It was a part of his evangelical church upbringing. Many people believed they were called to greater service. Nothing new here. Garfield was also torn by self-doubt. Freud would probably say there was nothing new there, either.

True. With the exception of Lincoln, every 19th century President between Jackson and Theodore Roosevelt was less than a stellar performer. The losing candidates were obviously worse, and other than Henry Clay, are names completely lost to history. But think about it: Less-than-stellar was exactly what was wanted in those days. Congress (particularly the Senate) perceived itself to be the most powerful of the three branches of government, and would not allow anyone to threaten its supremacy.

True. The word *available* comes up countless times describing political candidates of that era. It did not mean the candidate had nothing else on his schedule for the next four years. It meant the candidate was a) from the "right" part of the country; b) had exemplary credentials in his private, business and political life; and c) had taken no strong position on any subject to incur the wrath of powerful enemies. Garfield was available. Few other than his congressional colleagues had ever heard of him.

True. The "conniving" inference is usually based on the circumstances leading to his nomination in 1880. He was pledged to support the colorless John Sherman (although he personally preferred Blaine and opposed a third-term for Grant), and indeed, made the nominating speech. It was a curious ramble of high-sounding political blather, waving the bloody shirt for a half hour, and ending with a noble call for party unity. Nobody had the slightest idea whose name was being proposed. It could have been anyone. At the end of the speech, without elaboration, detail or personal recommendation, he announced John Sherman's name as the nominee. Many people believed he was actually nominating himself. Indeed, Roscoe Conkling, my four-times-great-Uncle-in-law Cork's "peacock with feathers a-fannin'," intimated Garfield was the *real* dark horse from Ohio. Conkling may have been a preening dandy, but he was an astute politician. There is enough smoke here to cause a small flame.

True. "Not capable of having an original thought..." Anyone with original ideas in the post-Civil War years would never have been nominated, let alone elected. It was a conventional age, and Garfield was as one with his contemporaries: a conventional man. In today's world, where we make a sport of building-up-just-to-tear-down, we want a President to provide strong leadership, so we claim. Garfield was, by nature, an accommodator, not a leader. But then, politics is a business of accommodations, isn't it?

Garfield accommodated in consenting to Chester Alan Arthur for Vice President. He accommodated in allowing the New York political machine to believe it would have presidential hands-off of patronage jobs in return for campaign support from Conkling and Grant. He accommodated to Blaine's disappointment by making him Secretary of State, and further accommodated to every political faction and voting bloc in order to choose his seven Cabinet members.

Stalwarts needed to be rewarded. Pennsylvania's hard-drinking and corrupt boss, Don Cameron, had delivered the state's electoral votes to Garfield. Cameron, by the way, was from a long line of corrupt political bosses. His father, onetime War Secretary, was fired by Lincoln, who remarked that "Cameron would steal anything except a red-hot stove." Cameron the Elder was indignant and demanded an apology and retraction, and Lincoln characteristically obliged, saying, "I'm sorry I said you wouldn't steal a red-hot stove."

Westerners and Midwesterners needed to be represented in the Garfield Cabinet, likewise the South. And New England. But that could be handled by Blaine of Maine. And, of course, the Half-Breeds who had supported Blaine and later championed Garfield's candidacy were owed rewards. And certainly New York, which had coveted the Department of Treasury, now that Blaine was ensconced in State. But in Conkling's New York, it would be like appointing the fox to run the henhouse.

The only non-controversial appointment (in a field of men nobody ever heard of or would hear of again) was Robert Todd Lincoln, named Secretary of War as a sop to Illinois' Stalwart Boss John Logan. Robert Lincoln was a nominal Stalwart and long-time friend and supporter of General Grant. There was magic in the Lincoln name to be sure, but the son of Father Abraham was only 38, and achieving a fine reputation on his own merits as an attorney. Everyone was pleased.

The new President tried his level best to please the Stalwarts. He approved a long list of New York appointments suggested by Conkling, believing he had fulfilled his pledge to "consider and consult" with the New York Republicans. Conkling might be livid about the "paltry" Postmaster Generalship for his State, but thousands of jobs were at the disposal of that office. But there was absolutely nothing Garfield could do to please Conkling short of handing the New York Senator the scepter of eminence grise. This was never going to happen, particularly with Blaine as Secretary of State.

If Conkling was furious about the paltry Postmaster Generalship, he went ballistic when he learned his arch-enemy, William Robertson, was named to the highest federal appointment in New York—Collector of the Port of New York—Chester Alan Arthur's old job. It was the spark that lit a raging inferno, and a crushing blow to the ego and prestige of the New York Boss, who suspected the sly and unsavory hand of Senator Blaine in that mischief. Conkling whipped himself into a frenzy, pulling out every parliamentary stop in his arsenal to block Robertson's nomination. It was now an open fight: Little David (the President) against Goliath (the Machine Boss).

Conkling invoked the tactic of "senatorial privilege," by which a senator can deny any appointment made in his state, without the need to justify his refusal. It was an old unwritten perquisite zealously guarded by senators. Garfield, a congressman for nearly two decades, and briefly a senator-elect, surely would never deny that courtesy. So Conkling cajoled and bullied his fellow senators to support his denial of Robertson, and as expected, no senator was willing to forgo his right to "senatorial privilege."

Parliamentary procedure can be very complex and complicated, so the President (with the expertise of Blaine guiding him most likely, pulled a rabbit out of his hat himself. He withdrew every other New York patronage nomination except that of Judge Robertson. The line was drawn. Moderate senators of both parties rushed to the President in a panic to persuade him to withdraw Robertson's name. Garfield refused. He had his epiphany. He had had enough of the Machine Boss and his cloying henchman, Chester Arthur, who no one trusted or had a good word for. He announced in no uncertain terms that he "did not believe it was the job of the President of the United States to be the recording clerk for the Senate." (I suspect this was the main reason his supporters-among-historians believed in his potential.)

Newspapers across the country were quick to grasp the situation and enthusiastically supported the President. They had also had their fill of the New York senator. And when Conkling, like a spoiled child, tendered his resignation, dragging his half-hearted New York senatorial colleague, Thomas Platt, with him, it became obvious New York had had its fill of Conkling as well. He was never returned to the Senate, nor involved in politics.

One of the office seekers who appeared at the White House nearly every day was a short, strange-looking man in shabby clothes. He would seat himself in the hallway, read the newspaper, and frequently "borrow" White House stationery to write letters. He would wait patiently until Joe Brown came out of his office, and then he would thrust himself forward with his request for an embassy consulship—preferably in Paris or Vienna. The twenty-four-year-old Brown knew that such an important post would never be given to this odd little man, but courtesy in the President's House was essential. Brown would turn him away politely, saying, "The President is not seeing any diplomatic appointees today." The little fellow in the shabby suit took it to mean, "He is not seeing anyone *today*. Perhaps he will *tomorrow*." He hoped.

The little man was staying at various cheap boarding houses in Washington, skipping out in the middle of the night when the rent became overdue, and moving to another one, preferably cheaper. During the day, he stationed himself at the State Department or in hotel lobbies where important politicians congregated. Sometimes he would spot one and press his application, seeking their support for his cause. It would come out at his trial, nearly a year later, many senators and congressmen indeed remembered this peculiar man with his absurd request for a consulship. Every one of them testified that "he wasn't all there," but they were also inclined to politely turn him *away*, rather than turn him *down*. That's why they are politicians, I suppose. They would say, "I'm not sure I can help," or "Perhaps the next time I see (whomever), we might discuss it." The little man would thank them, and consider he had made progress. He was becoming a "friend" of all these senators and congressmen. He continued to hope.

Charles Julius Guiteau, by all standards of modern

psychiatry, was insane. He was almost forty, with a long history as a loner, a drifter, and a person who seemed unable to make a career for himself, even though he had studied law and had been admitted to the Illinois Bar, which merely consisted of a brief oral examination.

He was short, wiry, homely and irresponsible. He fancied well-tailored clothing, although he seldom finished paying for it. In truth, he rarely paid any of his bills, owed everyone, and was continuously being evicted wherever he lived. He married, but was attracted to prostitutes. His wife divorced him.

After spending some time as an itinerant preacher and follower of evangelist Dwight Moody (who eventually discharged him), he gravitated toward politics in 1880. First he supported Grant, but after the convention, supported Garfield with equal zeal. He traveled from Chicago to the New York campaign headquarters to offer his services, but perhaps sensing his mental instability, Garfield's campaign managers politely rebuffed the offer. Guiteau then wrote a long, incoherent speech on Garfield's behalf entitled "Garfield Over Hancock." After pressing New York politicians daily and making a general nuisance of himself, he was finally scheduled to deliver his speech in Brooklyn. After five minutes of pointless rambling, Guiteau abruptly stopped, left the platform and never returned. The speech was never delivered again, nor published in any pamphlet or newspaper. But in Guiteau's diseased mind, his speech was crucial to Garfield's victory at the polls, and furthermore deserving of a rich reward from the new administration.

Two days after the inauguration, Guiteau went to Washington to claim his prize: a consulship in either Vienna or Paris. Living on borrowed money, he haunted the State Department, the Capitol and the White House, pestering everybody he could find to support his cause. He had little to do in Washington except loiter in the public buildings and hotels frequented by prominent men. He spent hours at the library, where he had free access to the daily newspapers. Few monitored the Senate battle more closely than Charles Guiteau. As months passed, and he was no closer to his consulate than he had been when he arrived in March, it began to dawn on him that perhaps he was losing ground. All his political "friends" who had been so courteous to him had not advanced his cause one inch.

On one occasion he had actually been admitted into Garfield's private office, but his outbursts and erratic behavior made his lunacy obvious. (It must be remembered that the Executive Mansion was open to the public then, and any presentable person who wished to see the President was allowed entry.) The President personally gave orders forbidding Guiteau from further access to the White House.

Later in spring, Guiteau chanced to meet Secretary Blaine in the street, and again pressed his cause. Blaine, preoccupied with urgent matters, lost patience with this strange disheveled man who kept annoying him with his ridiculous request. He told Guiteau never to bother him again.

It was the straw that sent Charles Guiteau's fragile reason over the edge. He was barred from the White House. Blaine had turned against him. He was being denied the reward he deserved. He had no money, was growing deeper in debt, and his prospects were dying. Conkling and the Stalwarts were in trouble. He lost hope.

There was only one way, according to the voices that began to affect his mind: Garfield must be removed. With Garfield out of the picture, Chester Alan Arthur would be President. Arthur had always treated him kindly at the New York Republican headquarters. Arthur always said "good morning" or "good afternoon" to the strange little fellow who showed up day after day. Arthur was his "friend." For certain, he would be promptly and generously rewarded. The Stalwarts would be back in power, and they would owe it all to him.

Guiteau's years as an itinerant preacher led him to believe

that the voices he heard, typical of many schizophrenics, were messages from God, commanding him to remove the ungrateful President. He began stalking Garfield, who seldom traveled with bodyguards. He purchased a snub-nosed .44 caliber revolver, nicknamed the "English Bull Dog," and practiced with it. He visited the jail, since he knew he would be arrested—at least until Arthur had him released. One Sunday as he sat in Lafayette Square, he saw the President leaving for church. He followed him, but decided against shooting him there lest he injure an innocent bystander.

Not long thereafter, Garfield escorted his ailing wife to the station when she left for The Elberon Hotel. Guiteau again had the opportunity to eliminate the President, but when he saw the frail Mrs. Garfield, he did not wish to subject her to the horror of seeing her husband's assassination.

Details of Garfield's trip to New England had been printed the newspapers: The President would leave from the American Railroad Station, the depot of the Baltimore and Potomac Railroad. This time Guiteau would not falter. The strange little man embraced his so-called fate, and prepared for the momentous occasion. He would become a celebrity and wished to make a proper appearance. He had his suit brushed and pressed, his shoes shined. He wore a clean shirt, and took care with his shave and haircut. He even wrapped his pistol in paper to prevent his perspiration from dampening the powder. He carried a letter of confession and a letter to be delivered to General Sherman. The die had been cast. Charles Julius Guiteau would have his name in the history books.

At his trial a year later, the crazy Guiteau (whose behavior was extremely erratic in hopes of justifying the not-guilty-by-reason-of-insanity plea) was asked if he killed Garfield. He replied that "he only shot the President—the doctors killed him." Guiteau was definitely crazy, but he wasn't stupid. It was an accurate observation.

Medical science in 1880 was in keeping with the horse and buggy. We cannot and must not judge it by modern technology standards. Doctors were still warring over Lister's controversial concept of germs and bacteria. But in Garfield's case, it was even more than medical ignorance. It was a Keystone comedy.

Garfield was shot at 9:20, the morning of July 2, 1881. He was walking through the ladies' waiting room of the train station with Secretary Blaine when shots rang out. One grazed his arm, the second penetrated his side. He collapsed immediately, but remained conscious. Guiteau was apprehended within minutes by the station's police officer, who literally "marched him off to the police station" a few blocks away. He offered no resistance. He had done what he set out to do.

As the shots were heard, people started running toward the waiting room. Mrs. Sarah White, the ladies' matron, had the presence of mind to run to the stricken man, sit on the floor, and cradle his head in her lap. The President was bleeding profusely, vomiting and showing signs of shock. Cabinet members rushed from their train compartments (they had already boarded), ran to the President, and then raced to the station's telegraph office to summon medical help and alert the world. Within fifteen minutes the news had been sent across the country. (No ambulance was called, mind you.) The Cabinet wives, along with the elder Garfield sons, were sent back to the White House.

The first doctor on the scene was Dr. Smith Townshend, a Washington Health Officer. Garfield was still on the floor with his head in Mrs. White's lap. He was conscious, but his pulse was weak and rapid, and he complained of "heaviness and numbness in his groin and legs, followed by tingling and then acute pain." They should have paid more attention to what he was saying. Dr. Townshend gave him some spirits of ammonia and brandy, which Garfield promptly vomited up. Townshend believed the President to be dying, but comforted him, saying he did not think the wound was serious. Garfield, more prescient than most, replied, "Thank you, Doctor, but I am a dead man."

Then the good doctor explored the wound with his unwashed finger to determine the path of the bullet, a common procedure at that time. No anesthesia. The pain must have been excruciating!

Fifteen minutes later—a whole half hour after the shooting (and still no ambulance), someone had the clever idea of pulling a mattress from one of the Pullman cars and carrying Garfield upstairs where he might be slightly more comfortable. (It was probably Mrs. White's idea, for all the common sense of the high-minded Cabinet members and Dr. Townshend.)

But first, the President had the presence of mind and coherence to ask his friend Rockwell to send for Crete, and even dictated the telegram.

Very shortly after Garfield was brought upstairs, Dr. D. Willard Bliss arrived. Blaine had summoned him, since he was the President's childhood friend from Ohio, and had been serving as his personal White House physician. The aptly-named Dr. Bliss's ignorance was surpassed only by his ego. Dr. Bliss also probed the wound, using a special instrument designed to withdraw a foreign object. Again, standard procedure. Naturally the probe was unsterilized and no anesthesia was given. All the probing accomplished was to create a false channel; from that point on, as the channel became deeper and deeper, all the doctors (and there were dozens of them!) were unanimous that it was the path of the bullet. They were also all wrong.

Within minutes of Dr. Bliss' arrival, in came Surgeon General Joseph K. Barnes, Dr. J.J. Woodward of the U.S. Army, and Dr. Robert Reyburn, a local physician who lived nearby—all summoned by one or another Cabinet member. (Woodward and Barnes, by the way, were odd coincidences of history, having participated peripherally in the autopsy procedures of Abraham Lincoln). They witnessed Dr. Bliss's attempt to withdraw his probe—which got stuck and was liberated after great effort (not to mention agony to poor Garfield). Then the wound was cleaned with carbolic acid, their one concession to sanitation, and a dressing applied.

Again it was Garfield himself, weak, and in terrific pain, who urgently insisted he be taken back to the White House. An ambulance was finally called. An hour had passed.

Garfield arrived at the White House at 10:45, and was immediately taken upstairs to the bed Joe Brown had ordered prepared. He was put to bed, still fully clothed. He would not be put into a hospital gown till after 5 p.m.!

By 11 a.m., doctors, reporters, public officials and friends of the Garfields were flocking to the White House. Nearly every doctor in Washington came to offer his expert advice. Most of these well-meaning medical men were given access to examine the President, who was in acute pain, nauseous, hemorrhaging, and in shock, with a rapid and shallow pulse of 112, according to Brown's first "official bulletin." There would be hundreds of "official bulletins" during the next ten weeks. The doctors poked some more, probed some more—all with unsterilized hands and instruments. It is a wonder the President didn't develop blood poisoning and die sooner!

One homeopathic doctor was alarmed at what he saw. "My God, General," he said to the President, "You should have surgical advice." Garfield, understandably testy by that time, replied, "There are about forty of them in the next room. Go and consult with them."

Exhausted, weak and irritable, Garfield told Bliss to take charge of the case, and dismiss the other doctors as he saw fit. While they consulted, the President asked Blaine, who sat beside him, "Why would anyone want to kill me? He must be insane. None but an insane person could have done such a thing." He was also concerned about his family, waiting anxiously for his wife to arrive. He was assured she was on her way—a journey delayed for hours when her special train derailed near Baltimore. Later in the afternoon, a tearful Hal and Jim were brought in, and the President comforted them saying, "The upper story is all right. Only the hull is a little damaged." He then instructed Hal to wire the elderly Eliza Garfield in Ohio to reassure her that her son was in good hands. Hah!

So far, the wounded President seemed to be the most sensible and coherent of any of them. I can certainly understand why some historians saw his potential.

But by 4 p.m. (still fully clothed, remember), Garfield was worsening. Demanding to be honestly apprised of his condition, he was told by Dr. Bliss that he was critical and probably couldn't last many more hours. "God's will be done," the President said, and prayed he would be spared long enough to see his wife again.

Finally (!) the doctors inserted a catheter to relieve his bladder, which immediately made him more comfortable, and confirmed no damage to his kidneys. They also gave him (finally!) a sedative to relieve the nausea and vomiting, and told him to "try to rest." Incredible! I can almost picture Charlie Chaplin, Fatty Arbuckle and Harold Lloyd playing the medical team.

At 7 p.m., Mrs. Garfield arrived, still weak from her own illness, and understandably worried about her husband. She spent fifteen minutes with the President, who began to instruct her on how to raise the children in his absence. She hushed him, saying he was not going to die, and she was there to nurse him back to health, just as he had nursed her a few weeks earlier. Thus reassuring each other, Garfield insisted Crete go to bed, and he dozed off.

After a few hours of rest, he felt slightly better, and again asked Dr. Bliss for the indications. Told there might be a small chance for recovery, he replied cheerfully, "Then we will take that chance."

At times through the night, Garfield's pulse rose to 158 and his temperature dropped two degrees below normal, indicating deep shock and internal hemorrhage. He was conscious and extremely thirsty, but unable to hold down any fluids. But miraculously, the internal bleeding stopped spontaneously around midnight, and Garfield could tolerate a few sips of water. And he could rest. He slept fitfully on and off, but he slept. The President made it through the night, to the relief — and surprise — of his doctors, who provided round-the-clock attendance.

On Sunday, July 3, an important visitor called at the White House: Vice President Chester Alan Arthur, who took the night train from New York after being summoned by Blaine, who feared Garfield might not survive the night. He paid his respects and was advised the president had rallied a bit and was resting comfortably. He spoke briefly to Mrs. Garfield, expressing his sincere concern and hope for the President's recovery. Then he attended a Cabinet meeting where he was all but ignored.

On Monday, July 4, Dr. Hayes Agnew of Philadelphia and Dr. Frank Hamilton of New York came to the White House. They were considered two of the finest surgical specialists in the country. While they did not stay permanently with the patient, as did the other "Keystone Docs," they came regularly for consultation. In addition, two others were included on the peripheral medical team: Dr. S.A. Boynton, Garfield's cousin, and physician from Ohio, and "Dr. Miss" Susan Edson, the doctor who had treated Mrs. Garfield during her bout with malaria.

The Garfields had known Dr. Boynton for years and trusted him; Dr. Miss Edson (and yes, that's how they referred to her) was included in a nursing capacity as a courtesy to Mrs. Garfield.

At last, the official medical team of "Keystone Docs" was announced: Bliss, Reyburn, Woodward and Barnes. The first guys on the scene. Hamilton and Agnew for bi-weekly consultations, plus Boynton and Dr. Miss Edson as "nurses." Most of their time was spent jockeying for authority, responsibilities and procedures, and whose name would be in the newspapers. Bliss—who was accused by many people of being extremely high-handed with the others—named himself "doctor-in-charge" and made assignments as follows: Dr. Barnes came twice a day for consultation; Dr. Reyburn kept the notes and the patient logs, and Dr. Woodward (assisted by Dr. Reyburn) took the patient's temperature, respiration and pulse three times a day.

They (with the help of Joe Brown), devised a chart of the morning, afternoon and evening vital signs, which were made available to the press, and thus the public. In the ensuing weeks, Garfield, when he was up to it, would ask Crete or Rockwell read the newspapers to him (over Dr. Bliss' strong objections), and he would learn about his own condition from the press. The doctors would never tell him the details. It seems Dr. Bliss was just as high-handed with the patient, who, coincidentally was President of the United States, as he was with the other doctors.

Garfield's injuries have been subjected to considerable medical and pathological retrospective. All experts concur on three points: First, given today's modern medical practices, Garfield would be expected to recover and be back at his desk in a month or six weeks. The autopsy showed two ribs had been fractured by the bullet, and as it traveled downward, nicked one or possibly two vertebrae. He would be recovered sufficiently to work, if not to walk. There might be some paralysis requiring physical therapy. His injuries are considered more serious than those of Ronald Reagan a century later, but Reagan was also twenty years older, and recovered easily and without complication. Garfield was only forty-nine years old and in the prime of health. There would be every expectation for him to do well.

Secondly, it is also concurred that if his second wound had

been left untreated (the first shot grazed his arm and had done little damage), Garfield would likely have recovered in due time—perhaps with the aforementioned paralysis. Thousands of Civil War veterans had been wounded in battle and carried internal bullets till their dying days—scores of years later.

Finally, most modern physicians agree the attending doctors did far more harm than good in their well-meaning ignorance. The medical world of 1881, the press, most of the country, and even the insane assassin himself, concluded the President was over-doctored.

So it should come as no surprise that the President developed septicemia—an infectious condition that riddled his body throughout. Without doubt it was caused by the repeated poking and probing by unsanitary hands and instruments, and complicated by threads of clothing that had become embedded in the wound. The doctors knew septicemia when they saw it and diagnosed it correctly, but they would have been horrified to think they had caused it.

By mid-August, Garfield was festering repeated pockets of infection. The doctors would drain one area, and in a day or two, like a leaking roof, another pocket would develop elsewhere. At least once, the patient (who truly exhibited a tremendous amount of patience under the circumstances), was given chloroform so rib fragments could be removed and some of the infection could be drained.

For nearly two months Garfield retained his natural good nature and optimism. He had taken a keen interest in his case, particularly the innovative "air conditioning system" that had been rigged successfully. He was also interested when Alexander Graham Bell tried to locate the elusive bullet with his metal detector. But as the pustules began spreading their systemic poison, he intuitively realized that death was a foregone conclusion. He had been in acute and unending pain. He had been given daily doses of strong opiates. He had been poked and prodded according to the well-intentioned ignorance of the day while the doctors and specialists argued the merits of antisepsis. And he had been starved. Literally. His weight dropped from over 200 pounds to barely 135. They fed him an ounce of the despised oatmeal, followed by equally loathsome lime water and milk. No wonder he was nauseous and unable to keep anything down!

In an attempt at nourishment, the doctors gave him enemas of beef broth. Actually there is some merit in the concept, when one thinks of medications being administered today as nasal sprays or skin patches. The doctors believed nourishment could be absorbed through the skin. In this particular case, it couldn't and wasn't. All it succeeded in doing was to subject the poor man to more lifting and turning and pain. Six strong men lifted him by the bed sheets and rolled him over nearly every half-hour to prevent bedsores. About the only thing that helped somewhat, was the bit of brandy he was given.

He was also starving for companionship. Other than brief visits with his three older children, contact was limited to Crete, his attending physicians, nurses and aides who turned him dozens of times a day. James Garfield was a gregarious man. He begged to see Blaine and Rockwell and some of his other friends. For the most part, the request was denied. Dr. Bliss was tyrannical in his insistence the President be kept isolated from anyone other than family—and the medical team. Once the infection started, even the rare visits with friends were stopped. He was not only sick, he was lonely.

Between the opiates, malnourishment, infection, pain and loneliness, Garfield sank into an understandable depression by early September. He became listless and unfocused. His usually curious mind was no longer responsive. And it was hot. One of the hottest summers in history, despite the first prototype in air conditioning.

The White House sickroom was also depressing. In the conventional medical wisdom of the day, the room was stripped of all but essential furniture: his bed with plain linen, a couple of chairs for the attending doctors and nurses, a bedside table and lamp, and a small desk and chair for the medical team to write their volumes of reports (and they wrote dozens and dozens of them!) The room was devoid of anything to give the poor man even a modicum of personal comfort.

———

Francklyn Cottage was an ideal spot to bring the dying President. It was about 50 yards southeast of The Elberon Hotel. The front faced the ocean, a mere hundred feet from the edge of the bluff. It was said that one could stand at the edge of the bluff and drop a pebble in the ocean.

It was a long, rambling structure, in a style somewhere between Queen Anne and a Swiss Chalet. (Most Victorian houses are a conglomeration, but somehow, it all seems to come together and make for a thing of beauty!) It was two-and-a-half stories high with seven gables. (Those Victorians loved gables, turrets and widow's walks!) The lower part of the house was painted sienna brown, and the roof and gables were a dark slate.

It had twenty rooms, including two large parlors and a huge dining room on the ground floor. The dining room faced the ocean, with broad full-length double windows that opened onto a wraparound veranda encased by a high railing. The way it was situated, the veranda was about six feet above the ground.

The main hall featured a flight of broad steps with shallow risers leading to the second floor. This allowed the President to be easily carried upstairs. A twenty-by-twenty room—much larger than his White House sickroom—would serve as his bedroom. Happily, a large window on the east and two windows on the south provided excellent cross-ventilation and respite from the late summer heat. Blinds and awnings protected the room from sun glare. Best of all, all the windows had an ocean view.

The kitchen was the kitchen of The Elberon Hotel. Charles

Francklyn had been using the cottage as rental property for some time, and the summer occupants preferred to use the hotel staff and services rather than employ a private cook. The Elberon had designed covered underground passageways to the adjoining cottages so hot food could be delivered even in inclement weather.

Not far from the hotel were a series of smaller cottages for smaller families or for children and their governesses — or other servants. The lobby of The Elberon Hotel was once again turned into a reception room, and friends of the President were once again recruited to accept cards and flowers and well-wishes from hundreds of concerned citizens who came to call.

Joseph Stanley Brown was on hand to deal with the army of reporters who flocked to Long Branch that September. As soon as word came that Garfield was to be moved to Long Branch, newspapermen from as far away as California made a beeline for the Jersey shore. Additional telegraph wires were installed so the thrice-daily bulletins could be transmitted cross-country within minutes. For the first time in history, the President's secretary became the liaison with the press. It would become a permanent assignment thereafter. The competent Brown, by the way, on the day of the shooting, had devised and issued press passes to a dozen reporters of his personal acquaintance and instructed them to share the information with their colleagues.

Joe Brown would earn his salary that summer.

The President's listlessness and apathy lifted. He took an interest in the plans for the journey. He would be moved from his bed, transported down the stairs to the front door of the White House, then moved to a wagon for the ten minute ride to the station (which would take more than a half-hour, keeping the horses at a slow walk). Then he would be lifted from the wagon, carried through the station to a waiting car, where he would repose until it arrived at the door of the Francklyn Cottage. Finally, he would be lifted once again and carried upstairs to his waiting bed. He likely sensed the hopelessness of his recovery, but tried to be encouraging, for his family's sake. Mrs. Garfield and the children were consistently encouraged by Bliss to keep their hopes high. If it was a Victorian custom for doctors to withhold medical information from the patient, it was triply customary for them to withhold it from women and children. Dr. Bliss was extremely conventional. So Mrs. Garfield and the children, naively perhaps, or perhaps because of their strong religious faith, insisted the cool sea breezes would restore the President's health, just as it had reinvigorated hers.

But despite primitive medical science, it was still an age of ingenuity. The forty years between the Civil War and the dawn of the 20th Century would see hundreds of inventions and processes that would change the lives of mankind forever. The embryonic cooling system rigged in early July for the President's comfort would be refined and redefined into today's air conditioning. The original premise was sound. The metal detecting device Alexander Graham Bell invented may have failed to locate the elusive bullet, but forty years later, it would locate minefields.

And, to provide maximum comfort during the arduous six-hour train journey, the first waterbed was invented. A large rubber mattress was fashioned—about the size of a double or queen-sized bed. It was then filled with water and affixed to carrying rods. Six strong men, three per side, would carry the President. Both in the cart, and again in the railroad car, the water-filled mattress would be suspended above the floor. The water would mold to his body and jostling would be kept to a minimum.

In the early morning of September 5, Harry and Jim Garfield bade their father a tearful farewell. They were leaving to start their freshman year at Williams College. The President had insisted the boys follow their original plans, and they would both write him several times before he died.

At the appointed time, the six "carriers" (Dr. Boynton, Dr. Bliss, General Swaim, Col. Rockwell, Col. Corbin and Col.

Rockwell's brother, for anybody who needs to know), lifted the dying man onto his water mattress, and carried him carefully down the great White House staircase and into the waiting wagon. The carrying "rods" were ingeniously designed to function as six wooden seats for his escorts once the litter was safely inside the train. The move was fine-tuned to the last detail.

Staff and servants lined up at the White House door to wish the President Godspeed. The move had been announced in the papers, and all along the route people lined the streets to pay their respects. From his waterbed litter, Garfield smiled and tried to wave a greeting. He was never a brilliant man, never a man of great ideas or leadership. But in his dying days, in his days of pain and suffering, he became a man of great character. The entire country was one with him, and he was never higher in their esteem.

The train was pulled by Engine #628, a coal burning engine of the Pennsylvania Railroad Company. Attached was the personal car of the president of the Pennsylvania Railroad, who permitted it to be completely gutted and refurbished for the President's maximum comfort. The seats had been removed and a false top had been placed a few inches above the roof for better cooling and air circulation. Screens had been affixed to the windows to keep out the dust. The inside was heavily curtained and carpeted. Dozens of boxes of ice were placed underneath the waterbed-litter to help keep it cool. His escorts took turns fanning him.

Several train trips had been made on the train during the past two days, and Drs. Bliss, Barnes, and Agnew rode back and forth from the Washington station to a Maryland station about five miles away, in order to test the waterbed. To their surprise, the faster they went, the less jarring occurred. Special engineers had taken a train to Long Branch to ascertain the timing, the route, the bumps, the stations, how long it would take, how fast the train could go, and dozens of other minor details—all in an effort to keep the President as comfortable as possible. They experimented with various speeds, and finally determined a top speed of 60 miles-per-hour would be best.

Two other cars were part of Garfield's train. One for Mrs. Garfield and Mollie, the Rockwell Family, "Dr. Miss" Edson, Joe Brown, General Swaim and the doctors. Another car held the baggage.

The engineer had been instructed to signal along the route that it was the President's train, and all other trains in the vicinity were alerted to watch for the signal and stop until Garfield's train had passed. (They didn't want the President disturbed by the noise, although it occurs to me the poor man might have welcomed the diversion.)

Washington to Long Branch was 238 miles by rail. The Presidential party left the White House at 6:45 a.m. The trip would take about seven hours, considering the train slowed down at more than 40 stations along the route, where a waiting populace was gathering to pay its respects. The train would stop three times: once, to dress Garfield's wound, once to take on coal and water, and another time to take on water. The dying man was bearing up extremely well and urged the engineer to go at top speed. Garfield was anxious to get to his destination. It was also a change of scenery from the sterile surroundings (about the only thing that *was* sterile) of the past two months. They arrived at 1:10 p.m. Garfield's color had improved, his pulse rate lowered, and his breathing was easier.

Through this entire ten-week ordeal, James Garfield never lost consciousness or coherence. Until the beginning of September, when blood poisoning had sapped his remaining strength, he maintained an interest in his case, despite his doctors' efforts to keep him in ignorance. And he consistently demonstrated not only good spirits, but common sense and judgment.

The judgment remained. Once situated in Francklyn Cottage, he told Dr. Bliss to tactfully dismiss the other doctors. He knew the end was approaching, and I suppose he figured enough was enough. Tact was completely alien to Dr. Bliss. The team of doctors quarreled right outside the sick man's room. Finally it was determined that Drs. Agnew and Hamilton would come regularly for consultation. No one seemed to trust or have a good word for Bliss' competence, either.

They had placed Garfield's bed so he could be propped up to view the ocean, which gave him great comfort. His wife and daughter spent time with him in short intervals. He could no longer concentrate for a longer conversation. He insisted Rockwell and Swaim, his two closest friends, remain nearby. He had lost an enormous amount of weight and was pathetically weak. Once he asked to be given a hand-mirror so he could look at himself. Over Dr. Bliss' objections (Bliss apparently objected to everything), Crete Garfield handed him the mirror, and he stared at it a long time. Finally he let it drop, saying he couldn't understand how someone who looked as well as he did could be so dreadfully weak. He tried to sleep.

He lasted until September 19 at 10:30 p.m. They said it was a ruptured aneurysm.

Shortly after midnight, the Attorney General sent a telegram to now-President Chester Alan Arthur in New York, informing him of the sorrowful event, and advising him to take the oath of office as quickly as possible. Arthur duly summoned several New York judges (first-come, first-served), and the oath was taken at two in the morning.

Of course they did an autopsy. The six attending doctors returned, along with several others, summoned for that purpose. They finally found the elusive bullet—in a totally different area than any of them had suspected. It had fractured a vertebra, and had lodged two inches or so below the pancreas, where it had become completely encysted, and would have done no further damage had Garfield been left alone. The long channel—the false channel the doctors had forged by their continual probing those first days—was filled with infection.

Once the funeral and burial and memorial services and official mourning period was over, the medical team submitted a preposterously high (for those times) bill to Congress, for what the newspapers would call "the longest house call in history." Congress, as well as the rest of the population, had lost considerable regard for the attending doctors, and they were finally paid considerably less than requested: Dr. Bliss, $6,500; Drs. Agnew and Hamilton, $5,000 each; Drs. Reyburn, Barnes and Boynton, $4,000 each, and Dr. Miss Edson, $3,000. There was no such thing as health insurance.

I was taught that a biographer needs to have a point of view. Of course, I am not a biographer; I merely did a bit of research to help Grandma Kate with her book. But I do have a point of view. I like James Garfield. He had his faults as everyone does, but he was a genuinely warm, friendly, sensible man. He was not a mental giant. Mental giants are seldom wanted and have a very hard time being elected. But he was not a mental pygmy, either. His biggest fault was wanting to please everybody—a common trait of a politician. But he had begun to show signs of becoming his own man, let the chips fall where they might.

Who knows what might have been had Garfield lived. Surely he would have not been a great man, in the sense Lincoln was a great man. But he would have made his mark, and I personally think it would have been a passing grade.

The train of events, beginning with Garfield's nomination the year before, and ending with his assassination by a "disgruntled office seeker" as Guiteau has been termed in the history books, was a momentous turning point. It would take another twenty years for a dynamo named Theodore Roosevelt to wrest supremacy from the Senate, but the foundation had been laid. Bossism would always a part of political life, but it was dealt a mortal blow. Chester Alan Arthur surprised everybody by also being his own man. His dependency on Roscoe Conkling dwindled and eventually dissolved. He supported the Civil Service reform the country insisted upon (after the legislative mess and its aftermath in 1881), and is considered by historians to have done a credible job.

When I die and go to heaven, I will look up Mr. Garfield and pay my respects.

Chapter 12

As we neared the ocean, Gran, Alice Ann Langer and I were silent, each of us—actually each of them—lost in their own memories. I had no memory; only a slight direction into the past glory days of a rundown town, although I was definitely impressed by Lincoln Avenue. I could use my imagination about the old grandeur.

"Is anything left?" Gran asked. "We are," Alice Ann replied. "And I think the old church is still there."

At the intersection of Lincoln Avenue and Ocean Boulevard, there was no Elberon Hotel or Francklyn Cottage. Alice Ann said there was a fire thirty years before and too much had been destroyed. In its stead were some slap-together summer dwellings interspersed between run-down monstrous houses and a long-neglected church across the way whose best days had long passed.

"The Elberon Hotel had been the smartest resort in town," said Gran, obviously seeing a vision all her own. "It had all the latest features. Bell pulls in every room. Room service. Dumbwaiters on every floor to carry baggage up and down. Underground passages so waiters could bring dinner trays to your room without going outside—if you were staying in one of the cottages. The finest you could have back then. The whole town was the finest back then—and The Elberon district was its crowning glory.

"Charles Francklyn was one of the wealthy industrialists. I don't know how well he knew the Garfields. Certainly not as well as the Childs' did, but I think they were all acquainted. Anyway, Mr. Francklyn didn't use the house much himself and was happy to lend it to the President.

"When Garfield's train pulled in that afternoon, I think the whole town turned out. We had been up all night, sweaty and tired and grimy, but we lined up all up and down Lincoln Avenue. Miss Peg and I had gone home around 6 a.m., took a nap till noon, and then dressed and came back. The Captain didn't nap.

"More than a thousand people lined both sides of the railroad track," Gran continued. "People came from all over the area. Children held flags and ladies held up bunting swags. Men removed their hats. And, above all, everyone was quiet, out of respect for the dying man. You could have heard a pin drop. Other than the Garfield family, I don't think anyone believed the President would recover.

"It had been a trip of several hours, and they said Garfield actually enjoyed it in his own way, urging them to go at top speed. Sixty miles an hour.

"At the station—I wonder if you remember this, Alice Ann— the engine had to be switched. The original one was too heavy for the track to the Francklyn Cottage, so they had to bring in a lighter-weight engine."

Alice Ann Langer shook her head. "I was ten. I don't remember much of anything."

"Anyway," Gran continued, "when they finally arrived at the Francklyn Cottage there was a slight hill maybe twenty feet from the door. The engine couldn't pull the train over that hump, and rather than carry the President the extra distance, about a hundred burly men pulled and pushed the train by dint of their own force—right up to the door.

"A fine, spacious room had been prepared, with floor-to-ceiling windows on the ocean side for a good breeze. The cool ocean air was a great relief from the sweltering heat of Washington—and the stuffy train."

"Grant's house is only five minutes from here," said Alice Ann, indicating a piece of shorefront property on our right. "Oh the happy afternoons I spent there, while my sisters and brothers played with the general's grandchildren," she sighed, as we walked over. "Fred Grant's house was over here," she said pointing across the way.

"Elberon is still a nice place," she continued. "They take good care of it. But it's the well-to-do families who own the homes. They don't get tourists. The people who live here during the summer aren't interested in boardwalks or amusement rides."

Grant's Cottage was only a block or two over the border between Long Branch and Elberon. As we stood in front of the house, I was struck by its simplicity. Even making an adjustment for seventy years of minimal care and upkeep, it was definitely a modest place in comparison with the opulent old "cottages" still standing, even the decrepit ones. The grounds were ample and the house set back sufficiently to have allowed the general his privacy. But the actual house was no larger than those for less prominent citizens. It was also visible from Ocean Boulevard. Anyone could stroll by and wave to the Grants if they were sitting on their porch, which, I was told, they loved to do.

But it had gone to seed. It was a disgrace to Grant's memory, as well as to Long Branch and Elberon, that their most distinguished residence should be so dilapidated. It was thirty or forty years overdue for painting, the gardens were overgrown, the shutters and roof sadly in need of replacement, not repair. I doubted it had been fitted for electricity or modern plumbing. I had gone to Washington, D.C. some years before and had seen the White House. I had taken a side trip to Mt. Vernon. I heard glowing stories of Grant's Tomb, that white marble mausoleum in New York. This weather-beaten old house bore no resemblance to its former resident's glory. Grant:

the most famous man of his time. The Hero of Appomattox. It was sad.

I suppose my expression was not lost on my grandmother and her friend.

"Not much to look at," Gran remarked.

"They've been trying to sell this property for years," confessed Alice Ann. "A few potential buyers made offers, but they all fell through. It'll be sold eventually. The family can't keep it up, and the town can't afford it either. Shore properties are expected to become very valuable since the war is over."

I can only imagine what twenty-first century towns would do with such a prize! If dozens of organizations would be eager to renovate an old train station, how ecstatic they would be to inherit such a treasure. Grant's Cottage! A "Summer White House." They would raise millions to restore it to its historic past, albeit with electricity, air conditioning and modern plumbing. They would refurnish it with period pieces gladly donated for the honor. They would put in a gift shop with postcards and souvenirs. It would be listed on every tourist registry in New Jersey. It would be a national treasure. But in 1947 it was an eyesore. An historic eyesore.

"Mother and I went the day after they arrived," Gran said. We knew the journey from Washington had been arduous for everyone and Mollie and her mother needed to get settled. Besides, like everyone else in town, we had been up all night and we were tired ourselves.

"The Elberon Hotel had set aside several rooms for the President's staff. General Swaim and Col. Rockwell were accepting cards and well wishes and bouquets. Practically every room in The Elberon had been taken by Cabinet members and staff and doctors. The reporters stayed at cheaper hotels.

I'm not sure if Grant was in town when we built the little track, but I know he was there the week before Garfield died. He stopped every day to pay his respects and inquire about his condition. Politics was laid aside.

"General Swaim was there when Miss Peg and I showed up. I had never met him, but when I said I was Louise Dunbar, Mollie's friend, he recognized the name. At just that moment, Col. Rockwell entered and saw me. He knew me quite well by then, and told Gen. Swaim it was all right to let us through. He gave me a big hug, greeted Mother with a warm smile and handshake, and she smiled and curtseyed slightly.

"'I want to thank you both so much for your kindness toward my daughter,' he said. 'Lulu is shy with strangers, and you have made her feel so welcome. She speaks highly of you both.'

"Well, Kate, I admit I felt a little sheepish hearing such glowing compliments when in truth I never liked Lulu Rockwell," Gran confessed. "And I also admit from then on, I always considered her shyness, and my thoughts of her were kinder. She died many years ago. Nineteen twenty-five or -six, I think. I sent flowers.

"Anyway, Miss Peg said some appropriate things, including that our house was open to the President's family and friends. Then Col. Rockwell said the best possible thing. He said The Captain had been largely responsible for the smoothness of the President's move.

"'He and I exchanged dozens of telegrams during the past few days,' he said, 'and I do not believe for a moment things would have transpired half as well if not for Captain Dunbar's excellent administrative skill.'

"I could easily understand why Col. Rockwell was the President's closest friend. They were both alike in their generous and gregarious natures.

"If you had handed Mother and me a gold medal, we could not have been prouder. We both knew The Captain had worked tirelessly to make sure everything was done quickly and efficiently. He had spent two solid days with little rest, running from engineer to surveyor to railroad supervisor; running from constables to veteran groups; running from The Elberon to the local merchants, making sure paperwork was filed, making sure traffic was detoured, making sure wagons were lined up properly, making sure everyone had whatever they needed to do their jobs, and making sure everyone who wanted to help was included.

"He notified our local newspaper fellow of the events, and made sure the reporters who were flooding into Long Branch had accommodations and were notified that interviews with railroad workers were strictly forbidden till after the President arrived. No detail was overlooked, no matter how small. And then, once Garfield had been settled at Francklyn Cottage, The Captain was on hand to help Col. Rockwell and the others 'entertain' the visiting politicians who flocked to town.

"The old quartermaster had come through his own proudest hour," Gran said, obviously moved by the recollection of her father's efforts. There's a citation somewhere in the family album, Kate, signed by President Arthur, acknowledging the Long Branch mayor for his efforts during Garfield's final days."

Gran stood silently for several minutes as we stood outside the Grant property. I have no idea what she was thinking, but I was trying to imagine what had once been the most sought-after residence in the whole country.

She continued. "The next day, Mollie and Lulu Rockwell showed up at our house. School had started for me, but when I got home, there they were in our front parlor drinking lemonade with Miss Peg. Mollie and I embraced, and she was quick to notice the new addition to my wardrobe. After The Captain and Uncle Cork turned me upside down trying to shake out the imaginary bullet, Miss Peg decided I was in need of my first corset, and the very next day we shopped accordingly. I was growing up.

"It was also apparent that neither Mollie nor Lulu really appreciated the futility of President Garfield's situation. They knew he was gravely ill, but truly believed he would recover with the benefit of sea air. Miss Peg shot me a warning look, and I didn't say a word. I had heard the talk in town as we built the railroad spur that night. We all knew the President was being brought here to die in a little more comfort.

"I didn't see much of Mollie those ten days before the President died. I had to go to school. My parents insisted there was nothing I could do except to 'be there' if Mollie needed to talk. She didn't want to talk much that week and I understood. Sometimes with deep, deep feelings, people clam up. I am like that, and so was Mollie.

"My father, however, was extremely busy being mayor that week. Every politician in the state came to pay respects and sign the book. Some came from Ohio—and even farther. I think everyone agreed the President would not survive. I think the President knew it too. The only ones who didn't seem to know were Mrs. Garfield, Mollie and Lulu. The Sunday before he died, the President heard the bells from the little church across the way and inquired the reason. Mrs. Garfield said everyone was praying for him. She told him Mrs. Childs was in the choir and had dedicated her solo hymn for the President's recovery. Garfield smiled. Mrs. Garfield hoped and prayed right up to the end. She was very religious about those things.

"Mollie only spoke to me once about her father's death—the actual events, that is. Her feelings ran very deep. It was many years later, when The Captain passed. She said her father tried hard to put on a strong face for her. They had moved his bed close to the huge windows and propped him up to view the ocean and breathe the salt air. He saw an old soldier walking guard on the bluff. Garfield told her the man saluted him and he had returned the salute. I had heard that story many times. The old soldier was a fixture in town and loved telling about it every chance he could, each time with more embellishment. In the last version, I think Garfield leapt up from his deathbed to hand him a medal.

"Anyway, Mollie said she could see how frail her father had become. He had lost seventy pounds and was a mere shadow. The last time she saw him, she fainted. She was embarrassed about it and said it was the one and only time in her life she fainted. It was the tight corset and her time of the month she claimed, but frankly, I think it was the shock of reality. The Captain and Miss Peg did not shield me from the inevitability of death. 'God's will must be done,' they had said." Gran paused and reflected. "I think it is better to be prepared.

"Finally," she continued, "the poor man's body could bear no more. He complained of a sudden terrific pain, lapsed into a coma and died within hours. Every church in town had a memorial service. I imagine services were held all over the country. Vice President Arthur, who was now President Arthur, came to pay tribute, as did Blaine and Robert Lincoln and the other Cabinet members. Grant was there and so was Sherman. Conkling, however, wasn't.

"The doctors insisted on an autopsy of course, and they finally discovered the bullet — in a completely different location than everyone had thought. It turned out that all the poking and probing had made a false channel, and nobody realized the true path was elsewhere. Of course since there was no such thing as X-rays or wonder-drugs at the time, no one was to blame. They all did their best.

"People lined up by the dozens outside Francklyn Cottage, and a few of them were allowed to enter and pay their respects to Mrs. Garfield. There was a funeral service right there at The Elberon and Reverend Young held a short service and preached a eulogy. We were invited, but we sat far in the back. The front rows were for the family and close friends and all the VIPs, including President Arthur.

"Then the funeral train was backed up to the side door of the Cottage and they loaded the President's coffin back on the train. Mrs. Garfield, Mollie, the VIPs and an honor guard of soldiers entered their special cars. The whole train was draped in mourning bunting. All the carpets and drapes had been removed and recovered in black cloth, with American flags interspersed between black crepe rosettes. I wasn't in the car, of course, but Mollie told me about it.

"We had sent a wreath, and so had Uncle Cork and Aunt Phee. And Uncle Walter. And most of the people in town, not to mention the Childs' and the Grants and the Shermans and Pullmans and all the rich summer folks. They needed an entire railroad car for all the flowers.

"When they were ready to move, the little Elberon church bell began to toll. The men removed their hats, and everyone bowed their heads in respect. Then the other church bells in town took up the toll, and Lincoln Avenue was once again crowded on both sides with silent onlookers all the way up to the main track, where the regular engine was coupled on to begin its mournful return journey.

"All the red, white and blue bunting and rosettes had been replaced with mourning wreaths and drapes. Everybody stood in silence as the train went by very, very slowly. It was so sad."

Gran's face was sad too. She was doing more than telling me a story of something that happened years and years ago. It was a sad occasion for the country, but more so for her. The Garfields were very real people in her life, and she loved them dearly.

"The train passed slowly through thirty or more towns along the way back to Washington," she went on, "and at each station there was a crowd, hats in hand, to stand in silence. Flags had been lowered to half-staff. Even in remote farms and fields, people gathered quietly as the train passed. Bridges were filled with bystanders. In Princeton, some of the students threw flowers on the tracks and kept the crushed flowers as souvenirs. All of Washington was draped in black, the White House included, and Garfield lay in state at the Capitol before being taken home to Ohio. I didn't see Mollie again till that Christmas, when I was invited to their farm.

"They buried him in the local cemetery in Ohio. We didn't go, mainly for the same reasons we didn't go to the inauguration. Too far, too expensive, too busy, and too hard on Miss Peg. But not long afterwards, they erected a big memorial in Cleveland.

I went to that ceremony. By that time, I was old enough to travel alone, and I stayed with the Garfields at their home for a few days. Then many years later, when Mrs. Garfield died in California, they brought her back to lie beside her husband." Gran fell silent. The story was finished.

Alice Ann had been as enraptured by Gran's story as I was, and we stood outside the Grant property saying nothing. I was struck by the complete lack of any commemoration of the site or the event of "Long Branch's proudest hour," and said so. Alice Ann Langer was quick to agree, and added there had been some effort to erect a memorial plaque—if enough money could be raised. Gran immediately offered to contribute $100 to the campaign, "in honor of Mollie's father."

Two minutes later, a car pulled up and tooted the horn. Alice Ann smiled and waved and announced she had a surprise for us.

"This is George Presley, Arthur Presley's grandson," she said. Mr. Presley parked the car and ran around to our side to help the two elderly women get in.

"Where are we going?" Gran asked. "We don't have much time. We've got a couple of stops to make before we catch the five o'clock."

"You'll make it easily," Alice Ann said. "We're only going a few blocks."

Minutes later, we were in front of a modest-sized house with a neatly kept yard. An elderly man around Gran's age was standing on the porch waiting for us.

"Do you remember Arthur?" Alice Ann asked. My grandmother shook her head.

"No, perhaps not," she continued. "He was in my class in school. You wouldn't have known him." The old man smiled and came down the porch steps to greet us.

"Arthur, this is Louise Stanfield. Louise Dunbar, then. You probably don't remember her, but her father, Captain Dunbar, was mayor when we were children. And this is her granddaughter Kate." We nodded and shook hands.

Alice Ann went on, "After you left last night, I called Arthur and told him we were going to walk the old Lincoln Avenue track, and I thought you'd both like to see it."

I drew the complete blank that had become a major part of my repertoire of facial expressions. Lincoln Avenue bore no trace of a track or train, or even a sign indicating what had occurred there sixty-six years ago, and here we were at least a half mile away.

Noticing my puzzled expression, Alice Ann explained. "After President Garfield died, they dug up the track. There was no need for it, and it was right down the middle of a residential street. The people wanted their property back. Then Oliver Byron bought up all the planks and ties and spikes as a souvenir. Do you remember him, Louise?"

"Good Lord, yes," said Gran. "He was a theatrical actor. I don't know how good or famous he was, but he lived here in town and owned a lot of property. Anyway, he had a cabin built from the old ties, and painted it red, white and blue."

The elderly man and his grandson escorted us around to the rear of his property and pointed to a very faded red, white and blue log cabin, about ten foot by ten foot, presently being used as a tool shed.

"And now I have it," Arthur Presley said. "My father was a carpenter, and Oliver Byron had asked him to build this back in '82. I think he used it as a little tea-house. When he died, his son kept it. And when his son died, he willed it back to my father, who willed it to me. I'll probably will it to my son or grandson. I have no idea what to do with it. But you're welcome to look around."

I don't know if Gran was amused, delighted or deeply touched, but her eyes filled with tears at the sight of the rundown red, white and blue weatherbeaten relic. It was in the same state of disrepair as nearly everything else in Long Branch.

"Oh, I definitely remember this," Gran said, gently touching the old splintering railroad ties that made up the walls. "I remember Mr. Byron saying since President Garfield was born in a log cabin, it was a fitting tribute." Then she turned to Alice Ann and the Presleys and added, " I'm so glad you brought me here. I'm probably one of the few people alive today who actually remembers the man."

⎯ ⎯

The taxi came to the Scarboro Hotel at three o'clock. The driver loaded our bags, and Gran directed him to a local flower shop where she purchased five bouquets. Then we went to an old cemetery on the west side of town. The sun had begun to peep through the clouds and the air had warmed considerably.

"I won't be here," she said matter-of-factly. "I'll be with Charlie in Pittsburgh." She made her way through the rows of gravestones as if she knew the route by heart. "I've been here many times, Kate, although it's been twenty years since the last time—when Aunt Phee died."

We stopped at a fair sized double headstone that said "Dunbar." On the left was the inscription "Beloved Wife and Mother." Underneath, it said Margaret Coyne Dunbar, and under that, 1842-1888. On the right it said "Devoted Husband and Father." Underneath was John Milton Dunbar, 1840-1901. Gran laid two bouquets at the foot of the tombstone. Her money hadn't exactly been wasted; the grass had been cut. However, the entire cemetery was in keeping with the overall sorry condition of Long Branch. Gran shook her head at the dilapidated headstones in the surrounding area. "Obelisks and double gravestones are more stable," she mused. "They don't tilt over as easily."

Then she took my arm, and introduced me to my great-grandparents who had died long before I was born, although after Gran's story, I felt I knew them intimately. We stood silently by the grave for a few minutes, each in our own private thoughts. I tried to picture them in my head: The Captain with his waxed-tipped handle-bar moustache and straight-as-an-arrow posture, and Miss Peg with her dark, serious eyes and warm smile. But of course, I was picturing the photograph on Gran's mantel. Except for the smile. Nobody smiled in the old pictures.

Then we walked over a few rows to another double gravestone where Gran placed two more bouquets. This one bore the inscription "United Forever in Eternity." On the left, Daniel Patrick Corcoran 1838-1904; on the right, Ophelia Dunbar Corcoran, 1842-1927.

It was easier for me to picture my great-great aunt and uncle. Gran's story had been so vivid. I could see Uncle Cork's reddish hair—like an Irish setter, she had said—and full beard and merry gray eyes. And I could visualize Aunt Phee with her rosy cheeks, bustling about and taking charge of everything. I wished, I truly wished I could have known them all in person.

Then we took the last bouquet and walked quietly to the other end of the row. There was a single headstone still standing straight among the dozens of tilted markers. It was engraved "Henry Francis Cobbs, 1861-1893." Underneath were the words "A finer man never lived." This was my grandfather. My real grandfather.

I don't pretend to know the thoughts in Gran's mind. I only know the tears were real, as she reached into her purse and pulled out her handkerchief. "It was true then, Kate, and it's true now. A finer man never lived. Charlie Stanfield was a wonderful man. But no finer than my Henry Cobbs. I am the only one left to remember him." She wiped her eyes and blew her nose. "And I loved him so dearly."

I had never even seen a photograph of him. Gran had those mementos tucked away, out of respect for her wonderful second husband, the "Pops" who had raised her children as his own. But she had said that Henry Cobbs was tall and lanky like James Stewart, so I pictured "Mr. Smith" or "Elwood P. Dowd" dressed in Victorian clothing. That seemed to work. Mother and Uncle Henry were tall and fairly lanky. Gran may have been the only one left to remember him, but his children, and now, I, a grandchild, carry a part of Henry Cobbs.

The cemetery is still there. When Gran died, I sent a check for perpetual care of their graves. There was no one else to do it, and I think she would have been pleased.

Chapter 13

On October 17, 1947, my grandmother was eighty years old. Uncle Henry and Aunt Rose gave a party for her, and the whole family was invited. Several friends and neighbors, representing nearly fifty years living in Pittsburgh, came to pay their respects. I had given Aunt Rose Hal's address and the addresses of the uncles. They sent telegrams of love and congratulations. I had also given her Alice Ann Langer's address so she could be invited. She sent a card and a box of candy. I wasn't there. I was in bed with the flu and a hundred and one fever.

Two weeks later, when I was feeling better, I called Gran and said I had a birthday present for her, and asked if it would be convenient to stop by. Even though I called every two or three weeks to say hello, I hadn't seen her since our trip. I was busy with school, and it was a little too far. She was delighted to hear from me and insisted on making dinner—Alice Ann's sauerbraten recipe, which was every bit as tasty as the original.

I had two gifts for her. The first was a large bouquet of flowers, which my mother had always insisted was a perfect gift for any occasion except an attack of hay-fever. The second gift was even better. Hal Brown had sent me a packet of snapshots he had taken when we were in Pasadena. Among them was a wonderful photo of Gran and the uncles the day they went to Knotts Berry Farm. The sun was shining, the flowers blooming, and they were smiling and obviously happy to be together. I'm glad people smile when they have their photos taken now. I had the picture enlarged, found a lovely frame, and gave it to Gran. If I had handed her a basket of rubies, she couldn't have been more pleased. She put the picture in the center of her mantel, and sniffed back a tear. "I know I shall never see them again, and I love them so dearly." She was right. She would be the last survivor.

Then Gran asked me about Hal, knowing I would share the progress of my romance. In the eight weeks since we left Pasadena, I had received a dozen letters and had written back promptly. He was planning to come east for Christmas. Gran invited him to our annual family Christmas dinner.

She also had a couple of surprises for me. First was dessert—a lemon pie, which she knew was my favorite. And, of course, coffee—but this time she used the delicate cobalt and gold Minton teacups that she had insisted were only for special occasions. And the coffee pot, cream and sugar bowl was the carefully polished silver service she had received from the Millses as a wedding gift. I felt honored.

Then she handed me a large manila envelope, brown and cracked from age. In it were several photographs I had never seen before. "My wedding picture when I married Henry Cobbs," Gran said simply, showing me a formal photo of a young girl with her hair piled high on her head, sitting in a chair, holding a bouquet. Standing next to her was a tall, lanky fellow in his mid-twenties with an enormous brown moustache. He looked nothing like what I had imagined; certainly not like James Stewart, other than the tall and lanky part. He was dark haired with light eyes, gray or hazel, Gran couldn't quite remember. But it was his moustache that overpowered everything. It was shaped like swag draperies. The upper lip hair was trained to slant slightly upward at the sides, perhaps a quarter inch, and then continued down his face like a panel on each side of his mouth—until it reached his chin.

Moustaches were out of fashion in 1947. The only people I

could recall having them were Charlie Chaplin, Hitler and Thomas Dewey—none of whom struck me as particularly handsome. Henry Cobbs' moustache was a work of art, hair-wise.

Gran probably noticed my astonishment, since she was quick to point out that moustaches and beards were very much in vogue when she was growing up. She pulled another photo from the packet. There was Gran and Henry standing behind two older people, seated on formal high-backed chairs. "My father and Henry's mother," she explained. "Your great-grandparents."

The Captain's wax-tipped handlebar moustache was a mere pittance compared to the opulence on Henry's face. Clara Cobbs, my great-grandmother, looked like a pleasant old-ish woman. Gran said she was only three or four years older than The Captain, but she could have been his mother. She had a sweet face, and rimless glasses, but there was something in those eyes that indicated she was not one to be trifled with. I suppose being a governess to eight or nine children brings out the disciplinarian. The Captain's eyes, however, looked sad. Gran had said more than once that Miss Peg's death had hit him very hard.

There was one photo I had never seen before, but I recognized Uncle Cork and Aunt Phee immediately, just by Gran's description. My great-great uncle had a full beard and moustache. The entire bottom of his face from his nose down was a mass of hair. And the light eyes were merry, despite the childhood memories that were sad, hard and hungry. Aunt Phee looked exactly like what my sister Margie always said about her: she was huggable. But then again, there were several photos of Aunt Phee in the family albums, albeit as an elderly woman. In this photo, she was in her mid-forties, and her dark hair was tucked up under a massive hat, full of feathers and flowers. And, despite the formality of the poses, I could detect a hint of a smile.

The next two photos were taken some time later. Gran seated with a baby—my mother—in her arms, and Henry standing. The other photo had Gran seated with a baby in her arms, and Henry—who had shaved the hanging panels of his moustache in this picture—was standing beside her, holding a toddler of about two. The baby was Uncle Henry.

"When I married Charlie Stanfield, I put these photos away, Kate. They were *my* memories, not *our* memories. And since Charlie and I were very happy, and since Clara and Henry had no memory of any other father than Charlie, who they adored, I thought it would be very inconsiderate to keep them in the family album."

"Have they seen these photos?"

"No."

"Don't you think they should?"

"No. There is no need. They know I was married before, and that their real father died when they were babies. But they adored Pops and he adored them, and I don't see anything to be gained." She paused, and added, "I look at these from time to time especially since Charlie died. You may have them if you like."

"You want *me* to have them?" I asked incredulously.

Gran looked at me as though I was insane. "Well someone has to have them," she said. "Besides, you should have them for the book." Then her expression became stern. "And I fully expect you to write it. It's good story worth telling. In another few years there will be no one left to remember that time. I don't even think the Garfields themselves know as much as you do now. None of the brothers were there that week. The older ones were at college, and Irv and Abe were in Ohio. Mollie is gone now, and I doubt she ever discussed it with her children. They were different from her, and she was a very private person.

"After Garfield died, the family became quite wealthy. Cyrus Field, the industrialist, set up a subscription for them and raised about a half-million dollars. I think Charlie was right. The country was ashamed of the plight of poor Mrs. Lincoln, so they were especially generous toward their second martyred President's family. Millions of people contributed. School children sent their pennies. I know our family made a contribution. Anyway, Mrs. Garfield never had to worry about money. All four of the boys went to Williams College, and they all had graduate education after that. Hal and Jim and Irv became lawyers, and Abe, as you know, was an architect. And Joe Brown did very well for himself too."

"Have you decided what to do with Mollie's letters?" I asked.

Gran took a deep breath. "I knew you were going to ask me that. No. I haven't decided yet. Mollie entrusted them to me, and I want them to go where they will be appreciated. I don't know who would appreciate them. So I think I'll just wait."

<hr/>

Gran held on to the letters until she died. When she was eighty-two, Uncle Henry, Uncle Walter and my mother decided she mustn't live alone in her big house any longer, so she went to live with Uncle Henry and Aunt Rose. When she was eighty-six she had a stroke. It became too much for them to care for her, so she went into the nursing wing of the hospital. Fortunately it was a rapid decline and she suffered only a few weeks. I suppose the only good thing about it was that she was unaware of what was going on. Had she been cognizant, the distress of it would have killed her. Living to a ripe old age is not always the most wonderful thing in the world.

In her will, she left Margie and Marlene and Chuck and Louis generous sums of money, jewelry, a Minton cup and saucer and a few small trinkets. I got a generous sum and the big trinkets: The Minton Set and the Silver Tea Service from the Millses. Mollie's gold brooch with the rose-cut diamonds. And the "Mollie cups." My sisters and cousins were happy to give me their baby cups; they had no use for them. I also got the family albums. And Mollie's letters.

I kept those letters for years and years, since I didn't know what to do with them any more than my grandmother did. She wanted them to go where they would be appreciated, and there was no one, except me perhaps, to appreciate them. The Garfield descendants didn't know nor would they care one bit that their ancestress was secretly a Suffragist and had been so deeply pained keeping it secret. That information would embarrass no one now. It might even make them proud.

Then, some years ago, when they established a Suffrage Museum in Seneca Falls, I decided the time and place had come. I contacted them, told my story, and sent a copy of one of the "Sarah Allen" letters, which they were able to determine was indeed the same handwriting as Susan B. Anthony. It was genuine. I suppose the letters might have fetched a considerable sum from collectors, but I didn't think Gran or Mollie would have wanted to cash in on Miss Anthony. So I gave the Museum the letters as a contribution, along with a tape recording of my recollections of conversations with "L.D. Stanfield," my grandmother. They were thrilled to have them and I imagine researchers will appreciate them. At the same time, I contacted the Garfield House in Mentor, Ohio. They still call it "Lawnfield" and it's run by the Federal Government. I think the family donated the house after all the uncles died. They were delighted to have the "Mollie-Louise" letters. Between the two correspondents, there were nearly 2,000.

I believe I found the best possible home for them.

I'm still waiting for the town of Long Branch to do something to honor its bit of history. I would be happy to contribute — if they hurry it up a little.

I did not marry Hal Brown. We kept up a serious correspondence for a while, but the long distance proved to be too great for a serious romance. Shortly before I graduated college, I met David Heller, a former captain in the Marines, who had completed his engineering degree at Lehigh College and, fatefully enough, had taken a job with my Uncle Henry, another Lehigh alumnus. Nature took its course, and we have been happily married for more than fifty years.

Hal Brown and I, however, have remained very dear friends. He also married about the same time I did; his wife Joan is a delightful woman. Every time the Browns come east, we make it a point to visit with them. On each of our trips to California, we hook up with the Browns, usually for a side trip to Las Vegas. Our children have met theirs, and now my grandson Peter, who is studying at UCLA, has become good pals with Hal's grandson Jeff. The friendship continues through the fifth generation.

Hal and I have also continued the tradition of "Mollie-Louise" cups. I sent monogrammed sterling silver cups from Tiffany's to his children and grandchildren and his three great-grandchildren. And he has sent monogrammed sterling silver cups from Tiffany's to mine. Tiffany's would be proud.

As a matter of fact, Sandra should be receiving a package shortly. She had twin girls two weeks ago. She named them Mollie and Louise.